# HATED VOWS

SOPHIA KARLSON

Cover Art: Qamber Designs

Edits: Leanne Rabesa

*For Amanda Holly*
*Who dared me to write a Mafia romance*
*and held my hand all the way!*
*This book wouldn't exist if it weren't for you!*
<3

# 1

# MATTEO

I've been summoned to this office many times. In the beginning, often against my will. Now I could walk here blindfolded, which is a good thing. One day it will be mine.

I knock on the double wooden door, and it opens almost immediately. A nurse in scrubs ushers me in. She's holding bagged blood samples in her hand, and I blink. Blood on the floor, on the leather couches, splattered against the walls—any day. Samples like that? Too fucking neat for the Don, also known as my father.

Our eyes meet across the warm expanse of his office and a shiver of premonition runs down my spine. Giuliano Scalera, Boston's most notorious, most hated, most dangerous Mafia Don, God of his own underworld, has aged a decade in the month I haven't seen him. The Don drops his gaze to where he's rolling down his sleeve and I eye the doctor, who is packing away his stethoscope.

I know not to speak until we're alone. This doctor and the nurse aren't our usual service providers. The faint scent of medicinal alcohol drifts over as the Don shifts in his seat and stands with effort.

"Matteo Scalera. *Mio figlio.*"

My son. Countless times I'd wished I belonged to anybody else in the world but this man. *Literally anybody else.* I still don't understand how a man could be so cruel to his own son, regardless of his own upbringing and the life he chose to lead. My brothers didn't escape his cruelty either, but I learned early on to shield them where I could.

The doctor glances up at me as he takes his medical case in hand and gives me a curt nod. "I'll call you with the results. You'll have a lot to discuss."

I step aside as the doctor makes his way out of the office. It's an old-school gentleman's study, all wood and leather, with bookshelves lining one wall. They are all just for show. The Scaleras aren't exactly a scholarly bunch. Center stage is the massive desk that hides built-in automatic machine guns, ready to shoot the place to splinters. Above the massive fireplace hang three sets of moose antlers, each shot at sniper range. Another reminder not to fuck with Giuliano Scalera.

The door clicks behind me and as if he's only become aware of my entry now, Bruno, my dad's aged mutt and constant companion, lifts his head from where he's napping on the Persian rug. Looking at his scruffy coat, you'd think the dog is more coyote than anything else, but his size suggests there's some pit bull and mastiff blood in him. As a young pup, he was wild and kept chained to the Don's chair. Bruno was too keen to bite, which was why the Don got him in the first place. Now the mutt blinks in my direction, eyes blind in old age, and rips a massive fart.

"Jesus Christ, Bruno," the Don says as he sinks back into his leather chair. "Spare us."

I chuckle, but we'll need more than Bruno to break the tension in the room. "So, who's going to kick the bucket first here? You or Bruno?"

My dad shoots me a grimace. "Don't joke, Matteo. I've been given my notice."

Fuck. I try to summon some sympathy, but that well is empty. That he's alive and has survived his life to this point is a miracle. But then, if you kill every last person that stands in your path, you get your way.

The last thing I need is the power shift and strife that comes with the inevitable death of the *Capo Crimini.* As his first-born, I'm the natural heir to the Don's empire. And I'll kill to keep it. It's the only way I know how to protect my brothers. "What's wrong?" I ask, making a vague wave in the direction of his body.

"Cancer. Stage four. Here there and everywhere."

"Why didn't you tell us?"

"When it's time, it's time. I'm not going to do chemo and all that shit."

I nod. There's no point in arguing with him. He knows what he wants. I also know he's called me here alone for a reason. All our operations are running smoothly. The Don has been good at handing over the reins, and now just sits at the head of the table, listening to our monthly reports and giving the odd piece of advice.

"When are you going to tell the others?" Everything in *Il Consiglio,* the umbrella name of our operations, has always run on a need-to-know basis, but I bet my four brothers don't know the Don is sick. Not that it matters. The last thing the Don can afford is to appear weak. He must be far along if he's held out until now and is breaking the news to me first.

"Sit, Matteo."

I wasn't waiting for his invitation. I'd hoped this would be a quick in and out. With some resignation I sink into one of the wingbacks opposite his desk, and the leather huffs with my weight. Bruno comes over and sniffs where my hand hangs over the armrest, and I stroke his head in greeting. "What's the plan?" I eventually ask when the Don just watches our interaction.

"I have three jobs I need you to wrap up for me. Business I've left unfinished."

*Unfinished?* That's new. *Il Consiglio* never leaves any job unfinished, and since his semi-retirement I've been the one to make sure there are no loose ends. Whatever these jobs entail, I already sense there's going to be blood.

"Okay." This is the last chance for me to prove to the Don that I'm worthy of taking over as head of *Il Consiglio.* Worse is, if I don't do what he asks, it will be one of my brothers that gets to clean up his dirty business. It took years to get them settled in their niches that don't require the sacrifices I need to make, and I'm keeping it that way. "Tell me more."

"Vow that you'll do this, Matteo. I can't rest until it's done."

A charged silence fills the space between us. It's one thing to make promises and know what you're getting into, but making a vow to do something when you have no clue what it is, is dangerous. I have no choice. "I vow to do whatever you ask, Don Scalera."

He nods. "Good. I need you to go deal with the Sicilian."

Fuck.

"That's the first thing." The Don leans back in his seat and laces his fingers together as he stares at me. "And then I need you to deal with the senator."

Now there's someone I've been wanting to scrape off the face of the earth for years. "No problem."

"You can't take him out, Matteo. He has paid for Alex's death."

"With the amount of money he owes us, with his backstabbing, I don't understand why he's still alive." I see the accounts every two weeks. For twelve years not a penny has been paid towards the two million the senator owes us.

"He hasn't dared cross me in twelve years, but now the time

has come for the final retribution." The Don swivels his seat and reaches into a drawer behind him. "He has protected her for years, but he owes us. It's time for his final lesson in the ways of *Il Consiglio*."

When he faces me again, he has a thick folder which he drops to the desk with a thud. "Natasha Armstrong. The single, final installment that will settle the debt."

I reach for the file and open it, and with a swift glance through the first few pages know what the Don wants from me. Ruin her. Use her. Make her pay for Alex's death until she begs for her own.

Pretty little thing too. "I'll make it happen." I'm known as the one that gets a job done, whatever it takes. And unlike most men, I'm not swayed by a woman's allures.

"Good. Play nice and make it happen off-shore for me, will you?"

I nod. Dealing with the Sicilian already means a trip abroad. This job might as well tag along.

The Don coughs and I listen closer. It's a cough he's had for months but now it has a harsher, wetter ring to it. I don't ask questions. Not of that kind. "What's the third job?"

"Bring me proof that the other two are done and I'll tell you. It's more of a personal nature."

"Bruno?"

"No. Bruno is a good boy. He'll wait for me to go before he does."

And like everybody else the damned dog will comply. I'm not going to get anything more out of him now. "What proof do you want?"

"Be creative, Matteo, it's always been your strength."

A compliment? Fuck. The guy must be really close to the end. "How much time do we have?"

"Four months if the doctors are right, but just get it done, will you? I want to rest in peace."

I want to laugh but plug it. *Peace*. What a notion. No such thing for any Scalera in this city, probably not even on this planet. It's as if our destiny was chiseled into the blood-stained stone of an ancient altar where human sacrifices used to be made.

"I'll prioritize it." I stand and notice how the Don is shrunken in his chair, seeming smaller than before. As his son, as his firstborn, I should probably walk around the desk and kiss him. At a minimum on his hand, graced by our insignia ring. But I can't get myself to do it.

I take the file and walk out. It's always only been a matter of time for his reign of terror to pass. Now we can hear the clock ticking.

Finally.

# 2

# MATTEO

When I get home, I walk straight to the bar to get a whiskey, but Burley, my bodyguard, is here and we need to talk. The Brit is a pint man, so I crack open a beer instead.

"Do you want one?" I ask, ready to toss one in his direction. Since my brother Dominic upgraded my security to top-of-the-line systems during a recent reno, I no longer need people around me all the time, but Burley is more than a bodyguard; he's a friend.

"Sure, boss." He nimbly catches it and I watch with some fascination how he maneuvers his thick forefinger under the tab to open the can. His name is so fitting. His hands are so big, there's no seeing the can anymore.

Burley has been with me for years. He's ten years older than my mere thirty-four, but he's become a fixture in my life and one of the handful of people I trust and rely on one hundred percent.

"What's the paperwork?" he asks as I make my way across the gleaming hardwood floor of my penthouse to the living area, Natasha's file in hand. I toss the file to the coffee table and strip off my jacket and holster. Placing the gun on the coffee table as I sit down, I reach for the one nestled against my calf as well.

"A project the Don has been saving for a special day." I reach for the file and spread the photos and intel out, glancing over some of the content.

"That's Armstrong's daughter."

"Yep." My team has been keeping eyes on her too, but I never thought the Don would save her for last.

"She's got 24/7 protection."

"As she should have. One of ours too, if I know the Don." There's a guy that's going to need a new position. Best I include that in my planning. "Having a security detail must fuck with her social life."

"Meh. That one's a real daddy's girl."

"You think?"

"She's never had a boyfriend. She goes to her classes, goes home, cooks healthy meals and plays hostess for her father's political antics."

"Replaced her mother then."

"Like a little lost puzzle piece."

There's a summary page. Natasha Armstrong, twenty-four, blonde, five foot seven, blue eyes, runs every day, potential Miss America or porn star material if she wasn't studying to become a doctor. She doesn't look the type—doesn't need to be the type. Her family has money. The millions they owe *Il Consiglio* were calculated opportunity costs, not actual cash. A deal may fall through but know this: *Il Consiglio* still takes its dues where we expended time and our own funds to get a project off the ground. "Never had a boyfriend, you say?"

"As far as I know."

The bodyguard circles are a small world, and like everybody else, they talk amongst themselves. "What are the chances she's still a virgin?"

Burley shrugs. "Unless Daddy messed with his little girl..."

He flexes his fingers, then cracks the thick digits, a signature ritual I've watched him perform a few times before he strangled someone who had it coming. *Il Consiglio* might be into organized crime, and over the decades have spread to numerous cities with hundreds of members, but there are a few things we don't abide. "Wanna bet on it?"

I smirk. This one is going to be a gambler until the day he dies. "Ten thousand bucks I say she lost it to some prick in high school."

Burley grunts and we shake on it. "So, what's the plan, boss?"

"I'm making a trip to Sicily to wrap up business for the Don there. This little one can tag along, and we'll see."

"Bit high profile, don't you think?" he says as he picks up a photo. "And way too sweet for the appetites I think you have in mind."

I counter him with the latest update that's been printed out. "She's got an internship this summer. We'll arrange a change of destination. Dominic can keep her socials going while she goes on auction and comes back, safe and sound, once the debt is paid up."

"You don't want her dead then?"

"The senator paid for Alex." And I stick to the rules. You kill one of ours, we take two of yours. The math is simple. "She's going to need travel documents if she's traveling with me."

"I'll get on it first thing," Burley says as he reaches for his beer.

I nod as Burley takes a last swig, then twists and crunches the can into a disc. "Thanks for the beer. The missus is waiting."

Lucky bastard. Every now and again Burley gives away his British upbringing, but this universal truth stands: the woman in his life comes first. He lives with his new wife in a four-bedroom apartment adjacent to mine. There is a connecting door for emergencies, but they have the same security level as my own place. Rosalia, who also works as my household manager, keeps everything ticking over smoothly. "I'll call my brothers in for a meeting tomorrow to set up everything we'll need."

Burley nods and we both stand. I head for the fridge, where Rosalia usually has a meal ready for me, as Burley makes his way to the front door. "Thank Rosalia for dinner."

"Will do. See you in the morning."

I'm still staring blindly into the fridge when the front door clicks closed some distance away. My mind is a bit of a mess. This thing with Armstrong has been on my own back burner for years. My younger brother Alex died in a shootout when Armstrong chickened out of a deal and blew the whistle on our cover. I walked away with two bullet wounds, but Alex... Alex died in my arms. To this day I can smell the mix of sweat on his brow laced with the tangy richness of blood as his life slipped away. The memory startles me awake at night and I'll grapple for my gun, ready to shoot my own image reflecting in the mirrored floor-to-ceiling closet.

They say it's survivor's guilt. I say I won't have peace until I've personally avenged Alex's death. I need to balance out this debt myself, over and above the Don's retribution. The Don has given me the green light. He must know how much I need to do this. His blessing is a gift and a curse because maybe he still thinks I won't be worthy of becoming the *Capo Crimini,* the Don of *Il Consiglio,* until I've put the past behind me.

The fridge starts beeping and pulls me from my thoughts. I close the door without taking out the plate of gnocchi Rosalia prepared. Instead, I walk back to the coffee table where Natasha Armstrong's file is spread out, ready to be memorized.

Best this girl starts praying. I'm about to rip her out of her comfort zone and show her how the world really works.

And for that, no amount of prayer can ever be enough.

# 3

# TASHA

"God, I wish I could spend the whole summer in this pool," Vee says.

I look towards her where we're lying on a twin float mattress, sipping mimosas we poured from a box, magazines tossed to the side. "You do? You wouldn't get bored?"

Don't get me wrong, I love relaxing by the pool like any other person, but for an entire long summer? I have more valuable things to do. For two months I can make a difference in some people's lives. I'm heading south to the US border to assist in the immigrant crisis. As my dad always says: put your money where your mouth is.

"After that semester?" Vee groans. "Jeez, Tash, I need a mental *health* break, never mind just a mental break."

I drag my fingertips through the water, glancing up to the veranda where my dad appears. He waves at me but doesn't say anything. What's he doing, making that funny gesture with his hand?

Weird.

I flop to my side and the water splashes, wetting us. The cool drops are welcome on my sunbaked skin. We've been floating around for more than an hour now. I'm all toasty but dread getting into the water to get out of the swimming pool. Whichever way I look, I see Mom's roses in full bloom and it's as if I'm floating in memories of her. Roses were her favorite. She planted them everywhere when I was still in elementary school and now their sweet scent perfumes the air. What she wouldn't give to see these now... what I wouldn't give to have her here.

Maybe the problem isn't with the pool. The problem is spending time in this house that has become a hollow echo of the family we used to be. There's nothing like the long summer vacation, which used to be filled with joy and love and adventure, to remind me how much I miss my brother, Kevin, and my mom, who used to be the center of our universe.

I blink at the surge of emotion that threatens to spill from my eyes. Twelve years and it still hits me out of the blue like this, my throat constricting, my vision blurry with tears.

Vee slurps at her mimosa and nudges me with her elbow. "Your dad has guests."

"What?" Having visitors isn't unusual. Dad is forever hosting lobbyists and other politicians at home, but never on a Sunday afternoon. Like *never*. If he has something going on over a weekend, it happens on the golf course or over expensive dinners and fundraisers I don't have to attend.

We've floated in a half circle, so that our backs are now facing the house. I go up on my elbow and peer over the backrest.

Dad is standing at the veranda's railing, a man by his side. They are holding drinks, seeming convivial, but something stirs in my stomach. The man next to Dad towers over him and must be at least six foot five. He's wearing a black suit jacket and a white buttondown, which only accentuates the tanned skin from the collar up to his cut jaw. That five o'clock stubble is... *Damn*.

I swallow as my gaze travels to a sensual mouth, which is pulled into an insouciant smirk. And then higher, to where a pair of dark eyes make me feel like I'm staring into two woodland ponds, the type that harbors mythical creatures you don't want to meet in the dark.

It's as if he skins me with his gaze and I drop back, feeling exposed. "I think you've got to go, Vee." Whoever this is, I'm not getting good vibes.

"Sure. I've got to meet Hank for dinner in any case." She sits up and the inflatable wobbles. We both giggle, but mine is forced. "Hold on to your drink, I'm going to—"

"No!" I call out, half laughing, half protesting at the cold water as I get dunked. Goosebumps sprout all over and I pop out of the water, gathering my hair from my face. My plastic glass floats along with our magazines like party corpses, and I just shake my head at Vee. "Thank God you did that, I wasn't relishing getting back in."

"I knew it. You're welcome." Her focus turns to the men standing on the second-story veranda, which is actually the ground floor. The pool is on the same level as our walk-out basement. "There're three of them now."

I glance up as I reach for the magazines and my body stills. That moment where fight-or-flight mode is triggered. Two more men have taken positions beside my dad and the unknown suit, but they don't have drinks. It isn't unusual for visitors to come with their assistants, but I get the feeling these guys aren't here to take notes.

For the first time I curse quietly as I toss the magazines to the edge of the pool. If Dad had told me there were going to be a bunch of guys ogling us while we were swimming, I would have put on a full bathing suit. Not the skimpiest black bikini I recently bought thanks to Vee's tastes in something this... sexual. I hardly feel comfortable wearing it in front of *her*, now

I need to get out of the water and strut my stuff as if this is my usual attire.

In fact, if I'd known these men would be here, I wouldn't have come out of my room at all. Timo, my bodyguard, is off on Sundays. Ever since Dad's career skyrocketed and his life became so public, I've been closely guarded in his slipstream, trying to survive and live my life, dodging the flying debris of his career.

"We'll go round the back; it'll be quickest," I say as I make my way to the pool's stairs and our towels. Thank God I have something to wrap around this much naked skin.

Vee is out first, not body-conscious at all. Let's just say she's covered a lot of ground where I'm still stumbling to find the starting blocks.

Vee tosses her towel over her shoulder and reaches for her handbag. "I'll just drip dry to the car. Need to shower when I get home, and shave, you know."

I know. *Down there.* No need to elaborate. I get out of the pool, and with every step it's as if the eyes on the veranda take me in, measure me, and assess my value. As if there can't be more to a woman than being a man's trophy plaything. I pick up my towel and turn toward him, giving him my silhouette, then forcing myself to give him more of a full frontal. *See, there, satisfied now?*

He doesn't look away and a steady blush creeps over my skin. It's as if he can see right through me. Every doubt, every longing, every fear, every last insecurity that comes from living my overprotected life. His gaze shifts. It homes in on my hardened nipples, still perky from the cold water. Water which runs in steady rivulets from my hair down the valley between my breasts to my sex, where his gaze lingers. I breathe in sharply and our gazes clash. For a full five seconds we just stare at each other, then he raises an eyebrow at me, a slow intentional cock of his brow that says *she's tolerable, but not handsome enough to tempt me.*

I'm the first to look away as I wrap my towel around my breasts, fingers trembling, heat settling on my cheeks. I really hope Dad doesn't expect me to entertain that asshole tonight. "You have everything?"

"Yep." Vee swings her bag over her shoulder. "He's freaking hot, but fuck. So not in our wheelhouse."

I ignore her comment and unnecessary cussing. "This way." I take my cellphone and we saunter off to the side of the house where a wide path leads to the gated front. As soon as we're out of sight, I huff a slow sigh of relief, but it doesn't ease the tension in my shoulders or stomach.

In fact, I tense up more when I see two black SUVs with tinted windows parked in our driveway.

My gut tells me to get into the car with Vee and bail the hell out of here. My common sense tells me that the only way these cars could have entered the property was if Dad let them in. Which means it's all fine.

"I'll catch you later this week?"

"Yeah, sure," I say, but I'm too distracted to think ahead. I see her off and make my way to the front door. If I can make it to my room and dodge that jerk and his entourage, my escape will be complete.

# 4

# TASHA

I take the few stairs to our front door and open it with the security code, clutching my towel to my chest as it slips loose from my breasts. I walk into the foyer, expecting it to be empty.

Instead, Dad is there, surrounded by two of the suited men I saw on the veranda. They are both physically big, but one is bald and his head shines in the chandelier's light. The other one is holding a small case in his hand, flicking the lid open and closed.

And then there's *him*. The man who stripped me with his eyes alone. He is standing to the side, a mere spectator to whatever is unfolding here.

"Dad?"

"Natasha." He clears his throat.

"What's going on?" Another man is coming down one side of the dual staircase, my rose gold laptop and tablet in hand. I take a step back, only to feel the half-open door cutting into my back.

"I messed up."

My gaze jumps from one man to the next. I freeze when I spot the guns, one pressing into my dad's side, the other aimed at *me*, hardly visible in the way the goon is holding it. My heart hammers in my throat as chills of pure fear spread over my skin.

"How... what?"

"If you want—" Dad breaks off. Tears are flowing down his cheeks. "If you want us to live, you need to go with these men."

*If you want to live you need to run.* But I don't. Not when the man with the gun pressed against Dad's side prods at him so hard that he stumbles. I reach out to curb his fall, but a hand shoots out and jerks me back. My phone drops to the rug with a soft plop as my towel loses grip and slides off.

"Not so fast, luv." The guy with the bald head has his hands wrapped around my biceps and squeezes. "Be a good girl and make this easy."

"No!" I heave forward, trying to reach Dad where he's managed to get on his knees, but I don't even move an inch.

"It's the right thing to do, Tash," Dad whimpers. "He has promised to bring you back... once... once I've paid up."

On instinct my eyes shoot to the man who still stands to the side, clearly the one in charge although he hasn't said a thing.

"Do you have any other electronics beside your laptop, iPad and phone?" shiny bald head asks, his voice a gruff scrape by my ear. He is such a huge guy, our bodies don't even touch, his grip so firm I can't move.

"No?" I'm begging now, my tone giving me away.

"Good. Let's go." They're the first words I hear the man in the suit speak, his voice deep and masculine, but he isn't even looking at me. He's looking at the other guy who has the small case in his hand and gives him a nod.

When I see the syringe I buckle, but I'm like a twig in the bald guy's arms as he pulls me into a straitjacket pose.

"Just one prick, luv, and it will all be good."

Dad is weeping and it's like nails scraping against the inside of my skull. I always do the right thing. I always put him first.

I've always done what he expects of me to keep us safe, to be what he needs me to be for his political career. What has he done? Surely this isn't something that will keep us safe.

A cold wipe of alcohol and before its scent can even reach my nose, I feel the prick of the needle in the soft flesh of my hip. My mind thinks heroin, or meth, but then a list of anesthetic agents flashes through my mind. I slip, but I don't fall.

Instead, there's a warm cradle of arms that catch me as Baldy lets go, and everything turns black.

# 5

# MATTEO

The coffee table is littered with beer cans, empty pizza boxes, and our collection of guns. I like having my brothers over. It's much more relaxed at my place than the meetings we have every month at the Don's. We make a point to get together at least once a week, but since the Don's revelation to me weeks ago, we've met more often.

We don't talk about his illness. Or eventual death. We talk about everything else. The Don's two requests have been a welcome segue to get together and plan instead.

Dominic runs our security and has his own above-board firm. Handy when you want to get dirt on people. A lot of the things his company installs for us aren't legal, but good for harvesting blackmail material if you do it right.

Stephano and Luca run our finances and night clubs along the East Coast. Some clubs are more exclusive than others, some serve a certain clientele, and over the years, those two have made contacts worldwide. They've always been early adopters and have branched into websites. Everything runs smoothly without much of their own involvement now, from fan clubs to auction sites. You fantasize it, they'll deliver it. Mostly.

As for Benedict, the baby, he's what the rest of the world calls a nerd. He is quiet and observant, until he says something that shakes the room. Growing up without a mom, in the brutality of the Don's household, probably got to him the most. I at least still have memories of her.

Not that I want to analyze any of my brothers. That we all need therapy goes without saying, except that's the one thing we'll never get. Who needs therapy if you can kill, fuck, and in general bulldoze through life as a member of *Il Consiglio*, as a Scalera, the founding family?

We've finished watching the NBA game, and it's time to focus on business. I reach for my phone and change the channel on my TV to a visual of my safe room's security camera.

"Nice," Benedict grumbles as he slumps back in his seat as the rest of them quiet. "Thanks for the reality check."

Natasha Armstrong is still passed out on a bare mattress on the safe room's floor.

"You sure know how to set the scene, Matteo," Luca says. "We can get bids just on this footage alone."

"I bet you can." I wasn't trying to set a fucking scene, but yes. A nearly naked girl held against her will in a basement somewhere? There's a bunch of psychos out there who would pay good money to watch her for a few weeks with the promise of fucking her at the end of it for a price. I wouldn't even have to drag her ass over to Sicily and Cannes, which is the current plan. "That type of thing won't cover two million."

For a long minute none of us speak. The money is beside the point. Alex isn't coming back, regardless of what we take from or do to the Armstrongs.

*Deal with the senator.* That's been put in motion, but ever since this afternoon, something else has been eating at me:

Peter Armstrong could have paid up long ago. That mansion-for-two has a market value of around five million dollars, and he could have downsized.

Bottom line: the man is a fucking coward. He let me walk out with his daughter in my arms without even reaching out for her. He told her leaving with me was the *only way* to stay alive. He *encouraged* her. The fucker didn't even put up a fight. Anger roils afresh in my stomach at the mere thought of it. Turns out I'm not the only one with a fucked-up dick for a dad. We're different sides of the same coin. Good and bad. Light and dark. Love and hate.

It shouldn't have been so easy. Dominic managed to override their security systems and we drove right onto the property as if we'd been invited to a cocktail party. Armstrong let his guard down. Twelve years is a long time to hold your breath. Eventually you think the worst has passed, but the Don plays a long game.

Know this: once you've entered the realm of *Il Consiglio*, you're in for life. Don't think there's an escape, don't think we forget, and don't think we won't come for you.

Stephano shifts in his chair and reaches for his beer. "Our site's ready whenever you are. We just need a few photos and we're good to go."

He's referring to their very exclusive auction site. The type where you get to bid by invitation only. Women come to them to sell their virginity to the highest bidder. It's the first time we've ventured down the lane of an unwilling victim, but all of us feel the same. The Armstrongs will pay.

"No facial photos. I'm not risking it." I won't let this snowball into something we can't control.

"That's fine," Stephano sighs. "But this part of you going to Sicily on your own—"

"Is not negotiable." I'm not dragging my brothers into the Don's vendetta. His feud with the Sicilian is an old one that started decades ago when there was a succession struggle. The Don had been established on the East Coast for years. The Sicilian came over, thinking he could just take what the Don had built for himself. Then the Sicilian broke the golden rule: he fucked with the Don's family. He killed my dad's first wife and baby. The Don returned the favor, killing the Sicilian's wife. How it happened, none of us know, but a bloodbath ensued for two years that only ended when the Don took a wife from the Sicilian's extended family. The wedding was the ultimatum and a truce: leave and you live.

The Sicilian returned to Italy, where he still had connections and a foundation on which to build his empire. My mother was the last pawn in a battle that took too many lives.

Deal with the Sicilian... *don't think we won't come for you. And if I can't do it myself, I'll send my son.*

Natasha stirs and every gaze in the room homes in on her. I check the time. About right. The injection was supposed to knock her out for four hours. She's going to be groggy and confused as she wakes up.

"Party's starting," Dominic says as he leans in to look at something closer. "What's she wearing?"

"A bikini." A very skimpy one at that. It accentuates her skin more than anything else with its many thin straps keeping the thing together.

"A bikini?" Dominic laughs. "Did you drag her out of the pool?"

"Nearly. She was wet. Ruined my fucking suit." I can still feel the slight weight of her in my arms, the way she fit my frame perfectly as I carried her from my private underground garage to the penthouse elevator, Burley in tow. The other bodyguards will hang out with the senator, to make sure he doesn't lose his shit. Poor fuckers. Talk about a long summer.

Natasha struggles to sit. She rubs at her eyes, then reaches for her hip where she got poked by the needle. She flops back and stares at the ceiling, then takes in her surroundings. There's nothing except the steel walls, the mattress, and a keypad by the door.

"Bids are dropping by the minute," Luca jokes after a while of her just lying there. "This is boring as shit."

I might as well show the little bird that she can flee the nest. I'm hesitating because once she walks out of there, I'm going to have to deal with her. Not my usual Sunday night. I flick the app open on my phone, enter several security codes and my thumbprint, and from the living room we can all hear the heavy steel door click open. It is after all in front of us, a few paces away from the TV screen.

At the sound, Natasha rolls onto her side, looks at the door, and blinks at the faint strip of light falling over the floor.

Her dad might be a useless fucking coward, not worth the air he breathes, but this one... the jury is still out on this one.

I'll give her the benefit of the doubt.

For now.

# 6

# TASHA

The sliver of light beckons me. I sit up again, feeling less woozy than the first time. I get on all fours and crawl to the door.

I startle and freeze when a man laughs and says, "That's it, baby girl, crawl to daddy."

My knees hurt on the hard floor, but I don't move, too scared of what I'll find on the other side of the door. For a minute I wait, but no voice comes. When I lean back on my haunches, the same voice chuckles and says, "Fuck, Matteo, did you script this? Is she acting? Sitting like a submissive? If we were on auction—"

"Shut the fuck up, Luca," another voice says, and a frisson of fear shoots down my spine as I recognize it. *Him.*

Matteo?

I glance at the upper corners of the room and in the dim light I spot the shine of a camera lens. My skin bursts out in goosebumps as I realize they can see me. Two men on the other side of the door. I hug my body and, in that moment, realize I'm still wearing my bikini—and only my bikini.

I've never felt more naked in my life.

I have nothing to defend myself with.

An eternity of time passes before I eventually realize they aren't coming for me. I can stay in here forever and die or go out and face what waits on the other side. And die. This ends no other way.

I stand slowly, leaning onto the wall for support, and with some effort pull the heavy door open. I blink at the sudden light flooding over my body. My gaze flits over the space. Double volume floor-to-ceiling windows and the soft pink summer light of the sun just gone. The dark and masculine interior of the walls, the steel and glass railings, the even bigger black leather sectional where not two, but five men face me. And *him* in the middle, flanked by his lieutenants.

I don't step out of the small comfort of the door jamb, clinging to it in fear as every pair of eyes inspects me. A blush bursts out on my skin as I feel the unabashed caress of several gazes lingering on my breasts, my stomach, and my crotch, where this scant slip of fabric barely covers my sex.

He pockets his phone slowly and as he stands our eyes meet. I shrink inwardly and want to fall back to the safety of the room behind me.

"Miss Armstrong. Thank you for joining us."

"Who are you?" I ask. Nobody answers, they just stare at me. "And what have you done to my dad?"

"Your dad's at home."

"I don't believe you! You killed him!"

"Believe what you want."

"It's Matteo, is it?" I ask, taking a step forward.

That annoyingly perfect brow cocks at me again. "Yes. Matteo. My brothers." He gestures towards the other men who are all still sitting, and as I take them in, I curse inwardly. They are all... *freaking hot* as Vee would say. *Vee.* I should have bailed with her while I had the chance. Why didn't I listen to my gut?

These men might be hot, but an aura of danger hangs in the space.

Nobody speaks. They all just stare at me until a resigned sigh comes from one of the men as he slumps back and another one reaches for a beer and raises it to me in a mock toast.

"You killed him! God! Why?" I shudder with so many emotions, foremost the one where I want to kill this Matteo asshole in front of me with my own bare hands. "Are you going to kill me too?"

Matteo smirks. "Only if you don't settle your dad's debts."

I flinch at his tone. He isn't joking. I might be young and inexperienced, but I'm not naive. "And how do I repay these debts? By you all raping me until you've had your fill?"

Matteo walks around the coffee table, his gaze drifting over me, touching my body, tugging at every nerve that leads down to my sex. He comes to stand in front of me and I tilt my head to look up at him, forcing myself to look him in the eye.

"We don't touch the merch," he says, his voice deep and soft, intimate. "Ever."

Merch? Like in merchandise? "What does that mean?"

He doesn't bother to respond, and my thoughts swarm to the obvious conclusion. *I'm* merchandise. Their *property*. To sell, barter, and cut up piecemeal as they please. Kidneys, liver, eyeballs... every part of me once they're done. The blush I had drains straight to my toes as the full implication of my situation hits me.

"Here, let me fix this for you." His dark brown eyes, which held mine this whole time, drop to my lips, then lower to my chest. My breathing stalls as he raises his hand to my neck and with one finger traces the line of my bikini's strap down to the triangle covering my breast. I shiver at his gentle touch, in such contrast to every situation my mind conjured up seconds ago. His finger dips underneath the fabric and my nipple hardens even more with anticipation of this tender invasion. I want to step back, get away from him, but as his fingertip brushes over my nipple, a debilitating rush of desire spreads over my skin, down to my sex. He catches the fabric and tugs it out from where it had folded on itself, exposing way more breast than intended.

He straightens the strap by running his fingers under it, then pulls away. "There."

I've never been touched like this, and the heat of his hand lingers as I open my eyes. I didn't even realize I'd closed them.

"Your dad's fine." He takes his phone from his pocket and swipes away, then turns it to me. The phone shows video footage of Dad, sitting by our dining room table, having dinner.

"That's not real," I whisper. It can't be. How can he be eating dinner when I've been *kidnapped*? When I'm here with five strange men who could at the drop of a hat gang rape me and then sell my organs.

"No?" Matteo speaks into the phone. "Let Armstrong give us a little wave."

He turns the screen back to me and I watch, stupefied, as my dad turns his head, and fork in hand, waves at me.

I grab Matteo's phone from him and want to say something, but I don't know what.

*He's having dinner. Without me.*

*He's sold me out.* My fingers tremble—if only I could make one call to get me out of here. But I already know we're out of our depth with these men. Dad isn't even fighting for me, even though all I've ever done was to please and obey him. *Be the perfect daughter and I'll be safe.*

A level of anger I'd never known existed erupts and I fling the phone across the room. "Fuck you!"

Men dodge. The phone hits the black marble kitchen island with an echoing smack before it bounces off and crashes to the floor. I turn to Matteo, clawing at him.

And then there's a scramble.

Matteo grabs my wrists and has them caged in one massive hand in a second. He pushes me until my back collides with the cold steel door of the safe room, his thigh pressed between my legs as he lifts me against the wall as if I weigh nothing. His touch is rough and brusque and so swift I'm almost winded. His free hand wraps around my throat, pressing up so that I'm forced to look at him. When his palm squeezes with just the right amount of pressure I know he could choke me to death if he wanted to.

"Understand this, princess," he hisses. "We don't do tantrums here." He grips my throat for emphasis, then brushes his thumb along my jaw, so tenderly I could cry. "If you want to be gagged and chained for the duration of your stay, I'll make it happen." He leans closer, his voice deeper. "If you need to be disciplined, I'll make it happen."

Several beats pass during which he only looks into my eyes, our chests flush, our breathing in sync. He stares at me with such loathing that I flinch. Nobody has ever looked at me with such hate before and I have no idea why.

"Nobody throws, breaks, or damages what belongs to me. Only I get to do that. Understand?" With these words, his thumb presses on my jaw, forcing my face to the side, exposing my neck. He leans even closer and his warm musky scent envelops me as his breath comes as a hot wave over my skin, which breaks out in goosebumps in response. He trails his nose over my hair, inhaling, then lower, his lips open in a sensual tease as they ghost the sensitive skin on my neck, making me forget where I am and who he is.

When he closes his lips and sucks, the heat of wet arousal seeps from my pussy where it's pressed against his thigh. I can feel him making the mark as he sucks my blood to the surface where it will leave a bruise.

I whimper and he stops, but he presses his mouth to my ear and whispers, "Last thing. If you were mine, I wouldn't be eating fucking dinner if you'd been kidnapped by *Il Consiglio*. I'd be tearing the fucking world down to find you and make sure you were safe."

Matteo lets go of me so abruptly that I almost stumble, but at the last second, his hands on my shoulders stabilize me.

"That should be gone by the time you go up for auction."

# 7

## MATTEO

I turn away from Natasha, infuriated. At her fucking decrepit dad. At the fucking Don who's forcing me to do this. At *her.* Little minx threw my phone across the room like an NFL quarterback. Does she even know who she's dealing with here? That I can break her with my bare hands?

Except when I touched her the last thing I wanted was to break her. Her skin was so soft, her body perfect in all the right places against mine, her fucking arousal so obvious there's only one conclusion here: this girl is untouched.

Why did that thought turn me on? I don't do virgins. I don't have the time or the patience. Ever since the day the Don took me to lose my virginity at a whorehouse, I understood that women are just a commodity. At thirteen I learned that you take what you need, pay, and don't ask for more. Scalera men get served. Scalera men get everything and anything we want in bed, but Scalera men don't love. We can't afford to.

Stephano and Dominic are standing guns in hand, ready to take action if needed. Luca has picked up my phone and is walking it over. Benedict is shaking his head at me where he's still sitting, unfazed. I indicate they can relax. Natasha Armstrong has more bite than bark.

Luca hands me my phone with a smirk. "It survived. Fun times ahead, brother. Sure you don't want us to help you out with this little one?"

"Merch, Luca, she's merch," I say as I check my phone. "Get that into your fucking head."

"Your kitten has claws, Matteo," Dominic says as he tucks his gun into the back of his jeans. "Good luck. You know where to get hold of me."

Stephano comes up to me as he pulls on his jacket. "Good show, brother. When do you need the doc?"

"Tomorrow. Need to confirm her potential value before we do anything else."

"Doc will be here first thing; I'll make sure of it."

I nod as I watch them gather their things. Fuck. They are leaving and I'm going to have to deal with this woman alone.

Benedict finally stands and stretches with a yawn, showing off a slim and toned six-pack under a white T-shirt. He reaches for his gun under a pizza box and slips it into the holster on his calf. As he walks past me, he says, "You're fucked, Matteo. And not in a fun way."

Yep, trust Benedict to see right through everything that went on there with Natasha. I watch them file to the front door, with soft smirks and witty remarks about the whip I cut myself bouncing between them. I block out the noise and turn to where Natasha is still leaning against the door. When my front door clicks closed seconds later, we're still staring at each other.

When I saw her step out of that pool, I knew that she was fucking beautiful. Sexy as sin. Too shy, feigning confidence, making her breathtaking. But between then and now things have shifted. She's hugging herself, and where her neck used to be an unblemished column of pure seduction, a purple bruise has spread and stained her skin. The mark I made. The one and only.

"W-what did you mean by auction?"

"You'll see."

She's shivering.

"Come," I say. When she doesn't move, I take two steps and wrap my hand around her wrist. "Come with me." I tug her along and she doesn't exactly protest but has to take two steps for each one of mine as I march her upstairs and into my bedroom.

"No," she whispers. "Please—"

"I'm not going to touch you, kitten," I say, the nickname coming all by itself, sprouting from Dominic's claws comment. I let go of her. "You have nothing to fear from me. Unless we have a repeat episode." *As for what I'll allow other men to do to you—*

Before that thought can go anywhere, I push open my floor-to-ceiling mirrored closet door, but I forgot. I stare straight at the photo of my mom I still treasure after all these years. In black and white, it's timeless. I ignore her open gaze, her sweet, secretive smile, and jump to the photo of Alex and me when we were nineteen and twenty respectively. We have our arms flung around each other's shoulders, laughing. That refocuses my resolve and I go on my haunches to rummage through a pile of old T-shirts.

"Here." I hand her a T-shirt I no longer wear and should get Rosalia to toss out. "Cover up."

She takes it from me, but she's not fast enough or maybe just clumsy and drops it on the edge of the bed. She's probably shaken now that reality has sunk in. Could be the aftermath of the drugs we gave her.

"Come on, kitten, nobody's going to hurt you here." I shake the shirt out and guide her arms through it, trying to ignore how fragile her female body really is, how easy it would be for me to just have her. Once I have the shirt over her head, I pull out the thick strands of her hair. It's soft and luscious and smells of chlorine.

"W-what... what did my dad do?" she asks, arms hanging limp by her sides. "I-I've never heard of you or know of anything—"

"You'll figure it out." I have to get away from her. I'm not going to tell her how Peter Fucking Armstrong's cowardly back-stabbing cost us Alex's life. I pull my phone from my pocket and dial Burley. He answers in one ring. "Can you babysit?"

"Already?" Burley grunts, but there's teasing in his tone. "Be there in a minute, boss."

"Call Stan over, I'm going out." I kill the call, toss the phone on my bed and start unbuttoning my shirt. "Look and learn, kitten."

With each button I reveal more of the tattoo that incorporates my two bullet wounds in a bigger picture of dragons twisted in a mid-air fight. At first glance. You need to look much closer and know the backstory to understand the finer nuances of the art on my skin and see what's really happening.

Her gaze travels over my chest, my pecs, the closed eye of the one dragon underneath my nipple where they've incorporated the bullet wound, up to the other eye of the second dragon which disguises the other bullet. And then her gaze drops lower, to where my trousers hug the V of my abs and my happy trail disappears. She fists her hands now, her cheeks peachy with a fresh blush. She eyes my dick print and yeah, sweetheart, you're not up for that.

Footsteps sound and Burley calls out to me. "Boss?"

"In here."

He comes to lean in the door and Natasha turns to look at him, her eyes going wide as she recognizes him from this afternoon.

"I'm going to my regular," I say as I pick a black shirt from my cupboard. "You know the drill."

"Sure thing. Enjoy." Burley beckons Natasha with his hand and when she doesn't move, I groan inwardly.

"Unless you want to watch me strip and shower, kitten, now's the time to leave."

That gets her going. For some fucked-up reason I can't help the twitch of my lips when she zips through the door and Burley closes it with a wink.

# 8

## TASHA

It's the same guy that held me this afternoon when I got injected and kidnapped. He is massive. Probably over three hundred pounds of muscle and flesh, ready to rip my limbs off one by one. His bald head shines and his thick neck folds at the base of his skull where tattoos disappear under his collar. I gauge him to be in his late forties by the wrinkles on his brow and eyes. He strips his jacket off, revealing two guns on his body, and underneath his white shirt I spot the edges of a bulletproof vest. He tosses his jacket on the leather sectional and eyes the mess on the coffee table.

"Did they feed you?" he asks, his voice gruff.

I shake my head. "No."

"Are you going to behave, or do I tie you up?"

My eyes flit over the room, but I already know there's no easy way out of this apartment.

"Bulletproof, soundproof, security all over, everything managed electronically. Don't even think about it, luv," he says as he stacks the boxes and finds one with two slices of pizza in it. "Fancy some *Frutti di Mare*?"

I can't eat but I must. "Thank you."

He nods with his head towards the kitchen island where Matteo's phone did some gymnastics earlier on. "Sit. And put your hands where I can see them."

I clamber onto a stool, relieved that my shaky legs don't have to hold me up anymore. I place my hands on the counter, in awe that my fingers are still trembling. This is more than a blood sugar drop. The interaction with Matteo, the heat of his hard body against mine did one thing, while his words did the exact opposite. And then he said the last thing I ever expected: *If you were mine, I wouldn't be eating fucking dinner if you'd been kidnapped. I'd be tearing the fucking world down to find you and make sure you were safe.*

The mere thought of those words makes my heart rate surge again but... *Dad.* That video footage he showed me couldn't have been live. It must have been staged. How else? Since Mom and Kevin's car wreck, we have been each other's lifelines. Now it's been severed and I'm afloat in a world where he won't find me. *Trafficked.*

I watch as Egg Head microwaves the pizza and switches on the electric kettle. The kitchen is state of the art, quiet drawers, empty counters, slick in black marble and stainless steel. Egg Head opens the fridge and it's fully stocked with what looks like home-prepped ready meals, milk, yogurt, and fruit. Seems my keeper eats at home most of the time.

"What's your name?" I ask as he takes out some orange juice and milk and pushes it in my direction.

"Burley." The microwave pings and he takes out the plate, his palm the size of it. God, those fingers.

"We'll be spending a lot of time together?" I ask, knowing I'm probably not allowed to fish for info.

"Better me than someone else." He puts a glass in front of me. "Now shut up and eat up."

I bow my head at the reprimand and focus on tearing the pizza into bitesize pieces, my stomach still too hyped to take food.

Burley goes around the kitchen island to the living room area behind me to gather beer bottles and cans. I've shadowed in the ER. I know how much damage you can inflict with a broken bottle. Or a knife.

I don't need a gun to off my kidnappers, but I don't know if I have it in me to kill someone. My whole career is based on saving lives, not taking them. I've never anticipated being in a situation where I'd need to fight for my own life, but now... I'm going up for *auction*, whatever that means. I don't allow my imagination to run wild yet. It's been a crazy day as it is.

Burley is back in the kitchen and tossing the cans and bottles into the recycling bin, which I can't see from where I'm sitting. Once he's done, he leans on the counter and watches me.

"Just one bite, luv, to get things going."

I squash my reluctance and take a bite and as soon as the juicy richness of the tomato base hits my tongue, I realize I'm famished. And this pizza is delicious. Nothing like the thick-based American slice I sometimes get for a hasty lunch. Delicate and fresh and the sweet seafood balances the tang of the tomato perfectly.

For a moment it's quiet as I eat, and even quieter when I take a break. Burley's eyes are on me, and then his gaze shifts to over my shoulder.

I feel him, but I didn't hear him, and I shudder with shock when Matteo's voice comes from right behind me.

"Let her use the last bedroom for now and we'll see how it goes."

He's snuck up to me so quietly, like a panther in the night, and like his prey, I freeze. An easy kill.

It's only when the front door clicks closed seconds later that I breathe. Hell, I didn't even hear him traverse the expanse of his living room floor to what must be the foyer.

Burley doesn't move or twitch. "Yep, luv, you've summed it up. Don't fuck with him. You won't live to regret it."

# 9

# MATTEO

Stan, one of our bodyguards, drives me to the club and I phone Stephano on the way there. "I'm heading your way. Are you there tonight?" When my brothers left earlier, it wasn't because Natasha had come out of the safe room; some of them had to work tonight.

"I'm here. Luca is at OBSIDIAN. What do you need?"

For a moment I hesitate. Sex has always been easy for me. But now, as the vague memories of the women who've served me roll like a film reel in my mind, I groan inwardly. Nothing appeals right now. "Let me see when I get there."

"Want me to arrange something?"

"No, I'll have a drink at the bar and see if it goes anywhere."

When I walk into LUNA, a high-end strip club that also stages scenes in the basement for paying clientele, I glance around the dark space. The subtle lighting usually does a lot for a man's imagination, but now I can't see beyond the used bodies that sway in the light. Sultry, oversexed, and processed to look like some cartoon version of the standard male fantasy. I bet there isn't a rack in this place that isn't fake.

All I see in my mind's eye is Natasha's perfect natural

breasts, and that rosy areola that peeked out at the side of her bikini top, her full nipple just shy of showing. Her reaction to my touch was novel. Her breathing stalled and goosebumps followed the trail of my fingertip, and that little shudder as I grazed a circle over the hardened peak gave everything away. None of the women in this club would have reacted like that to such a simple touch. They're too jaded.

I sit down at the end of the bar with my back to the wall and order a double whiskey on ice, watching the guests. I'm halfway through my drink when I curse. The little minx at home is taking up way too much bandwidth in what should be a session of stress relief for me. I finish my drink with one gulp and slam the glass on the counter. Maybe if I go to the dungeon my head will be jerked into the right headspace for sex.

"Don't have another," Stephano says as he comes up to me with hastened strides.

Of course he knew where to find me. Security knows who comes and leaves all the time. As they fucking should.

"What's happening?"

"Greg Martinez just walked in."

"You got to be kidding me."

"Seems he took our bait."

Fucking idiot. He's a dead man. Fucker left one of our strippers as good as dead nine months ago. We don't pimp these women; they're on the payroll like any other staff at a big firm. We'll never be into prostitution, but we can't stop the strippers from engaging in what they will after hours. Martinez disappeared but our network has got some reach and Dominic, Stephano, and Luca have been involved in a scheme to lure him back to Boston. Doesn't help that our wider network let it drop that Martinez killed a prostitute in Mexico. Probably not his first, but tonight he's done.

"What do you have on site?" I ask as I follow Stephano to

the back office, where security footage will allow us to track his movement in the club.

"Some G and roach."

When we reach the security office, we both home in on the screen where the team is following Martinez's movements. *Good job, Stephano.* He jumped on this like a champ.

"You think he's going to go for a BDSM scene?" Stephano asks. "Or do we spike his drink and not even get him to touch any of our staff?"

"Fucker doesn't get to touch anybody." That one likes sadism too much. "Give him just enough GHB to get him out of here. I want him conscious when you deal with him."

We both know what happens next. We don't 'deal' with fuckers like Martinez at the club. *Il Consiglio* likes to keep its workplaces clean. It's good for staff morale. After some recent renovations, I have a freeze-dry promession facility in my ten-vehicle private garage in the basement of my apartment building. Perfect to get rid of unwanted bodies. Fish like to feed on the powder the process produces, and one of our money laundering shops is a chain of pet stores that specializes in tropical fish.

I watch as Martinez orders another drink from a waitress who is dressed Playboy-bunny style. Some things never get old. "Make sure that one's spiked."

Stephano walks out and I watch as the whole thing plays out on the screen. When Martinez attempts to stand it's too late. Two bouncers are there to help him along.

As Dominic would say, "Party's starting."

# 10

# TASHA

Now that I've eaten something and Matteo has left—and has been gone for a solid half hour, thank God—my body settles. I'm still hyped but drained from the hours-long adrenaline rush. Burley made me some super sweet tea and I couldn't help the smile when he pushed it in my direction with a "Drink up, luv, me Nan's solution to every problem."

He's been watching me like a hawk, but somehow I don't feel threatened under his watchful eye. I want to ask him so many things, because a man this size who recalls his Nan with such affection can't be all bad, can he? He might not give anything away, but it's worth a shot. "What are the chances you guys brought some of my clothes from my house?"

Burley shrugs. "Zero?"

Okay. "Any chance we can fetch some?"

"Don't get cheeky, luv. The boss will sort you out."

Okay. I get the feeling I'm so low on the boss's to-do list, I might fall off the edge of the page. "And... and my laptop... and so on?" Like my phone? Anything that could actually get me out of here with just one call.

Burley shakes his head. "You don't need any of that where

you're going." He takes the cup from where I'm clutching it for support and places it in the dishwasher. "Now you're going to be a good girl and take a shower, and then I'm going to tuck you in for the night."

Coming from Burley, the words make me feel like I'm five years old. If Matteo said them, they would have played in my head laced with innuendo… and what's up with that? Honestly. Ever since he touched me, ever since he guided my arms into his T-shirt with such care, I've been nurturing a quiet but rather annoying tension there where I need it least.

"This way. Take the stairs and then to the left."

He makes me walk in front, and I lead the way up the glass stairs to the second floor, grateful that Matteo's T-shirt is huge and hangs lower than mid-thigh. It's soft and wash-worn and as soon as I'm alone, I'm taking this stupid bikini off with its straps that cut into my skin.

As we ascend, I take in the vast expanse of the apartment. It is an architectural masterpiece straight out of some design magazine. There's no clutter, and I realize with a shiver there's no place to hide either.

"Last door," Burley says as he herds me down the landing.

I walk into a room with a king-size mattress and views over the city. I'm still in Boston, but I'll have to look closer to figure out where I am. Burley comes up to me and presses a button to roll down blackout shutters.

"In here." He holds the door to the bathroom for me. There's only a shower, a toilet, and a hand basin. A bar of soap. No towels. About five squares of toilet paper on the roll. "Hand me your bikini. Too many strings on that one. And leave the door open. Shirt only."

The tension is back, shooting cramps into my shoulders and stomach. "Okay." Burley is playing 'nice,' but not really.

I fiddle with the ties of the bikini under the shirt and manage to take the top off without having to reveal anything. I step out of the bottoms and hand the lot to him, red hot with embarrassment.

"Better get used to it, luv. Be glad he gave you a shirt." He gives me a nod and sits down on the mattress. "Get on with it and make it quick."

My future is so uncertain, there's no way of knowing when I'll be able to shower or use the toilet again, so I make the most of it, conscious that Burley is listening to every sound coming from the bathroom. Once I'm done, I wipe the water from my body and squeeze it out of my hair as much as possible. I'm going to look a picture at this rate with nothing but my fingers to comb through my hair.

When I walk out, the T-shirt wet in patches, Burley is just where I left him, not even a phone to keep him entertained. He gives a reluctant sigh as he stands. "Best put you back in the safe room. You can't get into any mischief there."

I follow him to the door, but when sounds come from the lower floor, Burley freezes. He puts up a hand to stop me as he pulls out his gun. He pads over to the door and peers out. There's more of a commotion now, and he lowers his gun with a shake of his head. "Stay here. Don't fucking move. And whatever you do, don't watch."

# 11

# TASHA

Burley closes the door but doesn't lock it, although I can see the door's lock is on the outside. It's almost like an invitation. If he didn't want me to look, he would have locked me in.

I put my ear to the door and listen. Male voices, one of them that I recognize. Matteo. And his brothers? One or two others that make comments to his commands. I can't hear what they're saying.

My fingers tremble but I touch the doorknob, twisting it slowly. It turns smoothly and soundlessly, so I twist it all the way and give the door a quarter-inch push, waiting for the click. I'm so deliberately slow that the click doesn't come, and I manage to open the door until I can peek outside.

Beyond the glass and steel railing, I can't see anything except the double volume windows and the top of one man's head. I'll need to get closer, so I slowly sink to my haunches and open the door just wide enough to crawl out on my stomach. I try to hide as much of my face as I can behind a steel balustrade, but it won't do much if someone bothers to look up.

Not that they would. I bite down on my lip when I register

the scene in front of me, my pulse all over the place again. Matteo is standing in front of a man who has sunk to his knees, a black plastic bag over his head. Two of his brothers flank him. Burley is down there too, on standby, with two other guys who look like bodyguards. The kneeling man, who is already suffocating, has his hands bound behind his back with cable ties.

Matteo steps up, twists the plastic bag tighter until the man leans over, then plucks it off just before he swoons. The man drops to the floor and bangs his head, but he inhales with a grating rasp that sends a chill down my spine. I try to control my breathing, but I can't, it's too shallow and rushed as tears well up and drop to the hardwood floor.

They're going to kill this man.

"So how much did you enjoy beating up Tatiana?" Matteo demands as Burley steps up and jerks the man back onto his knees. His head sways, but he manages to stay upright. "You broke five of her fucking ribs, her jaw, her nose, her fucking pelvic bone, you fucking—"

The sound of steel-toe boots crashing into ribs echoes through the space and drowns the rest of Matteo's words as one of the bodyguards gets him from one side, while the second gets him from the other. The man folds over onto his face.

Part of me wants to scream for them to stop, run down and force them to have mercy, but more of me wants this guy to pay. Either way, I'm too drained by fear to even move, my throat so tight, even my own breathing seems constricted.

Matteo rolls his shoulders and cracks his neck. He reaches for the man's hair and pulls him up by it, until he is slumped on his knees, blood oozing from his nose and mouth. Matteo doesn't let go of him but holds his head in place. "And then you had the fucking nerve to fist her, until she bled from the broken pelvic bone onto your fucking hand." Matteo jerks the man's head. "Look at me, you motherfucker." The man groans, but blinks through the sweat that runs from his temples and forehead, until he meets Matteo's eyes. "How does it feel to be on the receiving end for a change, hmm?"

At the visual Matteo sketches, my body convulses.

With disgust Matteo lets go of his hair with a shove, and as if Burley just knows what he wants, he tosses Matteo a dish-cloth so he can wipe his hands. "Party's starting," Matteo says as he drops the dishcloth to the floor.

Wait, what? They're not done?

I cower back, hesitant to peek over the rim as the two unknown bodyguards approach the man where he's face down on the floor in a pool of his own blood. They kick him over and tackle his belt and zipper, then drag his jeans and boxers down to his ankles. His flaccid cock looks sickly grey in the dimmed light of the room. I'm waiting for someone to step forward with a knife and sever it, but instead they twist him around and shove him up so that he is kneeling in the classic child pose.

The men look at each other and Matteo nods to one of his brothers, who picks up a duffle bag. He unzips it and pulls out a giant dildo with a pointed tip.

Oh my God.

"Lube?" the brother asks, but as the circle of men chuckles, it's clear he's joking.

"Get going. I've got shit to deal with tomorrow," Matteo says.

Another round of smirks, but Matteo doesn't join in. The brother nods towards the bodyguards and one steps forward and places his boot on the guy's neck and presses down so hard, I swear I hear bones crunching.

The other goon comes forward and the brother hands him the dildo, which he places right at the man's anus.

"Stephano," Matteo says, and it's a command as if there ever was one. "For Tatiana."

I'm holding my breath as the brother, who must be Stephano, steps forward. He kicks the back end of the dildo with such precision that an earsplitting shriek rings through the space. The man's body resists. Of course it does. I cover my ears, but it doesn't help as Stephano kicks while the booted foot holds the man in place, until the dildo is well lodged up his ass.

Stephano steps back and wipes at his mouth with the back of his hand.

The bodyguard lifts his foot off the man's neck, but he doesn't move, whimpers spluttering the blood that seeps from his mouth.

"I ask you again, how does it feel to be on the receiving end of such unwanted attention?" Matteo says.

A horrifying wheeze follows as the man shudders, and then silence echoes through the room. The man has stopped moaning, and all I hear is ragged breath. There's a subtle shift in the group of men downstairs, but none of them move or say anything. And then I realize they're listening to *my* ragged, tensed-up breathing.

"The girl's watching, Matteo," Burley says, his voice apologetic. "I told her not to—"

"Good. Let her understand what will happen to Peter Armstrong if she doesn't deliver." Matteo doesn't look up or even acknowledge me, but I realize now he knew from the start that I was here, peering through the railing. With that he pulls a gun from inside his jacket and holds it out to Stephano. "Wrap it up."

Stephano takes the gun and aims, but his hand is shaking so much that he hesitates for a very long minute. "No," he says, then lowers the gun.

"For fuck's sake," Matteo grunts as he takes the gun from his brother. In one smooth move, without a pinch of hesitation, he shoots the guy in the back of the head.

The shot whispers through the apartment. Of course. Silencer. My stomach convulses.

"Get him out of here." Matteo holsters the gun. "Party's over."

I've seen some things during my studies. I've dealt with dissections, human excrement, all kinds of flesh, but nothing —*nothing*—prepared me for this. My stomach roils and I can't stop the surge. I vomit *Frutti di Mare* and watch in horror as it drips over the edge and splashes to the ground floor.

# 12

# MATTEO

I knew Natasha was up there. I spotted her reflection in the window without even having to look her way. The apartment was designed by a very clever architect named Bryce Sutherland, who has, as it happens, a bit of a background himself. He understood my needs. Mirrors where nobody thought there were any. Echoes where none should be. Trapdoors when you'd least expect them.

He didn't put a gutter for vomit by the railing though, and I should make a recommendation to him next time we meet.

Ignorant, reckless woman. By looking on where she should have turned a blind eye, she just twisted herself tighter in the spider's web. At this rate, she isn't getting out of it alive.

I look up to where she's sitting on her knees, still convulsing, but dry heaving. And she got some of it on my T-shirt.

I knew she was going to be trouble but not like this. "Get her to clean up this mess," I say to Burley, as I indicate to the other bodyguards to bag the corpse and take it into the garage. "And call the butcher. I need this guy processed and off the premises before I leave for Sicily."

"Got it, boss," Burley says and I turn my back on the scene, having no interest in what they do next. I squeeze Stephano's shoulder and indicate that he and Luca should follow me.

I close my office door once we're inside and go behind my desk to the cupboard where I have some bourbon. I pour three glasses.

"You okay?" I hand Stephano his drink. His fingers are still trembling, but it's in rage. He sinks into a leather wingback with a shrug and tosses the bourbon back in one swig without a flinch.

Inwardly I sigh. The problem with this type of vendetta is that it doesn't balance the scales. Stephano found Tatiana ten hours after the assault, bleeding away in a back alley where Martinez left her to die. She might have been a prostitute who went willingly with Martinez, but Tatiana is more to Stephano than he'll ever give away. He's been holding himself accountable ever since, hating the fact that he couldn't protect her, that he wasn't there to stop any of it happening. Worst of all, since Tatiana has been released from the hospital, she's refused to see him.

Scalera boys don't get to love—a lesson my brother is learning the hard way.

"He wasn't worth the fucking bullet, Matteo," Stephano hisses. "I wanted him to die like he left Tatiana for dead."

"And you did. The bullet wasn't for him, dickhead. Martinez was already dead."

Luca tosses a hand in the air. "How the hell did you know that?"

"He stopped breathing by the time the dildo breached his stomach." I take a sip of my drink, feeling no remorse. "The bullet was for Natasha Armstrong. To make her understand that we're not fucking around." *Look and learn, kitten.*

"The plan was to auction her off and then drop her off at home after the fact?" Stephano says, seeming more in control of himself. "She wasn't supposed to see any of this."

No, she wasn't. A mistake on my part. One I'm going to have to navigate.

"Why wasn't she locked up in the safe room?" Luca prods as I swirl the golden liquid, not ready to look my brothers in the eyes. "Don't turn soft on the girl, Matteo."

Alex, the way I remember him now after years of battling the image of him dying in my arms, flits into my mind's eye. Alex smiling. Alex laughing. Alex, fifteen and full of crazy as he jumps off a cliff in Portofino. "Nobody's going soft. Martinez just sucked at his timing."

"It's done now." Luca puts his glass down. "We're going to have to deal."

"Yes. Next time I hand you a gun to shoot a fucker, do as I say, not as you think." The Don is dying, and my brothers are going to have to step up. The last thing I need is for any of them to go soft on me, or on a job I expect them to do. "Now, if you can both fuck off, I can go deal with the situation."

Natasha witnessing a murder is the part of the situation I *don't* need to deal with now. For that I have time. I first need to pay attention to a T-shirt stained with vomit, and a perfect, beautiful, sexy body underneath.

A body I've been burning to get another viewing of, just to remind myself that it's off limits.

## 13

# TASHA

Burley beckons me downstairs, and my knees wobble all the way, but I heard Matteo's command. *Get her to clean up this mess.* This feels like digging my own grave. Not only have I witnessed a mob murder, but I bet wiping blood and brains off the floor officially makes me an accomplice.

Burley keeps handing me paper towels to wipe the floor with, and now has an array of chemicals on hand to eliminate any traces on Matteo's fine porcelain tile. Note: tile, singular. At least twelve by twelve feet. It must have cost a fortune. Given that the rest of the apartment has hardwood floors, I can't help the nasty suspicion that this tiled part is intentional. The town square for executions.

Where I only had my vomit on my T-shirt before, I now have droplets of blood splattered where I was careless, caking onto my skin. Thank God I've been sick already. Going at this without gloves is creeping me out. I toss another triple fold of paper towel into the brown yard waste bag Burley pulled out of a kitchen drawer, spray with hydrogen peroxide, wipe, repeat. The whole clean-up proceeds with alarming smoothness, and the one thing that keeps running on repeat in my mind is that this is what will happen to Dad if *I don't deliver*.

I don't even know *what* I'm supposed to deliver. Matteo is going to Sicily. Beyond that...

All I know is I'm not going to stand by and watch my own death unfold. I'm not going to be a willing participant to their games. Regardless of what Dad had done, of what his hand was in any of this—if he even had a hand—I have a mind and will of my own. I will fight for my life in every way possible.

Bottom line: I need to kill Matteo before he kills me.

The notion has been brewing in the underbelly of my mind, there where darkness stirs and curls up like smoke to where it manifests in my inner voice. I don't know when or how, but this man will be dead before he can even put a foot on a plane to Sicily.

My knees hurt from being on all fours on the hard tile, but I'm almost done. The apartment is unnaturally quiet, soundproof to the extent that the only thing I hear is Burley's breathing and the crackle of the paper bag he's holding. When the office door opens, my hands tremble in fear. I'm going to have to get a grip. I can't afford to fold like Matteo's brother when he had to pull the trigger. I've always prided myself on my 'surgeon's hands', never showing the slightest quiver, but now I'm like a conveyer belt in sorting mode.

I don't look up but watch from underneath my lashes as Matteo and his brothers walk past, not a single word between them. I wait for the final goodbye, but it never comes. There's only the echo of the door closing and then Matteo's footsteps as he doesn't sneak up on me but comes to stand with his black Oxford shoes in front of me where I'm still bent over, looking at my reflection in the tile's freshly polished surface.

"Enjoy the fire pit," Matteo says.

"Will do. Sorry about the witness, I—" Burley starts.

"Don't mention it again. If someone doesn't want to listen, someone gets to deal with the consequences."

*Whatever you do, don't watch.*

Did he hear Burley's command to me? Probably.

Oh God. I'm dead.

I don't move, don't dare to look up as Burley takes his bucket of chemicals, paper bag and towels and walks away. Neither of us moves and the silence between us stretches, but I can feel his eyes on me. I eventually lean back and look up at him.

I watch in fascination as he slowly licks his thumb and reaches for my cheek to wipe at something. Vomit or blood, who cares. His touch is so gentle, it's a caress, hypnotizing in deceptive tenderness.

"See, kitten, this is where things get messy," he says. "And as you've noticed, I don't like messy things."

"No, you don't." I close my eyes against his gentle assault because he hasn't pulled away. Instead, he's cupping my cheek, running his fingers along my temple to gather my uncombed strands behind my ear.

"This is the second time I've had to warn you," he says, his fingers lifting away only to gather more hair from my face. "Already you're making me break *Il Consiglio's* rules. There'll be no third time."

I nod, and he lets go. I swallow at the bile still in my throat, feeling sick again. A man with this much control is a demon, the devil himself, and who am I to even think I can better him? I swipe at my face, not at tears, but to erase the lingering yearning his touch has left behind. A yearning that reaches way beyond the fingerprints still tingling on my skin.

"Let's clean you up." Matteo holds his hand out to me.

And as if I'm making a pact with the devil, I take it.

# 14

# TASHA

Matteo lets go of my hand as soon as I'm standing but moves his hand to the small of my back. With a nudge he guides me to the stairs.

The silence is too eerie and unbearable in the maelstrom of questions in my mind. There's only one thing I really want to know right now, and I gather my courage. "If you don't mind me asking," I start as we scale the stairs, not wanting to rock the boat more than I already have, "what happened to Tatiana? Where is she now?" Matteo listed her assault injuries in bullet points, and they made me want to cry. Just one of those is horrible, but that combination? She must have been in the hospital for weeks.

"Why do you ask?"

"I… I want to somehow justify the *punishment* you handed out earlier." Which he did without a flinch.

Matteo stops at his bedroom door, which is on the opposite end of the corridor from the one I got to shower in earlier. "Wondering how I sleep at night, hmm?"

I shrug, but hold his gaze as he studies me, because yes,

handing out that level of brutality would give me nightmares. Not that Matteo got his hands dirty and shooting a gun doesn't count. No, he was the puppet master.

"I sleep just fine, kitten."

He opens his bedroom door and ushers me in. Frustration bubbles up in me. He hasn't answered my freaking question. "Tell me, please."

"Natasha—"

I shudder. It's the first time he's said my name and I can't. "Just Tasha, please. Everybody calls me that because the way people say my name always reminds me of the nanny Dad got me when Mom died and he couldn't cope. She drove me to school and back always asking *How was your day, Natasha?* All fake sympathy and total disinterest. *My Mom and brother just died, how do you think it was?* Those were the days before I got a bodyguard."

At this he blinks. "You talk too much. Should have fucking gagged you and kept you locked up."

"I talk because I'm freaked out and nervous and *kidnapped*. I just witnessed a brutal murder, you jerk. Then I had to clean it up! And I want to know what happened to Tatiana because *no woman deserves that*." And to be honest my pulse is all over the place with shock and with fear and with *him*.

Matteo grunts a sigh. "Fuck me. At least we agree on one thing." He takes me by the arm and marches me into his bathroom, which is overly masculine in black marble. My eyes are drawn to the beautiful black bath that stands center stage. There's space for two in that one. "Now strip and get in the shower."

"No!" I jerk away and he's forced to let go of my arm. I'm not sure what is going on in my head or why I'm defying him. It's as if I have a death wish or something and want to get it over and done with. But I know that deep down I want to push him to see how far he'll go with me. I've done everything he wanted me to do, but this is where I draw the line.

"What did you say?"

"I said *no*."

"Do you want me to help you?" His tone tells me it won't end well for me.

"*No*, I want you to leave so I can shower in private."

At this he drops his head back and laughs. It transforms his face. Laughter lines cup his mouth, and I can't help but stare at his perfect teeth. His dark eyes spark as he folds his arms over the wide expanse of his chest and leans back against the double vanity and just stares at me. "You, kitten, are playing with fucking fire," he says as the laughter dies from his eyes, his mouth still pulled into a cynical smirk.

"I figure I'm dead if I do, and I'm dead if I don't."

Matteo doesn't move from where he's settled against the vanity, arms crossed, in a perfectly cut dark wool suit and black shirt that doesn't show blood at first glance. I'm standing in front of him, chest heaving, freckled with all kinds of gunk, at an impasse. And he says nothing.

Oh God. I'm so dead.

I watch as the shadows on his face somehow darken and when he leans into me, his eyes burning into mine, I have the urge to run and hide. My question took him to a place I don't want to go.

"Understand this, kitten." A chill shoots down my back at the tone of his voice. "We work on a need-to-know basis at *Il Consiglio*. You don't need to know that Tatiana wasn't that guy's first, or his last. You don't need to know that the doctors did what they could for her, but that she has permanent damage that makes it hard for her to walk. You don't need to know that she's addicted to painkillers and meth and will most likely overdose at some point." Matteo uncrosses his arms and reaches for a strand of my hair. "What you do need to know is that he didn't only break her body, he broke her spirit too. And for that, he got fucked up the ass. If he didn't die today, we would have gone at him again tomorrow until he did."

I nod, sensing the residue of his anger at Tatiana's fate vibrating in his touch. I don't want to show any weakness in front of this man, but the day has been too much. I want to weep for Tatiana but force down my frayed emotions. Still, tears which have been sitting shallow for hours push up and I blink. I'm overly conscious of his fingertips playing with my hair, the gentleness of his touch, always incongruous with everything he says and does. "I'm sorry."

"Yeah. Me too." He gathers my hair away from my neck and his gaze drops to where he left a hickey earlier. He brushes his thumb over my cheek, catching a stray tear, and runs it down to the bruise on my neck. "Now be a good girl and strip so you can shower. It's late."

I bite my lip to compose myself, his incessant request jerking me back to the present. "I won't. I'm naked underneath."

"You are?" Clearly this is news to him. "What happened to your bikini?"

"Burley confiscated it earlier. It has too many strings, apparently."

Matteo nods. "Yup. He's a pro." He pushes off the vanity. "Don't be shy. Most college girls nowadays have an OnlyFans going on the side to pay for tuition."

"I'm not *most college girls.*"

"True. Living the high life with Daddy owing *Il Consiglio* two million dollars, if you wondered how you got here."

That same rage that swept up from out of nowhere when I tossed his phone across the living room hits me. "I have no life at all," I hiss, my voice strained. "And now I'm as good as dead, thanks to you."

"Well," he says, unfazed, "let's do something about that." He reaches for the hem of my shirt, but I fight his hands off, grossed out by the texture and smell of dried vomit and the blood caking the soft fabric that grates my inner arms. I reek.

"Don't. Please."

"You've got nothing I haven't seen before, kitten," he says, hands on his hips, feigning patience.

*He's toying with me.*

I drop my gaze, too embarrassed with no clue where to look. Earlier all five brothers were there and stared at me when I crawled out of that safe room in my bikini, but somehow it was different. I was in fight-or-flight mode and couldn't think beyond the next second's survival. Somehow I'm still alive and this is much more intimate, one on one, just us.

"I've never been naked in front of... of anybody before." Never mind a man. A man like *him*. Who looks like he eats pussy for breakfast. And right now there's a glistening of moisture between my legs that will give away way too much.

"Fuck me. I think I just lost ten thousand dollars," he grunts as he rakes his hands through his hair. "Why not?"

I have no clue what he's talking about and at the rate he throws dollar amounts around, who cares? "Because I hate my body." The words come out of nowhere and they hit me hard. The truth of it all surfaces, as if I'm on a precipice of life and death. Which this is. My mom's last words to me still haunt me. *You're fat. You can't be a senator's daughter and walk around like that. I'm taking you to a dietician tomorrow. We'll talk about it tonight.*

I take a step back. *Something* got him pissed. Fury etches his face and then he moves—fast. His hands grip the hem of the T-shirt and he rips it up, forcing my arms to lift, tearing it over my head, but then he pulls the T-shirt down, basically trapping me with it before my arms can slip free. He spins me around, my arms pinned at my sides as he fists and twists the material in one hand at the center of my back.

The cat is tired of playing with the mouse.

I'm out of breath at the sudden swift and precise attack, as if he's done this move a million times. I'm facing the mirror now, his body trapping mine against the vanity, the cold marble pushing into my hips. I'm conscious of the length of his legs as they hug mine, the warmth of his body as his gaze meets mine in the mirror.

"Don't say those words ever again," he growls. "Do you understand?"

I can't respond. Not while his free hand gathers my hair where strands spill over my chest, uncovering my breasts one by one as he looks on. Heat spreads over my face at my nipples' response, but I can't look away. He leans in and blows a cold stream of air that flows over my skin, down to where my hardened nipple puckers even more as the air ghosts over it. I sag against his chest, too weak to protest, too aroused to resist.

Matteo's breathing becomes ragged as his knuckles slide down my shoulder, over my arm to my ribcage, and then he trails his fingertips over my stomach, higher, so that he strokes the underside of my breasts. As he brushes his thumb over my hardened nipple, I gasp, wanting to reach out for him, but I'm trapped.

"You are pure perfection," he whispers, his lips warm against the shell of my ear. "Just look at you."

All I can do is moan. I've become aware of his erection where it's pressed against my butt, hard and long, and all I want to do is rub against it. Encourage it. Beg for more.

"Open your eyes, kitten," he whispers, and as if drugged I struggle to lift my lids, blinking at him in the mirror. "We're going to work on this. You're fucking perfection," he murmurs. "Do you understand?" When I say nothing, he brushes his lips along my temple. "Answer me, kitten. Do you understand?"

"Yes." My voice is small, my heart in my throat.

He lets go of the T-shirt and the tension in the fabric gives way as my legs almost do too. He holds me up though, his legs pressing me against the vanity for two seconds, allowing me to find my balance.

"Now, for the last fucking time, strip and get into the shower."

# 15

# MATTEO

She's merch, you fucking idiot. Get it into your head.

*Il Consiglio* started with staple operations of drugs and gambling to feed every addiction. To get involved with any of our merch would have been a death sentence. We might have moved on to more 'above-board' operations, but some rules still stand. Scaleras don't touch the merch. So not only is Natasha Armstrong nothing more than weakness personified, but she can also ruin the whole operation by messing with my head.

That perfect body of hers is going on auction and I have no business touching her, teasing her, watching her reaction in the mirror as if I'm starving.

I rip open my closet, breathing shallowly as I listen to the shower running in the adjacent bathroom. My hands burn to run down her body, to soap her down, to trace the line of her slit and rub and suck that sweet clit until she succumbs. I'm so hard, it's painful. It's been too fucking long.

I shrug my jacket off and loosen my belt and zipper. My hand fists my cock as I brace with the other against the wall, fighting the temptation to walk back into the bathroom and jerk off in front of her. The visual is there though, her reaction to me still fresh in my mind. My fingertips still echo with the feel of her soft skin and the contrast of that perfect hardened nipple I wanted to suck into my mouth. It takes only a few hard strokes for me to crash-land into a release that isn't even satisfying. All this is going to do is to keep the beast in check.

I cover up and reach for the T-shirt she wore where I tossed it into the corner for Rosalia to deal with. I find a clean spot and wipe up the cum that's running down the wall. My ears prick. She's closed the faucet. Time to work on Miss Armstrong's self-confidence. The idea of other men's gazes on her grinds against me, but the notion only makes me want to get my fill while I can. It's not as if I'll be touching her. What happened earlier can't and won't happen again.

My resolve is firm now that my dick is not, and I pad over to the bathroom and lean against the door jamb. She's reaching for a towel, water glistening on her skin, which is rosy from her hot shower. Her wet hair clings to her back where's she's rinsed it down, opening her up completely for inspection.

Every inch of her is pure feminine beauty, from the weight of her breasts that I can still feel against my fingertips, to the length of her legs and the sweet little slit that leads to heaven. How can she not love what she sees in the mirror when she looks at herself? Women are sometimes so fucked in the head.

The bathroom is thick with steam scented with my male products, all herbal and fresh alpine shit or something. Whatever they call it, it doesn't suit her. She's strawberries and cream. The kind I want to lick off her body.

When she becomes aware of me, her movement stalls where she's dragging the towel down the heated railing. Then she tugs it free and wraps it around her breasts with such speed, I have to suppress a smile.

"You'll see a doctor tomorrow," I say as she steps out of the shower.

"I will? Why? I don't need a doctor." She rolls her eyes. Actually freaking rolls her eyes at me. "I mean, I'm becoming a doctor and I know I don't need one... yet."

I should fucking gag her, but her ramblings are somewhat entertaining. I walk over to the vanity and pull open a drawer where I keep spare toothbrushes. I put one on the countertop for her.

"How long am I staying for?"

"Until the job's done."

"What does that mean?"

"Shut up and wrap it up, kitten."

She reaches for the toothbrush and rips it from its wrapping. This one has a temper that I might find a bit too amusing. "And what about clothes? Right now—"

I take the toothbrush from her, squirt some toothpaste on and push it into her gaping mouth. There. That makes her shut up. "Brush."

She does so, all the while glaring at me until she's forced to spit.

Fuck. Even that I find arousing.

"Clothes we'll sort out once we've established your base worth."

"My base worth?"

I ignore her question. If she hasn't figured it out yet, I can't help her. For a moment I toy with the idea of locking her back in the safe room, but then decide against it. The other room is on the same level, and if the doc comes first thing, it would be less involved to just have her there already.

"This way." I nudge her towards the door, take hold of the luxury throw at the foot of my bed in passing and guide her to the room at the end of the corridor. "In you go."

As she walks past, I tug down the towel and toss the fake fur throw towards the empty bed. "Sweet nightmares, kitten. We'll touch base in the morning."

I close the door and lock it. The last glimpse I get of her is how my kitten flexes her claws, ready to pounce, but then scrambles to cover her body. She's an innocent little kitten, finally finding her claws. That doesn't bother me. Natasha Armstrong might be fighting fit, but she'll never be a match for me or any of my men, trained as we are.

What plays in my mind's eye as I pad back to my own room is that naked body of hers and how she'll react to the feel of the faux fur against her skin. And whether she is going to seek her own release now that she thinks nobody is watching her.

I hammer back hard at the idiocy of wanting to look on, so I refrain from fetching my phone and logging into that room's security camera footage.

# 16

# TASHA

I'm ripped from restless sleep by the door that's swept open, harsh light flowing in. I jolt upright, clutching the throw to my breasts. "Don't! Please!" I blink into the sharp light that's blinding me, terrified to look beyond it. Several figures are filing into the room. Burley, who is holding the light, an Asian woman, and my host, Matteo. I cower back, my heart in my throat, not wanting to know what's going to happen next.

What time is it even? I don't know. Not with the black-out shutters still down. I tried to open them last night, but they seemed to be locked in place. I rub at my eyes with a groan. I've hardly slept. I thought I'd pass right out, but once I was alone my brain wanted to dissect everything that's happened. Visions of the killing scene haunted me, and then there was Matteo. His touch. His plans for me. The doctor who is coming to take blood samples so that they can match me with desperate people who need black market organs.

I swallow as Matteo comes to stand right beside me. I glance up at him, nervous, and at the same time wanting to fly at him and scratch. He is dressed impeccably in his usual suit, looking well rested. Asshole. Hot freaking prick.

My gaze jumps to Burley. He looks as if he slept like a baby last night. His gaze is flighty, not looking me in the eye, as if we didn't spend a good half hour bonding while cleaning brains and blood off that tile last night.

"Open the shutter," the woman says, and as Burley presses the button and natural light floods in, I curse. I was either too dumb or too rattled to get it right last night. Or maybe they unlocked the jail while I was sleeping. It must be at least eight o'clock already.

She's an older woman, grey at her temples where her hair is sternly swept back, and slightly stooping with age. She has a doctor's traveling case with her which she puts on the edge of the bed. Then she takes the light from Burley, pulls at something, and a telescopic stand folds out with little wheels at the end of it.

Ah hell. I know those. They have them standard everywhere where doctors get to dig. I drop back against the cold wall, a giant knot twisting in my gut. *That type of auction.* I should have known. I want to bury my face in a pillow at having been so naive, but I don't have one.

"This will take a few minutes," the doctor says, looking at Burley and then in Matteo's direction.

Burley nods and walks out of the room, but Matteo stays put.

"I'll watch," he says, and I curl up inside and die.

The doctor shakes her head with a grunt as she opens her case and pulls out sterile gloves. For the first time she looks me in the eye. "Lie back, legs open."

When I don't move, her cold hand reaches under the throw, touching my foot. I jerk away, only to feel Matteo's warm grip settling on my shoulder.

"You do this with the throw or without. With Burley restraining you, or not. Choose."

I close my eyes at his words, scoot down to lie on my back,

and obediently open my legs. A hot red flush is sweeping over me, and I cup my face with my hands to hide. At least they're not auctioning off my organs. Not yet in any event. This comes first.

Every time I've attended a patient's physical exam, whether this intimate or not, flashes in my mind's eyes. How freaking horrible. This one is probably the worst of them all, and I try to force my brain into medical mode to stop tears from seeping from my eyes. I won't be weak in front of *him.*

The throw shifts and cold air sweeps up my legs and higher, to my sex, all exposed to that stark light. I hear the doctor pulling on her gloves, but I feel Matteo's eyes on me, just like I did that first time he watched me from the veranda at our house. That feels like years ago now.

There're touches to my legs, urging me to open even wider, and I comply, forcing myself to relax to avoid any pain. There follows the confident approach of the doctor's fingers as she probes, the sound of her shifting as she looks properly.

"You know this isn't accurate, right?" she says as her fingers slide from my entrance. "Nothing is hundred percent, but from what I can gather, I'd say she's untouched. I'll write up the necessary letter."

A warm hand rests on my forehead, fingers caressing my hair. His callused palm, scented with the fresh-scented soaps in his shower, only hitches up my already frantic pulse. He is clean and I feel so dirty right now.

"Good girl," he murmurs as he drops something next to my head. A T-shirt. One that smells of him. His hand moves away, and I don't look. Not when I know he's covering my legs again. Not when the doctor pulls off her gloves and closes her case. Not when footsteps fall and the bedroom door locks again.

I turn on my side and curl into a ball, finally letting go of the bottleneck of tears.

# 17

# MATTEO

I wait at the railing where Tasha tried to hide last night as Burley sees the doctor off. Why I'm starting to think of her as Tasha, I don't know. Woke up this morning and my first thought was of Tasha and not 'Natasha Armstrong, daughter of the crooked politician who got my brother killed.' And now, after being in that room while—

Burley comes in from the foyer, and I descend the stairs and meet him in the kitchen. "Stan's here?"

"He's waiting for you."

"Her travel documents?"

"They'll be ready by Thursday."

Good. "I'm going to the Don's. Seems I owe you some money."

"Yeah?" Burley nods but he doesn't seem thrilled.

Confirming Tasha's virginity just set our plan in motion. There's no stopping now. "Get Rosalia's contact to bring her some clothes. Pretty things. Underwear. Evening dresses. Ask Rosalia what she'll need and make it happen. Put it on the company card."

"Yes, boss."

I sense his mood. It's foul, but so is mine. Trust the Don to fuck with my life by asking me to tie up his shitty loose ends. No pussy should be any man's loose-end solution. "And feed her. Can't let her lose any weight. She'll be too skinny for most men's liking."

"Yes, boss."

Fuck. When my most trusted bodyguard and friend starts *yes-boss*ing me, I'm two ticks away from blowing a fuse. None of this is negotiable, so I walk away and take the private elevator that has a couple of stops, some of them only accessible with a combination of high-tech security checks. There are perks to owning a building. When I walk into the garage, Stan has already pulled up the SUV and opens the back door for me.

As we drive through Boston and out to where the properties become larger, more exclusive and more like compounds, I go through the list on my phone. My mind is preoccupied by her, and before going into this meeting I need to make sure everything for Sicily is set up as I've discussed with my brothers. This trip isn't exactly going to be a walk in the park. Things could go phenomenally wrong. Once the Sicilian knows I've touched ground, I'll have to move quickly to get the Don's first job done.

*The Don.*

The exact moment I started referring to my father as *the Don*, and no longer as my dad, often plays out vividly in my mind. It was the last time I dared say no to him. Sometimes the scars on my back even sting, as if the whip connected with my flesh minutes ago. We went hunting, the one and only time he and I went on a dad-and-son trip. He wounded a deer with the exact intention of making it immobile so I could kill it by hand. I couldn't do it... until I did.

At age twelve I learned to never say no to the Don. After that whipping, I even ate the raw liver he knifed out for me, still steaming from the musky carcass. Warm, raw and iron-rich blood still tingles on my tongue, but over the years, those memories have become mixed with other tastes and smells.

I never defied him again. Not because I didn't want to, but if I didn't live up to his demands, my brothers would have to step in. I'm the first in the line of fire, and to my death I will protect them from him.

When I walk into the Don's office an hour later, Luca, Stephano, Benedict, and Dominic are already there, arguing about some red card handed to a player in a recent NFL game. The situation almost seems normal, as if we're a normal family, and when Bruno farts as I walk past him, I smirk.

"Bruno! Bruno, Bruno," the Don says, raising his hands with each repetition in exasperation. "Don't gas us out of the room, boy." He waves at the empty wingback that's been kept open for me and picks up a can of air freshener and sprays it liberally. "There, breathe easy."

It's quiet for a minute as I try *not* to breathe and take in my father's face. It's there, all right, the grey color of encroaching death on his skin. He doesn't stand so I don't see if he's lost weight or how weak he's become since our last face-to-face meeting.

"Let's hear your plan, Matteo," the Don says as he leans on the table and laces his fingers together.

"The Sicilian," I start, wanting to avoid talking about Tasha.

"Ah, Emilio Randazzo." The Don sneers with pleasure, finally uttering the dickhead's name. "The time has come."

I exhale slowly, disliking the interruption. "Plans are in place. I've scheduled a meeting with him which his agent confirmed, although fuck knows why he'd want to see me."

"He'll want to see you, trust me," the Don says.

Okay, whatever. "Dominic and I have a team on the ground that knows his location, so I plan to go in guns blazing." What can I say? Standard Mafia plan of action since day one.

The Don grunts. "Maybe take a slower approach. He's

meeting you as an equal. As my representative. Do to him as he would do to me."

Meaning torture the fucker. "Noted."

"What's your security like?" the Don asks, as if a request to torture a man to death is par for the course.

"Dominic is putting things in place," I say. "The mole will let us in and out and provide me with weapons once I'm in the compound."

"And my team's already on the ground, scouting," Dominic says. "And we've secured our premises and staff."

"I'm going in under the guise of meeting a realtor to sell the farmhouse. That's the word we'll be spreading."

"Good." The Don nods. "Your exit plans?"

"Getting them off our scent by traveling to Croatia, then taking the jet to Cannes from there."

The Don taps with his forefingers against his lips. "You might get stranded. Cornered. Don Trapani is an old friend of mine. From my school days. He's always told me to come on vacation and use his yacht. It's available to you and might be less conspicuous."

I shift in my chair. As inconspicuous as I'd like to be, using a stranger's yacht isn't exactly top tier safety. "I'll see."

"Understand, Matteo, you can trust Don Trapani. He also wants Randazzo dead."

Fuck. I just want it done.

"What about the girl?" the Don asks. "I hear she's at your place."

Whoever has spoken out of line is getting a bullet in the head. I glance around the room, to see who my dad's informant was, but I'm met with blank but equally shocked faces. Who the fuck is the mole in my house?

"Ah, Matteo. Relax... relax. Peter Armstrong phoned me last night. That's how I know."

I unclench my fists. "Did he? Before or after dinner?"

"What do I care? What are your plans for her?"

A weighty silence hangs in the room before I finally say, "The doc was there this morning. She's untouched, so Luca and Stephano will run her auction. You can go live on your auction site." I glance at my brothers who nod, but don't say anything.

"With our high-profile clientele, we should have bids coming in quickly," Luca says. "One of us will meet with Matteo in Cannes for the exchange. We have regulars that fly in, and Cannes is central. We'll make it easy."

"Excellent," the Don huffs. "To think Armstrong begged for me to have mercy. Mercy for his little girl. From me, who almost lost two sons thanks to him." The Don leans back and laughs, but it breaks into an uncontrollable cough and blood-stained spittle on the napkin he reaches for.

There's an anxious knock on the door which we all ignore. Probably the full-time nurse who is looking after him now. I hope for her sake she didn't hear anything more than his coughing fit.

None of us move to help him. When he finally wheezes in a breath, he stands, and in that moment, I'm reminded of everything I've witnessed in the years I've been this man's puppet. He still has it in him. That cruelty that knows no bounds, of which I've become a by-product, functioning like a robot. *Do as I say and do as I do* was the Don's motto I was trained on.

"There will be no mercy," the Don hisses once he's fully recovered from his coughing fit. "Twelve years I've waited. Now bring me proof, Matteo. I have no more patience for Armstrong's bullshit." The Don drops back in his chair and waves us off, chest heaving with exertion. I stand and nod. My brothers follow suit. We've been dismissed. We don't talk as we file out of the office and take the broad corridor to the impressive foyer with its double winding staircase and elaborate flower decoration on the center table.

We don't need to talk. Too much blood has been spilled in

his name, and not for the first time I acknowledge that I hate him. He killed our mother, the only being that ever cared for any of us. He cut the joy out of our lives intentionally to harden us for his service.

Two more things that I must do for him, and then I'm done.

Whatever the third thing is, I don't fucking care.

He can deal with that himself.

## 18

# MATTEO

I go to Dominic's office after the meeting with the Don. I pretend it's to review the security measures he's put in place for Sicily via his connections in Italy. We also need to discuss the oversight of my businesses he'll have while I'm gone, but honestly, it's to cool off after the meeting with the Don. And to avoid going back to my apartment.

Even if she is locked up in her room, I'll be conscious of her being there. What I didn't take into account when I hatched this plan is that Tasha is going to be in my space 24/7.

It's almost eight at night by the time I head back, and as I walk into my apartment, the buzz of female voices dies down. Four pairs of eyes turn to me, and Burley stands from where he's been observing from the kitchen island.

"Thought the ladies would be done by now, boss. It took some time to arrange, and Esta only arrived an hour ago."

My gaze jumps to Tasha, who looks down at her feet, blushing. I left her naked and frazzled this morning with another old T-shirt; now she's in a frilly summer dress that hugs her curves.

Rosalia's contact from the boutique clasps her hands together and looks toward her friend, uncertain. Burley comes to stand close to his wife, picking his side. I glance them over, saying nothing.

The place is a mess. A rail with at least twenty evening dresses stands to one side, and two more with day dresses, trousers and blouses, and one with underwear and silk pajamas make a square of private shopping in the space between the living room and the twelve-seater dining table. Three full-length mirrors complete the setting.

Rosalia steps forward, staring straight at me with a dare in her eyes. She's right. I asked and she delivered.

"Get out," I say. The boutique woman shoots a nervous glance at Burley and then at Rosalia, but Burley understands me perfectly and herds them along, probably to his own place next door to wait for further instruction.

Tasha doesn't move, clinging to the two dresses they were discussing when I came in. I walk past the evening gowns, running my fingers over the expensive fabrics, then make my way to the underwear and silks.

"Found anything you like?" I ask as I pick up a bra and panty set in virginal white.

She hesitates. "Yes?"

I hang the underwear back up and make my way towards the wine bar. Dirty dinner plates are stacked on the kitchen counter in a rush. She's been eating. Good. I reach for a bottle of red and two glasses and walk over to the sectional. I open the wine and pour, feeling her gaze on me.

I sit down with my wine and get comfortable. "Show me."

"Okay. Everything Esta brought is my size, so it's just a matter of picking a few things." Tasha glances around, seeming nervous. "I'm torn between this pink one and the bl—"

"Show me," I say again, and the command sinks in. She goes pale but turns away and hangs one dress up.

"I'll just go to my room to cha—"

"Do it here."

She bites her lip, ready to spew spit at me, which is rather entertaining. Kitten is catching on.

"Fine. After all, there's nothing you haven't seen before," she says as she drops the two dresses onto the sofa and in a smooth move pulls the one she has on over her head and tosses it to the side.

Fuck. She's wearing a lacy underwear set in pale pink, which only accentuates the purity of her unblemished skin. Her nipples harden under my gaze, becoming more pronounced through the bra's thin mesh and lace. I grind my jaw at the thought that she hates her body, but this is the type of thing that gives women confidence if handled right. She's going to need it when we're in Cannes, as she'll be the star of the show.

She pulls the pink dress over her head, struggling a bit because it's fitted, but manages and pulls up the hidden side zip. With a raised eyebrow she swishes her hips and the full skirt sways side to side. "What do you think?"

"Very, very pretty," I say, showing with a finger that she should turn.

"Really?" She complies, stops to look at herself in the mirrors, then completes the turn.

"Yep, you look stunning. It's a keeper. Next."

She smiles. "There are a few in the same cut, different colors though."

"Keep them all."

"I don't need—"

"Want me to gag you so you can stop telling me what you do and don't need?"

She shakes her head and unzips the dress, but I see the smile she tries to hide by looking down. I watch as she wriggles out of the dress, thinking that she'll need more than one of those because it's the type of dress a man will rip, impatient to get to her breasts.

Next she reaches for a pair of trousers, but I raise my hand. "No. Only dresses."

"Why?"

*So I can have my hand up your pussy whenever I want.* "You have gorgeous legs. Show them off."

Tasha groans as she hugs the trousers to her chest, effectively still hiding her body. "Stop messing with me."

I stand, walk over, take the trousers from her, and hang them back on the rail. I give the summer dresses a cursory glance. "We'll keep all of these."

Her eyes widen. "These dresses start at four thousand dollars a pop."

"And?" I ignore the consternation on her face and move over to the evening gowns. "Let's see you in a few of these."

She shakes her head with a sigh but comes to stand next to me, arms crossed. "Pick one then."

There's lots of black, which I ignore. This woman is meant to shine and not blend into the night. "Here." I hand her a red dress with a deep V-neck and a low back that spills into a full-length skirt.

"Okay." She doesn't sound happy. "I'm not sure about the bodice. I'll need tape for..."

"For?"

Tasha heaves an exasperated groan. "You'll see. Look and learn."

I want to chuckle but clamp it down. She steps into the dress, lifts the shoulders into place and then reaches for the back row of buttons. "I need help."

And the bra has got to go. "Here." I step behind her and, in the light, button up the row of tiny buttons that guides the eye to her rounded butt and the two dimples right above. It's a perfect fit, and when I'm done, I trail my fingers over her back to her bra's clasp and undo it for her. She reaches for a strap to pull it down her arm, but I stop her with a warning squeeze on her hip. Our eyes meet in the mirror. "Let me."

I'm toying with her now, playing with fire, but the temptation is too big. I hook a fingertip under her bra strap and ease it down her arm, watching her reaction to this simple touch in the mirror. She's dropped her gaze and goosebumps chase down my fingertip's trail. When I do the other side, she exhales with strain. I shift to reach the front of the bra and tug until it slips from her body, slightly protesting against the dress's fabric that kept it in place.

"Ravishing," I say softly, the moment even more intimate than intended.

Tasha looks up and into the mirror, a blush on her cheeks. "But if I turn even just a bit, a nipple will show," she murmurs. "Maybe Esta brought tape to hold everything together?"

I look down at her breasts, the focal point of the dress's cut, showing off the perfect cleavage any man would want to sink into. The wide plunge of the V-neck hardly stays in place, with the shoulders threatening to slip off. I toss the bra onto the sofa and shrug. "Try on the white silk."

"Matteo."

I'm at the little buttons again and have them loose in no time. I ease the dress off and she almost stumbles out of it as I force it to the side, ignoring her whimpered protest. She's naked in front of the mirror, in nothing but those lacy panties.

There's something heady about being fully clothed in a suit when a beautiful woman is standing so nearly naked in front of you, ready for the taking. Her own need is evident in every signal her body gives. Her eyes begging for more, even if she doesn't know it. Her need manifesting in that little wet spot staining her panties.

If she were any other woman, I'd be fucking her right now on the sofa, on the kitchen counter, all over the apartment, and making her come until she was spent with pleasure. Until she curled up in my arms and slept because she felt safe and loved and cherished.

But she isn't *any other woman*. She's the one woman I plan to ruin, the daughter of my brother's killer, my last revenge. The one woman on the whole planet I can't have.

"Try. On. The. Fucking. White. Silk," I hiss, my own frustrations getting the better of me. She moves, has the dress off the hanger and over her head, her fingers trembling as she hooks the corset in place and then drags the hidden side zip closed.

I'm back in control of my temper and gently gather her thick strands of hair in a makeshift updo. I stare at her in the mirror, at her flushed cheeks and eyes with tears in the shallows; the creamy skin of her neck, stained by my mark; her breasts, fully covered now but her nipples still hard and begging for attention. "See, kitten, you're so beautiful, you don't even need makeup."

Her arms are hanging limp by her sides, as if she's given up. "Where are we going? To Sicily? Is that where you're going to sell me?"

I don't answer. *Il Consiglio* works on a need-to-know basis and although she should know this by now, she chooses to be slow to catch on when it comes to that.

"You're going through with this plan then? To sell me? To be used like Tatiana was used?"

At these words, my anger and frustration flare. I twist her hair tight, and it pulls at her scalp. She flinches with a gasp, hands rearing up to stop me, but I catch her one arm and trap it behind her back with ease. Her head drops to my shoulder to accommodate the tension and to avoid any pain, her free hand clutching mine where I have fisted her hair.

"If you know what's good for you, you'll never mention Tatiana again," I say close to her ear, watching her struggle to avoid the pain of a locked arm.

"You're a monster," she hisses, meeting my gaze head on in the mirror. "And I'm going to kill you."

I want to laugh. Kill me? Let her try. Let her bring out her claws. I lower my mouth to her exposed neck and bite into it, careful to leave only a temporary imprint on her skin. I drag my lips up the delicate column, tugging at her earlobe with my teeth, in pleasure that's equally mine and hers. "Oh, kitten, I can't wait. In fact, I'm looking forward to it."

# 19

# TASHA

Matteo eases his hold on me, and I gasp in relief, tears flowing freely now, but I keep them quiet. If I could just stop being so *weak*. The man is ruthless, fast, and so freaking strong he could have dislocated my shoulder with just a bit more pressure. As if he knew the exact limit he could physically push me, he hurt me just enough to make me understand fighting is futile.

I'm shaking by the time he steps away from my body. My useless, treacherous body which can't seem to do anything but react to him, oscillating between fear and arousal, but arousal winning every time. This morning he was there, caressing my hair, telling me I'm a *good girl* for being pure, and it was all I needed to hear. Today I was dunked into a heated hell of thoughts and desires that circled only around *him*. His possessive hold on my head, his calm presence when I needed it, my freaking disgusting need to please him even more once the doctor confirmed my virginity.

As if I kept myself pure for *him*.

I have no idea where any of this is coming from. How he managed to get into my head like this in such a short space of time. Manipulating my thoughts, my body, that all I could think of was him the whole day.

I listen to him move away, the soft huff of the leather as he sits down again, the scrape of the wineglass as he picks it up. I look up into the mirror, watch him watching me.

"Join me," he says, pointing to the glass of red wine on the coffee table.

*I'd rather burn in hell* comes to mind, and I've made a promise that I'll kill him. People like me only murder sober. He didn't confirm anything, but I'm learning that silence is an answer too. Usually a yes. I'm going to Sicily to be sold to some sex trafficking ring they have a stake in. Once I've left American soil, I might as well be dead.

Rather him than me.

"I don't want to spill wine on this dress by accident," I murmur. It's exquisite. The white silk brushing like butterfly wings against my skin despite the weight of the fabric. The cut molds to my body. The way he looked at me tonight left me breathless. I've never felt more feminine, more beautiful, or more like a goddess before. A virginal bride for the slaughter.

"Then take it off." Matteo pulls his gun from the inside holster, hidden by his jacket. As he waits for me to strip, he places it on the coffee table. An invitation.

People like me murder in more than panties alone.

Not that a gun would be my weapon of choice. I've never held a gun in my life, but I don't need one to kill someone. "May I be excused?" I ask, refusing to fall for his bait. "I need the washroom."

He says nothing, and assuming that's his silent yes, I pick up my bra he dropped on the sofa. I reach for the few underwear sets we set aside when Esta arrived, as well as some rather sexy but functional cami and shorts pajama sets Rosalia raved over. I hold them up in a bundle. "May I?"

He takes a lazy sip of wine as he studies me, contemplative.

"Sure." He pulls his phone from his inner pocket and it's as if I've been dismissed.

Since I've been kidnapped, I've had eyes on me the whole time, or I was locked up in the safe room or in that hideous corner closet with no way to escape. Now he lets me have free rein? Too good to be true, but I'm not waiting for him to stop me. I rush up the stairs to the second floor, all the while watching him.

His voice is soft as he speaks into the phone, clearly over his earlier burst of anger. Tatiana is a sore spot for him, which is also in sickening contrast to the plans he has for me.

I feel his gaze on me and stop outside the door to my room to look down, eavesdropping while I can.

"No, everything except the black evening gowns. No trousers or blouses. Everything else stays." There follows a pause. "No problem. Put it on the card. Good night."

Crazy infuriating dead man. He most probably just spent over two hundred thousand dollars on clothes I plan to never wear.

# 20

# TASHA

Once I'm in the privacy of my room, I drop the clothes on the bed and slip out of the dress. I spread it out on the bed and smooth down the fabric. As I zip it up, I feel the inside where it has a built-in corset which guaranteed that perfect fit. My fingers explore the corset bones where they're stitched into the fabric. They are long and sturdy but built in, and it's going to be a job and a half to get them out with no tools. With a small prayer, I beg whoever sewed this dress for forgiveness should I even go there.

Next I turn to the collection of bras on the bed. They are all underwired and there are two corset bras that might give me easier options.

I glance around the room, into the corners for a camera, but I see none. Not that I would. This place is state of the art. Hidden cameras are guaranteed. I'm going to have to do this in the dark, under the throw, and will see if the bras give me what I need before I desecrate the dress.

My plan is outrageous, but it's my one and only plan. One of the bras has adjustable straps that come off for wearing a strapless dress, and I take one and tie up my hair. Thank God for that. I take a quick shower, drip dry and then put on some silky PJs. If I close my eyes and block my thoughts, I can imagine being home for a split second, as if the past few days hadn't happened.

Wishful thinking isn't going to get me anywhere. I slip under the throw and reach for the underwear, finding the weakest spot in the stitching and working it with my teeth until I can pull out the long wire supporting the bra. Most of them are metal, but there are plastic ones as well. When I have a fistful, I start snapping off the dipped tips on the ends. I run my fingertip over each break, looking for sharp edges.

This is so dumb. At most it would give him a paper cut. Far from deadly. Now if I had taken the wineglass, I could have broken off the stem and would have had a real sharp object. I need something that would stab into his neck, right there where you feel someone's pulse through the thin, delicate skin. I'll aim for one of the carotid arteries, depending on his position. I suppress a groan. Even a pencil would be better than this botched knife, and I'll only have one shot.

I can't give up. Who knows when we leave for Sicily. I work the corset bones on the two bras, and these give me hope. The bones are metal, and once snapped, give a nice sharp edge. When I run it along my inner arm, it pierces my skin and a warm trickle of blood drips to the mattress. Bingo.

I gather the bones together in a way that they make a short blade of sorts and tie them together with another bra strap. It's the stuff of cavemen, and I suppress a desperate and rather hysterical giggle. What I would give for a scalpel right now, but this is what I have.

The whole time I've been listening, and no sounds have come from the rest of the apartment. I swear every wall in here has sound-cancellation built in. One thing is for sure though: nobody has locked my door from the outside yet. I would have heard.

Must be an oversight or it could be intentional, but this is my chance. I guess around three hours have passed since I came to my room, and my fingers are raw from working the wires. It must be midnight or even past midnight by now. I slip out from under the covers and place my feet on the floor, careful to make no noise. I have my makeshift weapon tied to my wrist, ready to grab hold of it and stab. One shot at an eye will also do the trick—anything really to disable him for a few seconds so I can either grab his phone and make a beeline for the nearest hiding place to phone 911, or stab at his neck until he weakens enough from blood loss that I can walk out of here by myself.

My hand is on the doorknob; my heart is in my throat. I twist the knob, a millimeter at a time, so slowly that I'd be able to sense the least bit of resistance and could stop should it make a sound. The door latch slides open without a single protest, except for the slightest click I pray nobody heard.

I push the door open and wait.

Nothing.

I stare out into the corridor and the railing from where I watched the execution. The house is hugged in darkness, but some moonlight shines through the floor-to-ceiling windows. I haven't had time to even see how you get outside to the veranda and his rooftop garden. I pad out into the corridor, on high alert. The adrenaline in my veins is making me jittery, and thinking of what I'm about to do doesn't help. I glance down to the lounge where the clothing rails still stand. From here the evening gowns look like corpses, bodies of women sacrificed. *I've got you, girls. I'm taking this one for the team.*

There's no sign of Matteo. My filled wineglass still waits on the coffee table, his glass empty next to mine. The bottle left standing. Negligent. Or another invitation. I can break that and stab him to death without even trying.

One step at a time, I creep down the corridor, sticking close to the wall. The place is eerily quiet, but I don't get the feeling that I'm being watched. It's only about thirty feet from my bedroom door to his, and by the time I get there, I'm artificially calm. His door isn't closed but stands open an inch.

I press my forefinger against the door and its weight resists. So freaking heavy, must be made out of metal or something. Before I push it wider, I recall the layout of his bedroom. I've been in here twice, but both times I wasn't paying attention. His bed stands center stage, with mirrored floor-to-ceiling closets reflecting the light that pours in from the windows.

Without a sound the door pushes open, and I curse the faint ribbon of light that falls into the darkened room. Drapes block any light from the outside. If he were awake, he'd see my silhouette. The body under the covers doesn't move though, his length stretched out on his back, long legs just fitting on the mattress. He's tossed the covers off to his hips, revealing that chest and the striking tattoo I still need to dissect. Maybe I will, for real, cut him up into little dragon scales. I swallow at the notion, nausea twisting in my stomach. I don't get queasy easily and I'm not squeamish, both excellent qualities in a doctor, but this isn't what my training is preparing me for. If I were to cut him up, the urge to stitch him together again would be even bigger.

I take a step forward and pause, listening. His breathing comes even, calm. Peaceful. *Wondering how I sleep at night? I sleep just fine, kitten.*

Asshole.

I palm my makeshift knife with a firm, decisive grip. I take small, painfully quiet steps until I reach the end of the bed. The need to exhale loudly is overwhelming, but I keep my breathing shallow and through my nose. A few more steps, and I'll be at his head. My eyes have adjusted to the dark room, and I can see him perfectly now. His head on the pillow leans slightly to the side, opening his neck for me.

I have one shot at this. Just one.

Two more steps.

Pause.

Two more.

Pause.

And then I'm there, my hand slowly rising so I can put some bodyweight into the stab. I'm shaking now, chills prickling my skin, the reality of what I need to do blinding me like headlights. My hand trembles and it's as if the collection of corset bones rattles in my palm.

"Do it, kitten," he says, deadly calm.

I let out a horrid squeal in surprise, but he doesn't move.

"Never hesitate. It'll cost you your life."

Seconds pass, in which he waits, giving me a chance to do what I came for, but time slips away like sand through my fingers.

And then he has me, hands gripping my arms, jerking me down, tossing me with ease onto the bed, his big hand fisting both my wrists as he pins me down, his leg trapping both of mine with a weight I can never fight.

"I've been waiting for you, kitten," he murmurs. "You took your sweet time."

I'm out of breath, my chest heaving. I want to scream but cold hard metal pushes at my throat right there where I wanted to slice him open and let him bleed out. He saw right through me. There's no way I can kill him, or anybody for that matter.

"Time for a little test, don't you think?" he says as he slides the gun down my neck. "Let's see how well you know your anatomy."

# 21

## TASHA

"But first, let's disarm you." He rests the gun on my chest, the cold metal pressing down on my breastbone, and reaches for my makeshift knife where it's tied around my wrist, his other hand still pinning me down.

"What is this thing?" he asks as he works the bra strap loose that holds the contraption in place. I close my eyes, bracing myself for his ridicule. His chest presses against my side, his body warm where I'm a rush of goosebumps at his delicate touch to my wrists. He is so close, his skin smelling shower fresh from that soap of his, mixed with his own scent I find so intoxicating. And there it is, the unmistakable print of a long, hard, and thick cock pressing into the soft curve of my hip. The mere feel of it makes slick arousal seep to my panties.

How can he even concentrate when he's that hard? How did I even think I'd have it in me to kill this man... Never mind his strength and cunning, every cell in my female body is programmed to procreate with him, not kill him.

"Interesting," he says as he plucks my creation free and lifts it up to study it in the dark. "Innovative. Brave." He tosses it to the side, and it drops with a weak clang against the mirror to the floor. "Let me guess your plans for it." He picks up the gun where he left it and I shudder as his fingertips caress me in the process. He presses it to my neck again, gentle, careful. "You were aiming for the jugular or carotid here," he murmurs as he slides the barrel up and down my neck. "Or were you aiming to go lower?"

The metal glides down my chest, between my breasts, and he prods the gun just underneath my sternum, where a sharp knife could kill a man in seconds.

"No," I manage, wishing I had an off switch so I could block out his voice and what he is doing to my body.

"No? So many options here. Subclavian, cephalic, pulmonary... and then lower..." The gun's muzzle leaves a cold trail where he traces it over my skin, his breath following as he murmurs the words, a deadly game of anatomy if ever there was one. By the time he reaches my navel and circles it at leisure, my breathing comes in strained hitches, because he's heading there, to where my body craves his touch.

When he slides the gun over my hip, over the hillock of my pelvis, my hips roll of their own volition.

"Fuck," he smirks as he answers with a grind of his own, his rigid cock riding my silky shorts with just the thin flat sheet separating us. He stills again, dragging the gun down my groin. I whimper, a weak, futile protest.

"Shhh, kitten, we're still busy with this little lesson you signed up for."

He shifts his leg and with the muzzle makes me lift mine.

"The femoral artery, just here." Pressure, right where I know where to cut the upper thigh to hit the artery. "Deadly," he murmurs. "Handy to know when you have a knife. Part of your plans?"

I breathe out a *no* that's more a moan than anything. The muzzle is mere inches from my pussy. It's the fear, the adrenaline, the intensity of him that has me so aroused, the wave of an orgasm is already building. The metal rides down my inner thigh, and then he pushes it against the fold of my knee. It's a command I don't even register, just comply with. I lift my leg higher, splaying open for him. I'm nothing but a wanting hormonal mess right now and I hate myself for it.

When he runs the muzzle down to my sex, a rush of terror invades me. What if he fucks me with the gun?

"Not my style," he murmurs as if he read my mind, but draws a circle with the muzzle around my pussy, then runs it up and down my slit where I'm wet and so freaking needy I want to push up into the muzzle's touch.

"Matteo," I beg. I need him to stop.

"Like that, don't you?" he murmurs, continuing the slow, delicate strokes, and my pelvis curves and dips into the motion of its own treacherous volition, seeking the release he's promising.

"Answer me, kitten," he says, sterner, but not stopping.

"Yes," I breathe, unable to lie, helpless, with each stroke needing more, despite not wanting to give in to him.

"You're going to come for me like this?"

I don't want this man to have any power over me, least of all over my body and never with such ease. "No."

"No?" His tone says it all as the gun stills, its weight pressing down on my clit with such erotic pause that I need to remind myself to breathe.

"I'm not coming for you at all." I swallow, tense with a building orgasm that's been put on hold.

He laughs, his body shaking where it's still trapping mine. I get the drift. Nobody says *no* to Matteo Scalera. "Challenge accepted, kitten." He secures the gun and tosses it to the far side of the bed. He lets go of my wrists, but at the same time he lifts up, grabs the hem of my delicate silk cami and rips it with his fist.

"Matteo!" I cry out, so drugged by lust that I'm slow to

respond. I struggle, wrestling against his weight. By the time I get a slap in, he is straddling me in a mess of sheets, has my cami torn off my body, and is grabbing my wrists to tie them together with what's left of a thousand-dollar PJ set.

I jerk my wrists down, but I'm trapped, tied to something on the headboard I didn't see. I bite down on my lip as realization sinks in. I've messed up. Where he should have been dead by now, instead he's going to torture me.

Matteo leans to the side and switches on the bedside lamp. "So you can see better, kitten."

"I don't want to see any better, thank you." But I can't help staring at his chest, the dark shadow of the tattoo that graces his pecs, abdomen and arms, the veins that run down his biceps to his forearms, sitting so shallow I could have aimed for one of those.

He could do anything to me now. I'm at his mercy and I'm not sure he has any.

"I should fucking gag you," he says as he runs his knuckles along the edge of my jaw and down my chin, then spreads his fingers and circles them around my neck. There is no pressure, no squeeze, but the option is there. Instead, he caresses the bruise he made on my neck, almost contemplatively, with his thumb. "But you're entertaining. And I want to hear you moan my name, kitten, when you come." He leans closer, shifting and putting divine pressure on my body. He ghosts his lips from my temple down to my mouth, but he only sweeps them over mine as he murmurs, "Because come you will."

# 22

# TASHA

He kisses me then, right there underneath my ear, and continues to tease languid kisses down my neck and across to my other ear, until an involuntary moan escapes my lips.

"You're so soft, so delicate," he whispers as his fingertips caress my cheek, sliding over my lips. He runs both hands down the column of my neck, the gentle touch breathtaking and in such contrast to the rough calluses on his skin, the way he is, the things he does.

His caress travels south, down my chest and between the valley of my breasts, my nipples begging. When he circles the tight buds with his thumbs, I close my eyes and bite down on my lip, my hips bucking against him where he still straddles me. Nobody has ever touched me like this before, and this is an expert, gentle assault, something I'd never have expected from him.

"Calm down, kitten," he murmurs as he shoves away the sheet.

Oh God. He is naked. His erection—*holy shit*, his *erection*—juts into the air, bobbing with its size and weight with every move.

He lifts off me to settle on his side and cups my cheek, making me look at him. "I promised you're safe with me, didn't I?"

"Yes," I whisper, dazed. It's true. He hasn't hurt me once. Even when he held me when he warned me never to speak of Tatiana again, it was if he was holding a bird with delicate bones.

"Then trust me." He stares into my eyes as he gathers a stray strand of hair from my face. "I keep my promises."

I can't fight this. I can't fight my attraction to him. Not when he is like this, caring, gentle, and not the monster who executed a man in his living room. I relax my arms where I've been straining against the rope he's made of my camisole, and as if he senses my complete capitulation, he drops a kiss to my inner arm.

He lifts on his elbow, and I want to reach for him, cup his face, drive my fingers into his thick dark hair, trace the lines of his tattoo and kiss him back, but I'm tied up.

"You don't get to touch me, understand?" he says, the command clear in his voice.

"I can't, even if—" His hand clasps down on my mouth, quieting me.

"Even if you could, you don't, understand?" he says, peering into my eyes.

I nod, confused. He lifts his hand and I bite my lip as he starts to slide his knuckles down my chest, still peering into my eyes, into my soul. I close my eyes, not ready for what I'll reveal, and sink into the high that is Matteo Scalera.

He caresses my skin for such a long time that I'm completely weak with desire when he finally cups a breast and sucks a nipple into his mouth. The sensation is new, warm, a sudden sweet shock that travels right to my sex, making me jerk my hips up, my body seeking friction.

"Soon, kitten," he murmurs as he drops his hand to my

pelvis, resting it on my mound to still my hips. The weight is divine and when he starts to circle his palm with just the right amount of pressure, I know it's a matter of minutes, seconds maybe before I crash into orgasm.

He trails his lips between my breasts, taking the other nipple in his mouth, seeming only invested in *my* pleasure. My pleasure which is slowly building, futile to resist even if I didn't want to come at this man's hand.

Matteo shifts and gets onto his knees, and I startle at the size of him, at how unfazed and confident he is with being naked. But then, his type is allowed to show off. He's ripped, all lean muscle, six pack and the dark dragon tattoo with two spots of shiny scar tissue catching the lamplight. Bullet wounds… as eyes of the dragons. I search his body for more but get distracted by that V that leads my gaze to his shaved focal point.

I want that. I've never craved cock before, not like *this*. I want to touch him, taste him, grip him and watch him as I ride my hand up and down its impressive length.

I flex and release my fingers, fisting my hands in anguish that I can't reach out for him. He is oblivious as he doesn't even look at my face, focused on tracing the line of my shorts before he dips his fingers under the elastic and mutters, "These need to go."

He tugs at them, and I raise my hips so he can slide them down, panties in tow. He balls the fabric up, presses it to his nose and breathes deeply. "No wonder you're driving me fucking insane. How wet are you, kitten?"

The visual of him with the soft lamplight on his body, holding my panties to his nose, is almost too much.

*"Turning the Sahara into the Amazon, sir,"* I want to tease, but wouldn't dare.

His hands on my inner thighs kill any answer as he settles between my legs. My impulse is to close up, but he is spreading me open, and I know I'm not ready for this. Everything has been new tonight, but this... this might be too much. I strain against his hold, wanting to clam up as much as I want to see and feel what he plans to do next.

"Matteo," I protest, but he doesn't care or listen. His hold is firm, his mouth on my skin, pressing kisses to my inner thigh, his nose trailing the sensitive skin between my leg and pussy. When he finally licks along the length of my sex, to the side, off center, I jerk my hands, straining against my bonds, my hips quivering in response.

"What am I going to do with you," he whispers as he smooths his lips over my mound, placing a soft kiss in the center, then teasing the tip of my slit with his tongue. "Are you always wet like this or is this for me?"

I shudder at his words, at the reality that this is all him, but I refuse to give him that satisfaction. I feel him smirk with the heat of his breath as he makes his way down the other side, licking, torturing me by avoiding my clit. I'm digging my fingers into the soft fabric of the cami, working it, struggling to free myself and stop him from doing more.

My body has other plans. My pelvis presses up, seeking more from his lips, his tongue, the rough scratch of his stubble even more arousing against my delicate skin.

His hand slides down my inner thigh and pushes my lips wide open, and then he dips his head to circle his tongue around my entrance. I gasp, suddenly desperate to get away from the intensity of his delicate, deliberate assault. My thighs quiver but he is holding me open, pinning me down, refusing to grant me any reprieve. He groans as he shifts gears and grips my butt, and then laps at me, his tongue gliding over my clit and back. I arch into his mouth, release building up from deep inside of me.

I tug once more and my one hand slips free, then the other.

"Matteo, please." I can't help it. I can't stop myself. I can't think of anything else but to reach for him and rake my fingers into his hair, wanting to connect with him. He sucks my clit and the release I've been denying myself ever since he captured me rips and shatters through me in a thousand shards of pleasure. I cry out his name and he doesn't stop, he keeps at it until I've ridden out the wave, my hips trembling, my legs quivering against his hold with the intensity of my release. Without a doubt there'll be bruises.

My fingers caress his hair, conveying what I can't in words. It's only when he looks up, dark shadows over his face, that I pull away. He grips my hands, keeping them away from his body as he sits up.

"You don't listen, do you? You're a little rebel and it's going to get you hurt or worse." He wipes at his mouth, and my legs finally slump together in exhaustion. "I should fucking spank you for not listening."

# 23

# MATTEO

Fuck.

The temptation to discipline her is only outweighed by the temptation to fuck her. Good and proper. Plunge into her and make her mine.

*Mine.* The one thing she can never be.

She's as good as dead but I haven't figured that out yet, neither do I want to think that far or what that would entail. Not when her sweet juices still cling to my face, or while the orgasm that ripped through her has my cock screaming for my own release. Her chest rises and falls with every breath as she comes down from her orgasm, the glow in her eyes telling me what I already know.

She wants more. She wants my cock. It's obvious in the way she's studying my body, her hands straining against the grip I have them in, eager to reach for me. I glance down at her, at the beautiful glow radiating from her, the fine sheen of sweat on her skin like silver fairy dust.

She is so fucking beautiful, it hurts. The way she reacted to my touch was like a drug, drip-drip-dripping into me with every caress, every stroke, wanting me to go slower, watch her for longer, drag her pleasure out until she couldn't take it anymore. She isn't used to begging, but I'll teach her how... And she will love it.

To have a woman like this—to worship, to love, to pleasure—

Her hands in my hair—

I kill the thought. My type doesn't have women like this. Pure, unblemished, unchartered by a thousand cocks that dug their souls out. My type fucks and leaves.

Best I remind us both of that.

"You were shot, twice," she says, her voice soft. "Your tattoo—"

"Yes," I say, pulling at her wrists, forcing her upright. I've been stabbed too, but those marks are on my back. And whipped. Sliced open by thin leather, the scars now part of my dragon's tail.

"The dragons' eyes are your bullet wounds."

I should have gagged her for real. "Yes."

"Who are they?" she asks when she's finally managed to scramble to her knees, facing me. "Your dragons?"

That question should help my fucking cock to cool off already. Instead, it wants to toy with her belly button. *Wrong hole, asshole.*

"Too many questions, kitten." I jerk her towards me and gather her hands behind her back, relishing the pressure her body gives mine when it traps my cock between us. She struggles back, staring up at me, eyes wide, lips open with the shock of being so easily manipulated and tossed around. She is a light little thing, and I've been doing weights for decades. That she's still caught off guard is kind of funny.

Her breasts are squashed against my pecs, every curve a softer echo to my male body's planes and ridges. For a man with a job to do, she's fucking poison. I need to nip this in the bud. Which means this sweet, rounded ass that my fingers are brushing against won't get a spanking tonight.

I take in her face, her rosy cheeks and full lips I haven't kissed yet. Not only would that be idiotic, but it would also be pure madness, like downing poison straight from the bottle and begging for more.

I need to get this done and get her back in her room, this time locked up, not waiting for her to show her hand, fun as that was.

This is going to be vile, but it's time for a reality check.

"Here's what's going to happen, kitten," I say, ignoring the desire that pulses between us, the need we both still have for each other. "One, you're not going to try to kill me again. You're never to have blood on your hands. Plus, I might not be this nice next time." True. How many potential murders end up in orgasm? None to my knowledge.

She blinks and drops her gaze to my chest for a second, then stares back at me under her lashes.

"Two, I'm the only one who gets to ruin your underwear. No more shredding your bras, understand?"

She sucks at her bottom lip, giving no indication that she understood anything. Fucking tease.

"Three, you don't get to touch me, ever. Understand?" I'll drill a fucking hole in her head with the times I'm going to have to remind her of that. She's not going to listen to me, not with that wanton need in her eyes.

"Why not?" she asks, a full-on staring contest going on now, so frank and... *cheeky*.

Too many rebellious questions. "You don't need to know why. Just follow the rules." She strains against my hold, and I hug her tighter, forcing her to be still.

"Four. Your virginity is up for auction to cover your dad's debts to *Il Consiglio*. Bids are already coming in—"

"Fuck you," she spits out, and it's the second time I've heard her curse. It doesn't suit her at all. "My dad will pay! He's looking for me!"

"No." He isn't. Peter Armstrong is too scared and weak, wanting to save his own pathetic hide. He is offering her up like a sacrificial lamb. "You're going to be bought, paid for, and fucked by someone who isn't going to give a flying fuck about how you like it." The visual makes my stomach churn, but I can't stop now. "The men on our list have been vetted to a point, but there are some real crazy fuckers out there."

Tears well up in her eyes, and I steel myself. The vision of Alex dying in my arms, that panic I can still feel rushing through my veins at being helpless, unable to stop him from dying, helps harden my resolve. I clamp down hard on the tightening in my chest at what I need to say next. She struggles, but I hold her until she tires and stills in my arms. I lower my head so that my lips can rest against her ear, and her breathing comes haltingly, in panicked hitches.

Not long ago I was tugging at that delicious little lobe, treasuring the goosebumps that spread over her skin at my touch. This is going to leave chills of a different kind, and I have to force myself to carry on. "When that time comes, kitten, when he fucks you and you tear and bleed and hurt, you're going to separate your body from your mind. You're going to block off what's happening to you physically, and you are going to think of tonight instead. Understand?" I take a deep breath, inhaling her scent and for the last time treasure this moment of holding her close. "You're going to remember who made you come first, and that's going to be your saving grace."

She sags against my chest and tears drop to my skin, quiet and warm. I gather her wrists in one hand and cup her cheek with the other, forcing her to look at me.

"I hate you. So. Fucking. Much," she whispers as our eyes meet.

"Good. Keep it that way." I brush at her cheek with my

thumb, careful that she doesn't snap an aggressive bite or spit at me, both valid reactions, but the fight seems to have drained from her. "Do you understand, kitten?" I ask again, digging my fingers into her hair and pulling her head back so she's forced to look me in the eye.

"Fuck you," she hisses, trying to rip her head free despite the pain it must cause her.

I don't let go but nod. "Attagirl."

# 24

## TASHA

It's been two days since I've seen Matteo.

After our midnight crash course in anatomy and how to make me come within minutes, he'd marched me to the safe room, where I spent the rest of the night locked up. I fell into a listless sleep, only to be woken by Rosalia in the morning. She didn't speak to me, only handed me a clean T-shirt to wear and indicated I should follow her up the stairs to my other room, which was stripped bare. Only a mattress on the floor remained, with basic toiletries in the bathroom, all my ruined underwear and the beautiful white dress gone.

Ever since then I've been a prisoner, feeling really kidnapped by the mob. I've been drifting through bouts of boredom, sleep, and anxiety attacks that made me hammer on the door. Nothing. It's as if I were abandoned. The only thing that keeps me going is the meals Rosalia brings to me, Burley following in tow, always on standby and watchful. I can see how people go mad when they're locked up in isolation.

A knock on my door makes me look up from where I'm huddled on the mattress, rocking myself. I've become used to that knock, three in quick succession, a pause and then another knock. I still. The tears come and go, born out of frustration and the knowledge that I've been abandoned by my dad—the man whom I did everything for. He has contacts, he has influence, he would know where Matteo lives, or he'll be able to figure it out. No SWAT team has stormed this fortress yet, and all I can think of is that Dad is out of his depth and got mixed up in some real dirty business.

For all I know, Dad is dead.

I've been sitting so long in this same position that my legs cramp when I straighten them. I'm halfway up when the door swings open and Rosalia stands there with a tray, Burley holding the door for her. They are such a contrast too. Burley is basically a giant, where Rosalia is delicate with soft doe eyes and a secretive smile. A smile I haven't seen since we had an hour of stupid girly shopping in this apartment, as if I were a Mafia queen and not a pawn.

"Breakfast," she says softly. "And some clothes." A bag is swinging from her arm. "You're to shower and get dressed."

"Why? Where am I going? Sicily?" The end of the road for me. I've wracked my brain, wondering how they're going to smuggle me out of the country, but then I realized they'll have everything in place to fly me out as if I'm going on vacation.

Rosalia steps into the room and puts the paper plate with peeled boiled eggs and croissants down, then drops the bag onto the mattress. She avoids my gaze as if I'm Medusa.

"Rosalia, please!" I'm getting desperate, reaching for her, but Burley steps closer, his eyes empty as he stares me down.

"Half an hour," he says and his wife scoots past him into the corridor.

The door clicks closed and the lock turns. I know nothing. I expect the worst and have nothing to do but wait for it to happen. Waiting is a killer in itself.

I pick up the bag and empty the contents onto the mattress. I almost cry when I spot a hairbrush, proper shampoo, conditioner, and very expensive body wash tucked in with some gorgeous golden ballet flats, a set of underwear from Esta's, and the pink dress I tried on for Matteo.

*That man.*

He's had me in a total mind funk the past few days. Matteo left me with nothing to do but to relive every moment with him, every touch and every caress, only to now shatter me with the promise of sexual assault to eliminate my *dad's* debts.

I've done nothing to deserve this, but I'm starting to understand I'm part of a much bigger vendetta here. Collateral damage in some old men's feud.

It takes me only minutes to force down the food. Starving myself won't conserve my strength, and I haven't given up yet. Going to Sicily means there'll be road trips, flights, new locations: every one of them an opportunity to run and try to get away from him.

Half an hour later I'm ready, my hair still wet, but for the most part I should look presentable. When the door unlocks and Burley holds it open for me, I walk out and stare over the railing into the open plan living area. Matteo and three of his brothers are sitting at the dining room table, papers spread out before them, having a companionable morning coffee.

Assholes.

Matteo glances up and meets my gaze. If I could spit and know it would splatter on his face, I'd do so.

Burley has me by the elbow, directing me to the stairs. "Just so you know, luv, your dad is being held at gunpoint," he says softly. "If you don't do what Matteo says, he'll be executed."

He doesn't need to add that I'll be next. My knees cave, but Burley has me. I don't know how I get down the stairs, but I'm shaking by the time I get to the dining table.

Matteo stands, his gaze boring into mine, and if I weren't in shock, I'd tear at him with my *kitten claws*. He pulls out a chair for me and takes over from Burley, supporting me with a warm hand on my waist as I lower myself into the chair. A hand that has no business touching me so possessively.

He gathers my hair so he can rest his hand on my bare neck and leans over to whisper, his warm breath a caress to my ear, "You look beautiful." He straightens. "Good morning, wife."

"What?" I've never been more grateful for a chair to hold me up. I'm not married. Am I? "Wife?" I spit out. "To you?" I glance up at him where he towers over me. "When? *How*?"

Several other thoughts zap through the sudden maze in my head. No more virginity auction? Thank God.

Did Dad *sell me* to this man? *How could he?*

And then, probably the most frightening thought: what would it be like to be married to the Mafia? *To Matteo?*

"Just on paper, kitten." Matteo lets go as he sits down. "For now." He reaches for a cup of coffee and takes a sip. The brothers, who just look at me with sickening humor in their eyes, seem to have enjoyed breakfast together. Remnants of a continental breakfast are pushed to the side, making space for an array of documents. Passports... a marriage certificate... what the *hell*...

"Would you like some coffee?" Matteo asks as he reaches for the French press.

"To throw in your face, yes," I blurt out.

Deep chuckles circle the table.

Matteo shoots me a sideways glance, but it doesn't stop him from pouring me a black coffee and pushing the creamer in my direction. "Surely you don't want to start your honeymoon like that, kitten. All claws. Ruining that perfect dress."

"Honeymoon?" I close my eyes, trying my best to be immune to his compliments. This asshole turns on the charm like a tap. "Let me guess, to Sicily, to meet your charming fucked-up extended family?"

"She catches on quick," Stephano says as he gathers the papers out of harm's way.

"It's selective," Matteo says, placing the coffee in front of me.

The coffee's aroma wafts up my nose. It's been days since my fix and every cell in my body begs for a caffeine kick. I don't reach for it though, suspicious of everything.

Matteo leans over and brushes his shoulder against mine to reach for an iPad I hadn't noticed before. "Have a coffee with your dad, Tasha. Let him wish you all the happiness."

What the actual—

Matteo unlocks the iPad and it immediately lights up to video footage of my dad, at *our* breakfast table by the bay window, overlooking the beautiful garden and the pool, all of which seem as far away as an undiscovered planet right now.

"Dad?" I call out, wanting to grab the iPad, but Matteo rests a warm hand over mine.

Dad looks up, his eyes rimmed red, looking terrified. It's only then that I notice the other person in the video and the automatic rifle he has in his hand. There's no sound, but my dad speaks. I try to lipread, but all I make out is *Tasha... I love you,* but that could be wishful thinking.

"Come on, drink up, we have a plane to catch," Matteo says. "A plane which you are going to board without giving me any trouble, understand?"

"*Understand*?" Rage engulfs me, but I can't do anything but fist my hands so hard that my nails bite into my skin. "Perfectly."

"Good girl. Bottoms up."

I'm starting to hate so many words. His vocabulary is very limited when it comes to me. I glance to my coffee. This might be my last one on American soil. It might also be drugged.

I want to be drugged. I don't want to know what happens next.

Without further thought, I take the cup and swig the lukewarm coffee down in one gulp. I bang the cup down on its saucer and stand so abruptly that all the men around the table startle and have their hands on their guns in a split second.

"What?" I say, glaring at them. "Let's get this fucking show on the road."

Right now I'll do anything to stop them from tormenting my dad. He has aged a hundred years in the days I haven't seen him, and I now know why he'll never come for me. They've threatened to kill me if he does, just as they threaten to kill him if I don't comply. For now, going through the motions seems like the only way to stay alive.

Stephano drops his hand away from his gun where it's hidden in his jacket. "You should gag this one."

"And tie her up," Dominic adds.

"Better safe than sorry." Benedict is still sitting. Clearly it takes more than a female tantrum to stir him.

Matteo hasn't moved but stands with the same level of control I've come to know from him. When he turns to me, there's a sparkle in his eyes. He reaches for my face, and his fingertips are feather soft as he gathers my hair behind my ear. The touch blazes down my body right to my sex where every memory of that night flares up, making me glow with unexpected and unwanted longing. *For him.*

"The person who gags my wife, or ties her up, gets a bullet in the head." His tone is even, measured, and terrifyingly calm.

I don't doubt for a second that he'd actually kill someone for simply gagging me. His words do something to me that I can't even understand. He's ignored me for two days. Two whole torturous days after what he did to me, after what he made me feel. After what he's promised to do to me when we get to Sicily.

Asshole.

Gorgeous, hideous, beautiful, tortured asshole.

Stockholm syndrome must be real because I'm standing next to a madman I'm falling for. I must be losing my mind.

## 25

# MATTEO

I ignore my brothers as they glare at me and gather the passports and travel documents Burley delivered last night. Matteo and Tasha Scalera are going on a two-week honeymoon booked on a private island in Greece, with a quick stopover to visit my ailing grandparents in Sicily. They were too old to travel for the wedding, so I'm taking my beautiful bride to see them instead.

"Matteo," Dominic starts but I stare him down. I'm not in the mood for any words of wisdom now.

"See you on the other side." I put my hand on the small of Tasha's back and she moves in sync with me. She's still riled up, her body tense. She's also clever and knows when to fight and when to let go. I won't let my guard down, but the real-time video footage of Peter Armstrong shifted the gears in her head. Every emotion played out on her face, and she understood the situation perfectly.

Tasha isn't going to resist now, and the drug in her coffee is going to numb her just enough to function. Once she's on the plane, she'll probably pass out, and when we arrive in Sicily, she'll be too confused to recall what happened.

I need her zoned out. I don't need her to *chat* all the way to Catania. Just watching her walk down the stairs with Burley had me questioning my life choices. But I have no life choices. I have a job to do, and I'll deliver. In two weeks, all of this will be over. Time is ticking for the Don, and I've made promises to my father that I will keep.

With my hand on her back, I steer Tasha to the front door where Burley is waiting. By the time we get to the SUV, she's already less tense. By the time we get to the private jet departures' lounge, where there's border control, she's perfect. All sweet and docile, and ready to collapse. Our check-in is quick. Flawless. Money is a shiny wet glaze over everything. I fucking hate that it's so easy.

I hate Peter Fucking Armstrong more for crossing *Il Consiglio* in the first place.

We're up the stairs and into the aisle of the jet when Tasha stumbles. I'm right behind her and have her in my arms. "Here, kitten," I murmur. "I've got you."

"I'm exhausted," she whispers, her hands on my arms as I ease her down into her seat.

"So busy with the wedding," I say as I buckle her up. "Just for takeoff. I'll move you to the bed after."

"What?" She looks up at me, but not really seeing, confused. "Where're we going again?"

I glance up to the front of the jet, where the pilots are doing cross checks. The air hostess is preparing drinks in the galley. Burley and three other bodyguards are sitting down, flanking us. It's our jet and these are all our regular staff but trust only runs so far—nobody but my closest inner circle can know what's really happening here.

I sit down next to her and reach for her hand. It's willing and limp in mine. Her head lolls to the side and she tries to focus, slumping against me. "Matteo," she sighs. "You're here."

"Yes, kitten." The dose might have been a tad high. I lean

closer, my lips at her temple. "Almost forgot the most important part." I reach into my inner pocket and pull out three rings, putting mine on first. I waited for the right moment to slip hers on her finger. Firstly, my brothers would give me hell if they knew I took these out of the family vault. Secondly, this hellion would toss a million dollars of diamonds out onto the runway if she had a second to spare. Now I get to slip them on her ring finger, and she doesn't even resist.

She holds up her hand and watches in drugged fascination as the diamonds sparkle in the overhead lights.

"You spoil me," she murmurs, a smile playing on her lips. "For someone you plan to whore off in a few days' time."

There's my fire eater. And she's not completely out of it yet. "I see the idea is growing on you. Don't get any ideas, kitten," I say softly. "Where we're going, they'll cut your finger off to get those rings and ask questions later. If they ask them at all." Also, and this is something she doesn't need to know, but these rings are a type of insurance for her, should things go wrong.

Not that I plan for them to go wrong, but I'm not stupid. This trip has risks. Once we've landed in Catania, things are going to happen fast. The one good thing about Randazzo is that he's old. Like my father, he's gotten this far by killing those who stood in his way. There's enough bad blood between Randazzo and his subjects that most of them want him dead. Handy to know if you're planning a coup.

Tasha's head bobs. She's too short to get comfortable and the bucket seats won't allow her to rest her head on my shoulder. I suppress the urge to stroke that soft cheek. The captain comes over and makes sure we're ready for takeoff. I give him the go-ahead and half an hour later we're in the air.

Once we've reached altitude, I stand, unbuckle Tasha from her seat and gather her in my arms. The jet has a separate bedroom cornered off with a bathroom en suite. It's excessive luxury for a plane we rarely use outside of the US, but now I love the privacy and comfort.

Burley stands and goes ahead to open the bedroom door for us. "You're good, boss?"

"Yes. We're not to be disturbed."

Burley nods and the door closes behind me with a click.

I lay her down on the bed and make sure her head isn't in a funny position. She looks rather angelic like this, but I know she has twin devils sitting on her shoulder. I like it more than I should. I like messing with her more than I should too.

She's just merch.

Merch that's going to give me a hard time if I don't keep her in line.

Time to mess with my kitten's head.

I take her shoes off and place them next to the bed. Then I lift the skirt of her dress, loving the look of the panties I chose for her on that sweet pussy. It's all mesh and no gusset, showing off her skin and the tip of her slit. The waistband has got white flowers embroidered along the edge, short stems leading the eye south. Yep. I'm a pervert. I want to touch her, pleasure her again like the other night, and my cock is all for it, but she's too drugged to even notice. There's zero fun in that.

Instead, I hook my fingers around the hips of her panties and gently tug them off. She moans, a wasted protest. I press her panties to my nose, disappointed when there's only the slightest hint of her essence on them. Fuck it.

I pocket them and lower her skirts so that she's decent. For now.

I smirk. Nothing like a virgin arriving in a foreign country where there's a bit of coastal wind on the tarmac, realizing that she's naked underneath that skirt that could fly up like Marilyn Monroe's under a New York City subway vent.

She'll be too conscious of it to do anything but keep her skirts pressed down.

Satisfied that I now also have the perfect gag on hand should she actually need one, I go back to the cabin to fetch my laptop bag. For a moment I consider sitting down at a desk to work, but then decide against it. Someone needs to keep an eye on her and none of these bodyguards are getting close to her sleeping, half naked.

I go back to the bedroom, kick off my shoes, strip to my white dress shirt and roll up my sleeves. I settle next to her on the bed, lounging back like a lazy dick who works from bed. Her head is right there by my hip, her hair spread like a silky invitation. She's a distraction I can't afford.

With a grunt I open my laptop and the WiFi connects automatically. My email is already open, and I glance down the new messages in my inbox. There's the usual pile of junk from people I'm going to ignore, but Dominic's one-liner pops out like a stab in the eye in all caps:

SHE'S FUCKING MERCH, YOU DICKHEAD. WE DON'T TOUCH THE MERCH.

*You're fucking hard for her, brother. Don't go soft. She's going to be the death of you. I'm still pissed you're doing this alone. Phone me.*

I don't bother to reply.

# 26

## TASHA

I blink. I'm sunk into a cloud, my head heavy, but the tapping on a keyboard doesn't sound like an angel chorus to me. I open my eyes. Matteo. Right here, my face almost pressed to his thigh where he's sitting next to me.

I roll onto my back and stare at the ceiling with no clue where I am.

"Good, you're awake," Matteo says.

Immediately my heart rate speeds up. I can't recall much, but I know this wasn't *my* plan. "Where are we?" In a hotel somewhere?

His hand comes to rest on the side of my head, his thumb on my temple, and he strokes stray hairs from my face. "We'll land soon."

That touch that's always so gentle, as if he cares. I pull away and struggle up, tuning in to the soft hum of the jet. I look at his laptop screen. Spreadsheets? "What are you doing?"

"Working."

"What work do you even do?" Now I'm doubly confused. This guy doesn't work the usual nine to five normal people do.

He smirks. "I run some of our businesses. You'll be glad to know they're legit."

Things are starting to come back to me now through the fog of my obviously drugged brain. "You mean you don't just rape and pillage."

Matteo sighs and closes his laptop. "And yet I've done none of that."

No, but kidnapping and murder is more like it. I don't say anything, not wanting to push my luck. I eye his laptop. There's internet on that laptop. On this plane. What I wouldn't give for five minutes to send out a 911 into the void.

There's a knock on the door and then Burley's voice: "Thirty minutes to landing, boss."

Matteo stands, his tall frame towering over me. His shirt-sleeves are rolled up, showing off his tattoos. My pulse flutters at the thought of him, of those beautiful hands that held me open for his tongue. He stares at me as he rolls his sleeves down and heat spreads over my face. It's the way he looks at me, as if he's been thinking of eating me out this entire flight and has run out of time.

"Use the washroom," he says. "Last chance until we're at our estate."

I manage to swing my feet to the ground, but my head is still swimming. He has his arm around my waist and helps me to the washroom.

I grab hold of the handbasin for balance and he lets me go.

"The door stays open."

Matteo steps out, but I don't even have the energy or compulsion to fight him. I make my way to the toilet and reach under my skirt for my panties.

What?

I lift my skirt up. There's nothing. "You!" I call out, immediately knowing it was him who stole my underwear.

"Me?"

"Asshole!" I sink down on the toilet, not even caring that he could walk in any time. As I pee a hand appears around the door, swinging my panties from a fingertip.

"Missing something?" his voice comes, a smile in it for once.

I've never heard that tone in his voice before. It's almost as if I can hear the boy who played pranks on his brothers. He loves messing with me.

It's like that first day at the pool, when I had to get out while he was watching me. My confidence wants to fold, but I'm going to work it like a pro. "I walk around without panties all the time."

"Yeah?"

*No.*

"You won't mind if I keep them then."

"Nope." I pop that p for good measure. When I'm done I wash my hands, the cool water somehow sobering. My hair is a mess and I open the mirrored wall cupboard to find a collection of toiletries in there. Blades for shaving—

"Get going."

I startle. Matteo is leaning in at the door, my panties gone, his face serious again. I reach for the hairbrush and run it through my hair, only now noticing the diamonds on my finger as they catch the light. Holy hell. "Whose was this?" I ask. It's not the design that gives away its age, rather the worn white gold of the wedding band that hasn't been polished in a while.

"My mom's."

"Matteo—"

"Don't lose them. If anything goes wrong while we're in Sicily—"

"What could go wrong with a virgin auction?" I ask as I put the hairbrush back. "Except me no longer being a virgin?"

He steps up behind me and has my back against his chest with my arm trapped between us, his other hand on my throat, pressing and pushing up so that I'm forced to look at him in the mirror.

"You have plans then?" Matteo hisses. "To fuck one of my bodyguards and lose your virginity? Hmm?" His hand glides down my throat, releasing the pressure, gentle again. "Let me warn you, kitten, that as a common prostitute you'll take decades to pay off your dad's debts, even if you fuck twenty guys a day." His hand glides lower, over my breast and my nipple, which is already hard at the tease of his breath on my skin. "What we plan is one night only with a billionaire who pays and doesn't ask questions."

He's staring at me, his eyes angry, and I'm flushed with the heat of his words, at the visual he's creating in my head. His hand tugs at my skirt, lifting it. Then his fingers are warm on my thigh, his thumb stroking the soft skin, ever closer to my sex. "Which would you prefer?" he whispers into my ear as his thumb finally strokes over my mound, teasing the tip of my sex. "Serving twenty guys a day for years or one perverted prick for one night only?"

His thumb slides between my lips where I'm wet and wanting, desperate for more of him. I'm whimpering now, the cruelty of his words in contrast with the gentle caress he runs over my sex, dipping in to tease my clit.

"Look at me in the mirror, and tell me, kitten."

Now another finger is circling my clit. A minute more of this and I'll come. I lean back into him, wanting to come so badly, wanting to go all the way *with him*. I bite my lip, trying to resist, but he shifts his other hand, putting pressure back on my neck.

"A whore for life, or a whore for one night, Tasha. Choose."

Now I want to cry, wrecked by his expert touch, broken by his cruel words, the way he murmured my name. "Yours," I whisper, my eyes begging as I stare directly into his, "for one night."

The idea has been building in my head. He's so rich he

won't even miss the change. And with the way he's touched me, everything about him... If I'm brutally honest with myself, I *want* it to be *him*. Ever since the other night it's been all I've been thinking of when I'm not overwhelmed by anything else.

A look of disgust flashes over his face, and he retracts his hand. I moan as the delicious build-up in my body stalls.

"You're just merchandise to me, kitten. Don't you ever forget that."

*We don't touch the merch. Ever.*

Matteo watches me in the mirror as he licks the shine of my juices from his fingers. The gesture is so sexual, so erotic, that a fresh gush of arousal seeps from my sex. "Plus, you flatter yourself. Your little auction isn't the first order of business I'll attend to in Sicily."

Oh God. Somehow words come back to me. Something about people cutting off fingers to get to these rings, without asking questions. There's much more to this trip than just my auction. I've been such a naive idiot to think otherwise.

He slides his hands down my arms. "Now you're going to be a good girl and walk off this plane with a smile on your face, holding my hand like a good little wife so we can get safely to our estate. Understand?"

"Yes." And even if I didn't, I won't do anything dumb like run. I might flash anybody my aroused sex.

In the end all I could do was focus on keeping my skirt down with one hand, while walking so close to Matteo that the other side got pressed down by his leg, clinging to him as the breeze swept over the tarmac. Matteo knew the weather was going to be like this. Sunny and hot with a breeze. He picked my dress especially for this and then—*ugh*.

We don't even go near the public terminal, where there's a crowd I could blend and disappear into. With this pink dress I'll stand out like a running target should I bolt. Not that I *can* run; although my head is clearing, my body is dumb with a lagging dose of drugs. An SUV with blacked-out windows waits for us, with two other cars as our entourage.

Another chance slips through my fingers.

I'm starting to suspect this is a chess game and he is ten moves ahead, whereas I'm only a pawn with very limited moves.

# 27

# TASHA

Once the road from the airport leaves behind an industrial zone, it heads into the country. For a long while we pass through farmland, vineyards, olive groves and small towns, scattered houses that thin along the way as the landscape becomes more rural. Then the road descends and we're hugging the coast, the beautiful blue of the Mediterranean only outshone by the blue of a midsummer sky.

"Where're we going?" I ask.

Matteo is sitting next to me where I'm strapped to the middle seat, Burley's bulk walling me in on the other side.

"The family farm."

It's the only answer I get, so instead I focus on the road signs, trying to remember the names for all I'm worth. No money, no phone, and not speaking the language are all just one side of my colossal problem. Dressed like this with these diamonds on my fingers I scream money, so the chances of anybody buying that I got kidnapped by the mob is ridiculously low.

When we reach a six-foot-high stone wall that runs for over half a mile, unease spreads down my spine. Cameras and electrical fencing look out of place with the rest of the idyllic Sicilian landscape. An imposing gate opens as if on cue when we reach it, and I lean forward to see better.

Family farm. My ass. The driveway leads through an avenue of ancient palm trees, beyond which rolling vineyards stretch as far as the eye can see. The ocean is no longer a faraway horizon of blue, but right here, so close I could touch it. The lane opens to an old stone house with a circular fountain and a stately roundabout for a drop off and go. The house has small windows and shutters, but they're deceptive as the house has been expanded on one side into a sprawling manor which promises to have breathtaking views.

As the car stops, an older man, probably the butler, comes through the open double door and smiles as he descends the stairs.

Matteo pops his door open, and the man rushes forward.

"*Signor Scalera, benvenuto! Siamo così felici di ospitarla finalmente alla Villa Vista.*"

"*Grazie, Massimo,*" Matteo says in what to my ear sounds like perfect Italian. "*Siamo felici di essere qui.*"

My jaw drops, and Burley winks at me. "Didn't expect that, did you luv?"

My fake on-paper-only husband who guards my virginity for a blood exchange just got hotter by at least ten degrees. Matteo holds out his hand to me, and I slip mine into his. A soft squeeze and a gentle caress of his thumb over my hand seem to put in words everything he hasn't told me. *Play along, my love, for here, as my wife, you'll be safe.*

"*Questa è mia moglie, Tasha.*" Matteo smiles at me, warmly fake. "My wife, Tasha."

"Massimo," the man says as he bows somewhat formally. "Welcome, Mrs. Scalera. An honor. If you need anything, just ask."

His words are so sincere, I weep inside. If only he knew—

He probably knows. Whatever this gorgeous place is, it's going to be a prison for the duration of my stay.

Matteo nods at Massimo and soon we are inside the house, which is refreshingly cool, if dark in comparison to the outside. A waiter hands me a cold cocktail and with one glance I get the drift. This isn't a normal house; it's run like a hotel of sorts.

Matteo hasn't let go of my hand, and now leads me through the foyer to the dining area which overlooks a veranda. Further away there is a rim-flow pool and then, what looks like a direct drop into the ocean.

"Do you own this place?" I ask as the waiter opens the French doors that lead outside to the veranda.

"It's the original Scalera farm. Long ago it was only a house with a small vineyard; now it's run as a hotel. We're the only guests this week." He looks around, seeming as curious as me. A handful of tables with white tablecloths wait for customers under pale pink umbrellas. Beautiful roses circle the veranda, their scent hanging heavy in the heat. My throat constricts with the memory of my mom. She would have loved this place.

"You've come here before?"

"No. I've only seen it in photos, videos, building plans."

"Why?"

"To come to Sicily would break the truce."

"Truce?"

"Between the Scaleras and the Randazzos." He sighs as he leads me across the lawn to where a low brick wall marks the end of the property. "You ask too many questions, kitten."

I know I ask too many questions, but he has been humoring me. Matteo holds back but gives at the same time, as if he needs someone to talk to. As if he is carrying a burden that he can't share with anybody, except the woman he is going to kill at the end of it. Dead bodies don't talk. And *my* fate is sealed. I've witnessed a brutal killing in his apartment. There's no way he's letting me walk free with that information.

We've stopped at the short wall, and beyond it, two yards of shrubs cover the soil before it drops off into a hair-raising cliff. I lean over to have a peek but can't see more than the deep water that foams up and retreats. Boats are out at sea, some close, others further away, dreamy and otherworldly compared to my current situation.

I've seen his world. Breaking a Mafia truce can only mean one thing: bloodshed.

"Why are we here then, Matteo? And why did you drag me along?" He could have auctioned me off a hundred times in the US somewhere, or Mexico. My dad could have paid up—

It's too late for that now. I get the feeling all the money in the world won't satisfy this man and wipe out my dad's crimes.

"I'm here to end it once and for all." He raises my hand to his lips and presses a kiss to my knuckles, a move that to any onlooker would seem swoon-worthy. It has my heart in my throat, my pulse aflutter, my sex reminding me that he almost had me orgasming on the plane and that I still want him to finish what he started. That I begged him like a fawning idiot to have me, all of me. "I need you as a red herring, *mia cara*, to make them think I come with goodwill. For a day or two, at least."

A red herring. I've been reduced to nothing but a smelly, rotting fish. A new low. "Fine."

"So here's what's going to happen—"

"I understand already. You don't need to ask me if *I understand.*"

He lets go of my hand, and I give him my shoulder as I take a sip of my drink, really wanting to toss the glass into the ocean, where the water sprays against the cliff wall, about sixty feet below.

"I should gag you with this, drag you to our room, and whip that wet pussy into submission for your fucking insolence," he says, deadly calm, as he shoves my panties into my hand.

"Unfortunately, we're being watched, and when it comes to my *wife*, I don't put on that type of performance for my staff."

He takes me by the shoulder and the command is there as we turn back to the house. "I have work to do and don't need to worry about your naked little ass while I'm at it. So, you're going to be a good girl and stay in our room. Notice, *mia cara*, you're being guarded, so don't do anything stupid."

Matteo's fingers slide down my arm, a deceptively tender caress, controlled, and not for the first time I'm reminded of the power he wields in his touch alone. This is all for show. My gaze flits around to where I notice the security detail for the first time. Men on the roof and far along the short wall, holding machine guns. By the side of the house, further away up the vineyard. They're everywhere.

We make it back to the foyer in stubborn silence, but my mind is racing. All I want is to beg for him to live up to his word, to *drag me to our room, and whip my wet pussy into submission for my fucking insolence.*

I might be a virgin, but ever since he touched me, it's as if innocence has been stripped from my eyes.

All I can see in my mind's eye and all I want is the thousand ways in which Matteo Scalera can make me come.

# 28

# MATTEO

Burley shows us to our room on the second floor of the old house. He has scraped it for any potential murder weapons, real ones or ones that could be manufactured from scratch. As we walk inside, Tasha's breath catches.

"It's so quaint."

It's so fucking small.

I wanted to be in the house, and Dominic's team who inspected the space earlier this week deemed this room the safest. Never mind my own security, I'm not risking Tasha's.

While I watched her zoned out on the plane, I kept thinking of my baby sister. She would have been around Tasha's age if she hadn't been stillborn. When I'm forced to be quiet like today on the flight, my mind often drifts to my mom, and a softer time in life when she was the barrier between us and the Don. When she died in childbirth everything changed. Six boys, at the mercy of a maniac.

I follow Tasha into the room, watching as she wrings her hands, her gaze taking in the double bed. The *only* bed.

Too small for my tastes, unless you're really up for *cuddling*. Not my wheelhouse.

*Yours. For one night.*

Fuck. She knows how to mess with my head. Swinging between innocence and lust, then being so fucking sassy, I should really discipline her. She's a back-chatting rebel, but I'll never have it in me to hurt her. Not hurt her like some men do, thriving on female pain. Mom suffered enough. And we didn't even know half of it. Tasha isn't my sister or my mom, but fuck knows she's the first woman I want to protect with some force I've never felt before.

It must be because this job is the Don's vendetta, and not my own. I'll always want retribution for Alex's death, but on my own terms. Not the ones prescribed by *him*. The Don has left his mark on me, not only on my body, but in every choice I make. And the choice to go ahead with this virgin auction is starting to eat at me. For years, I've been using women only for sex and quick pleasure. But now here she is, crawling under my skin.

It fucking pisses me off. I need to focus on this job, get it done, so we can leave for Cannes. Stephano will be there, dealing with the auction, and I will hand Tasha over to him on a fucking silver platter.

"I'm going out." I'll deal with this one-bed situation when I'm back. I'll have to deal, since I'm *married*, with a ring on my finger to 'prove' it.

"Where? Why?"

Fucking questions all the time. "I have meetings." With people who have smoothed the way for me to kill the Sicilian.

"What do you expect me to do? There isn't even a TV in this room."

Nice and old school. "Enjoy the view. Burley will be outside your door. And the windows are being watched."

"I'm already bored!" She sits down on the bed with a huff, but I ignore her, reaching for the doorknob to stop myself from doing something I shouldn't. *Yours. For one night.* There's no way

I can sleep in the same bed with this woman. I'll fuck her so hard she won't have any memory of ever being a virgin in the first place.

I'm halfway out the door when I hear her lips smack behind me, followed by the very distinguishable blow. I turn back to face her. Did she actually just blow me a fucking kiss? "What was that?"

Her eyes sparkle. "Nothing."

I hitch my brow. "You're sure?"

She sucks her bottom lip with a shrug.

I want to laugh—fucking *laugh*—at her baiting me like this. With a determined inhale I turn back to the corridor, where Burley has pulled up a seat to guard her door.

"Hurry home, honey." Tasha's voice sounds through what seems like the whole house.

I freeze in my step. Burley's eyes meet mine as something between infuriated delight and maddening frustration boils up in me.

I count to ten. "Let them know I'm going to be late."

"Yes, boss," Burley says as he stands and picks up his chair. "You're not to be disturbed."

Damn right I'm not to be disturbed.

I turn back to the room, closing the door softly and locking it.

Tasha still sits on the bed, hands together on her lap, eyes now wide as she sees me stalk back into the room. I unbutton my jacket, slip it off and toss it to the chair by the antique dressing table. I don't break eye contact with her as I roll up my sleeves one by one. She licks her lips, clearly nervous now that she's poked me to my limit.

I come to stand right by her legs, forcing her to look up at me. "Just for the record, you asked for this." Begged for it, to be precise. I cup her face, stroking that soft cheek with a featherlight touch, smoothing my thumb over her lips. Lips that I want to kiss. Lips I've been wanting to kiss since that night when she tried to stab me.

*Merch, you fucknut.*

*Merch that needs to be tied up and gagged and disciplined.*

Her hands are on my thighs, brushing up to where my cock is already bulging in my pants. It's as I suspected. She needs to be fucked. This horny little virgin has needs. I take her hands and peel them off my legs. Fuck knows, I can unzip and take that virgin mouth, let her suck me off.

"You don't touch me, kitten. I thought you *understood*?"

"Why?" She strains against me where I have her wrists, her blue eyes dancing with evident pleasure at having me here, entertaining her.

"Because." I lean forward, forcing her onto her back as I raise her hands above her head. Her chest heaves in anticipation. Good.

As soon as she's on her back, I straighten up. Her legs dangle to the floor now and I reach for her ankles, lift and twist her in one smooth move so that she's perpendicular to me. Her shoes drop to the floor with soft thuds, and I bend her legs up, exposing that perfect pink pussy as her skirt falls to her chest.

Fuck. She's wet.

She's going to be even wetter soon.

I run my hand down the back of her creamy thighs, ghosting over her pussy. She clenches. I do it again, and this time as I ghost my palm over her sex, she actually presses up to meet my hand. "Matteo—"

"Fuck, kitten, so needy," I hiss. I have her by the hip and toss her over, forcing her onto all fours. Her skirt falls back to cover her sexy ass and with an irritated growl I rip it out of my way. I don't wait. I don't tease. I hold her with a firm hand on her neck, forcing her face down so her ass is good and proper in the air. Then I slap her several times on each butt cheek, watching with great satisfaction how the skin turns pink.

"Matteo," she moans as she squirms, but I'm not done.

"Moan my name a bit louder, kitten, so the whole house can hear." I now focus on her pussy, on that sweet little clit that tempts me. I slap her again, this time making sure my middle finger hits her clit so she can come. I slap her again and she moans where her face is buried in the covers, her hands clenched.

She's close. Again. But this time I follow it up with a slow sweep of my fingers over her clit, circling that sweet spot until she shudders in release with a moan.

I unbuckle my belt with one hand, still keeping her in place with my other hand on her neck. She is spent, her face flushed with the force of her orgasm. I want to fuck her so hard. Drive my fingers into her body and work her g-spot until she comes again. Then, and only then, will I give her the satisfaction of coming on my cock.

But I can't. I won't take her virginity in a mad moment of lust. So instead, I ease my hold as I pull out my cock, fisting it hard. This needs to be quick, although I could spend the rest of the year toying with her. I run my hand down her back to her naked butt and slip my fingers to her sex as I ride my hand. I go higher, to that tight little hole I could have with nobody knowing. Her virgin ass could be mine.

She quivers at my touch, leaning into my hand. Fuck. She's into this. The thought only drives me to jerk off harder, my thumb pressing against her tight little hole as I spread her own juices, tempted to finger her there. Her breathing is heavy, her body willing. The visual of her like this, open and offered up, tips me over the edge. I spray cum over her dress, her back, her sweet ass, watching her face. Her eyes are closed, her mouth open as she whispers my name, sensing my release. I close my eyes as I grunt, dropping my head back. Cum pulses until I'm emptied out.

Fuck, I always feel overdue when I'm around her.

I watch her a moment, coming down from my high. I can give her one more orgasm. I can go down and dirty on her, lick her until she begs, but I'm playing with fucking fire. As soon as she touches me, I'll lose all control. And at some point she *will* touch me, and I won't have the willpower to push her away. I release her as I fix my pants, zipping up, my cock pleased but not yet done either. So be it.

Tasha drops onto her back, her expression saying everything. She's shattered but whole. That feeling of falling over a cliff and not crashing to the ground but flying.

She watches me as I buckle up my belt and I can't take my eyes off her. She is fucking beautiful, glowing with spent pleasure. This woman needs to be fucked, often, and by someone who knows how. She might only now be realizing it for herself.

"You've ruined my dress," she murmurs as she touches the ragged edge of the torn fabric.

"That's why we got all of them."

She sits up, fingering my cum where it's glossy and white on her inner thigh. "You got semen all over me."

"And?" There's an adjacent bathroom fit for a queen if I recall correctly. "You sass me again, you're getting it down your throat."

She blinks, understanding slow to sink in.

"Yes, kitten, I'll gag you with my cock and you'll fucking love it."

I grab my jacket and make for the door. As I close it behind me, she's muttering, in that cheeky tone of hers, "Promises, promises, Matteo Scalera, promises, promises."

# 29

# MATTEO

The Don has several files on Emilio Randazzo, the Sicilian. Thick ones, full of letters and documents, photos, and details of people he's killed or had killed, information about his businesses in Italy and beyond.

The only link the Don still has with Randazzo is a birthplace which both men deserted for more lucrative soil. The Don split from the Cosa Nostra to form *Il Consiglio* on the East Coast, refusing to burn bridges along the way. Randazzo, on the other hand... The man is a worse psychopath than the Don.

Where *Il Consiglio* has gone above-board as far as possible and has steered clear from anything under eighteen, that seems to be Randazzo's specialty. Desperate immigrants crossing the Mediterranean disappear, become anonymous organ 'donors.' Girls and boys are fed into the European sex trafficking rings Randazzo seems to have a stake in.

Sicily isn't the bedrock of his crime ring, but he has retired here, out of the fray, under the protection of the Bratva and 'Ndrangheta he's in bed with. Without their protection, there's no chance in hell that the Cosa Nostra would allow him to nest here in his old age.

His goons are spread across Europe and killing this man would make chaos erupt through his operations. It's a good thing every police agency in Europe has been on his case too. I'll pull the trigger; they can deal with the aftermath.

The fucker needs to die. Only one problem: I have no idea what he looks like.

Like any crime lord who has blood on his hands and too many enemies to count, his images have been wiped off the internet, and there weren't many to start off with. All I had was a grainy black and white photo to go on, taken on the day of the Don's wedding to my mom. Yep, the Sicilian was there, giving Bianca Randazzo away. Mom told me once she wasn't Randazzo's blood relation, and I never unearthed the whole intricate web around the Sicilian, Don Scalera and Bianca, his 'donated bride.' Before I had a mind of my own to dig into family history, she had passed away.

All I know is that Mom was part of the truce between the Don and Emilio Randazzo, a human barrier to guarantee no further bloodshed between the families. The photo only shows Emilio Randazzo's profile, a mustache hiding his mouth as it droops down the sides, a diamond earring in his lobe. He has a notch in his ear, a triangular cut-out, as if someone marked him like cattle.

That's a lot to go on, but not enough.

I walk into a restaurant in Catania, one of those popular family places that caters for tourists. The space is already filling up with families after a long day at the beach. Younger kids are nagging, older kids are finally on their phones, blocking out the rest of the world. It can't get safer than this. My security detail has been all over the place, and the men I have with me have been under Burley's watch for years. I'm good.

Tasha is safe.

The mere thought of her makes me groan. No amount of

'disciplining' is going to tame that one. It might only make her wilder. Which is a fucking turn-on.

A man rises from a corner table, and I recognize him from various intelligence reports Dominic's team has been working on the past few weeks. My mole is one of Randazzo's right-hand men, one of those who has been crossed too many times. Asked too much of, pushed too far. A mole the Don has been nurturing for years. Groomed almost. Yep, the Don plays a long game.

We shake hands, not acknowledging each other by name. He's on my team now, as we've guaranteed him protection when shit hits the fan.

I sit down and he takes an envelope from his inner jacket pocket. "Keys, remotes, codes, house plan, garden map, guard rotation, everything your brother asked for. Also, weapons caches. There are several marked."

"Thank you." Walking into Randazzo's compound is going to be the easy part; coming out is always the fuckup waiting to happen.

I open the envelope and peer inside. Photos. I pull one out halfway, just to see what I'm working with. I blink. Emilio Randazzo. The Sicilian. An old man now, smiling at the camera in a way that makes a shiver run down my spine. His face is turned slightly to the side, showing off his diamond earring and the notch in his ear. This old man's face is familiar in a weird way I can't pinpoint.

I've seen him before, I just don't know where. It's more than just a synapse connection my brain has made with the wedding image from the Don's files. I shove the photo back into the envelope. "This is enough to go on."

"Good."

"You'll be there?" I ask, knowing this guy is risking his life as a security detail going rogue.

He nods and I stand. Our business is concluded for now. Normally I don't trust men off the bat, but this one defected to the Don years ago. He's been feeding the Don information for years and has earned our trust. Best of all, this mole was primed by Randazzo himself: in our world, you don't kidnap a man's older sister, force her into prostitution, and think a much younger brother forgets. A brother you've left for dead. We all make mistakes and at some point, they catch up with us. This one is the Sicilian's catch-up.

Tasha is mine. A mistake waiting in the wings to fuck me over.

As I walk out into the early evening heat, I nod towards my crew who have blended into the surroundings. The car is waiting. I can go back to her and the old family house and relax. My 'meeting' with Randazzo is planned for tomorrow. He might already know that I've landed. That a Scalera has entered his sacred Sicilian territory. He could preempt me by killing me before we can ever meet face to face. In fact, I know this is what the Don would do. Kill first and don't bother to ask questions. I might come in 'peace,' but Randazzo didn't get where he is today by taking things at face value.

I don't trust myself around Tasha, not after what happened earlier, and her sassy *promises, promises* she threw at me. That mouth needs cock and will get it if I don't hold back. I won't be able to stay away from her, and that's what I need now. Distance. Going back to the house, even with all those empty rooms, isn't an option.

The night is young, and so am I. Fuck, this might be the last night I'm alive. Shit could go south tomorrow, and I'm not bulletproof.

I get into the back seat and lean over to the driver. "Take me to a night club."

"What type of night club?" the driver asks, his eyes meeting mine in the rearview mirror. "It's a bit early."

"One with strippers and other services."

The type of club that doesn't keep hours and the last type of club a newly married man in love should be visiting. Not that I care. I'm only living up to my reputation.

May the word spread so that the Sicilian can know I'm the real deal.

## 30

# TASHA

It must be midmorning already. The sun has been up for hours.

And still no sign of my husband. He's been gone the whole freaking night and I'm not ready to face any of the staff. What would they even be thinking? First night on honeymoon and the husband is missing in action.

When Matteo left, I thought he was only going to be gone for a few hours. At first, I was shy to look Burley in the eye when he came to my room with a new dress and some PJs. He knew exactly what had happened and who knew what Matteo had told him as he left.

Burley brought some snacks and tea to my room and later asked me if I wanted to have dinner on the veranda. That was a guilt-lined invitation. Even he felt embarrassed that Matteo had left me to my own devices. I grasped at the opportunity, and even though Burley's conversation was sparse over dinner, it was better than nothing. I couldn't even lure him out when I asked him how he met Rosalia.

After dinner, we walked to the end of the garden, to the small wall with the ocean below to look at the sunset. I felt like a target. Guards watched my every step. The sea seemed a bit wilder, as if the tide was coming in with the wind sweeping against my skirts. There wasn't much else to see, except the boat lights out on the dark water. Proof of other people. Safe people. *Normal* people.

Everything is controlled. I have access to nothing but what I need in the moment. It's driving me nuts. I've never felt more isolated in my life.

Burley bid me goodnight, but I rolled around in bed for a long time, waiting for Matteo's return. For a sign of life. I know I'm not the first order of business for him, and that he has a vendetta to come and settle. But what if he gets killed in the process? At that thought my heart thumps against my ribcage, as if there isn't enough space for it, and tears burn at the back of my eyes.

Matteo has wrestled with death a few times and come out alive. I must have more faith. On that first day, every cell in my body wanted him dead. Now? He's become human. My connection to the outer world. I'm locked up here, and what will happen to me if Matteo is dead? Burley, without a doubt, has instructions to deal with me.

I'm just merch, and when the merch goes off, well, you write it off and toss it. I'm as good as dead and I've known this for a while, but I still have fight in me.

A knock on my door forces me to sit up. I'm tired from restless sleep, waiting for a husband who isn't real, worrying over a man who plans to kill me.

"Tasha," Burley's voice sounds through the door. "Breakfast."

"Okay." I get up and take a quick shower, then put on the same dress from yesterday. If breakfast is served on the veranda, then I'll take it. I'll do anything to get out of this room and the confines of the boredom that comes with it.

When I try to open the door, I find it unlocked. Burley is waiting outside and as he studies my face, I know exactly what he sees. Dark circles under my eyes from worry over a man who isn't worth it.

"Where's Matteo?" I ask.

"He spent the night at a hotel." Burley drops his gaze, but I've started to learn what his little signals mean.

He's embarrassed about the situation and doesn't agree with it.

"Don't tell me he was with another woman," I murmur, rage and jealousy boiling up in me in equal measure.

"I don't know. Could've been *women*." He looks down at me, his face stern. "What's it to you in any case?"

I shrug, pick up my shredded dignity and walk down the corridor to the stairs. Burley falls in step next to me, matching my pace. He doesn't touch me, doesn't command my body like Matteo would have at this point. I miss it. I miss *him*. And I'm jealous of whoever had the pleasure of getting served a Matteo Scalera orgasm last night. Or two. Or three.

I'm properly pissed by the time I sit down at the table we had dinner at last night. The pool is sparkling blue in the bright sun, the roses' perfume drifting over in the slight breeze. This place is idyllic. My seat faces the ocean and from here the slope of the manicured lawn to the small wall is almost inviting a sprint. My body is anxious with bottled-up energy. I usually exercise every day, be it a run or swimming laps or doing a class at my local gym. I'm fit. Fit enough to take the plunge.

I'm dead either way. That jump isn't that high. And when you're between a rock and a hard place, your choices are limited.

I eat my breakfast. I am after all endowed with common sense. I'm going to need the energy, but I toe off my shoes underneath the table, quietly so nobody hears.

It's when Burley settles back with his second cup of coffee, relaxed by the sun and a false sense of security, that I make the split-second decision.

I stand and at the same time start running. I bolt away as fast as I can, sprinting with all the energy I can muster for the wall. Immediately there are voices that call behind me, but I know Burley won't be able to catch me. He is big, but I'm fast. I only need to get over the cliff.

There's a commotion, shouting between the men as they don't know what to do. All the bullets in the world and they dare not shoot. The man who kills Matteo Scalera's wife is dead meat.

I make it to the little wall and scale it quickly, watching in rising panic as two guards on either end of the wall rush in my direction. They're close, they'll have me in seconds.

I'm at the edge of the cliff, looking down. I sway with vertigo, almost falling back. My heart beats everywhere. My throat, my head, my stomach. There's a fisherman's boat right there, two men in a motorized boat that will help me. Surely they will help me.

I take two steps back, then run and hurl myself into the air, swimming with my arms to get away from the cliff.

My skirt flips up to my face. I hardly register it before I bring my legs together and slice into the cold water. I plunge deep, but there's no bottom.

I heave up, using my arms to swim to the light.

As I break the surface, I drag in a deep life-affirming breath. I'm alive.

And I'm finally free.

# 31

## TASHA

I glance around, my hearing still dulled by the plunge I took. High above me, men are shouting at me as they cautiously lean over the cliff. I don't care to hear. Already the speedboat is coming in my direction. Soon I'll be gone and not a bullet wasted.

A man on the speedboat tosses a lifebuoy out to me and I'm grateful that I can stop kicking. I'm frantic as my dress's fabric is heavy when soaked and I'm weak with the shock of what I've done.

I actually jumped.

The men on the boat are calling to me now, speaking in fast Italian, as they maneuver the boat closer to me. I watch them as they glance up the cliff to where Burley is screaming my name.

I can't stomach looking in his direction. Matteo is going to kill him for letting me slip through his fingers.

A hand reaches out for me and pulls me from the water. I'm beaching on the boat's floor like a whale, relief seeping into my veins.

I actually jumped.

I'm free.

The two men talk to me at speed, gesturing with their hands, but I don't understand as I just try to catch my breath. One of them touches my shoulder but I pull away. "I'm fine. I'm fine." Adrenaline is rushing through my veins. I'm only vaguely aware that the boat's engine is going again, that we're heading away from the cliff.

My dress clings to my body, a second skin. Matteo's mom's rings are still on my finger, and for a short second I'm tempted to toss them into the sea. But then I recall the way Matteo said *my mom's*, how something in his eyes told me not to probe. That man has so many soft spots, weak points in his armor that he's exposed to me.

I sob, suddenly and uncontrollably. It's relief and regret and heartache all in one.

I had no choice.

Eventually I look up to where one of the men is waiting for me to calm down. He holds out his hand to me. The other man is at the helm, and we are hitting the swell at the speed we're going, making it hard to stand.

The man helps me up and I pull at my clingy skirts, the salt water already itchy on my skin. I need to keep my balance by leaning slightly forward with the speed of the boat.

"Scalera?" the man asks as he points at my chest. "You. Scalera?"

"No," I say, confused. How can he know Matteo's name?

It's only then that I notice the gun that he is holding in the other hand. A cold chill invades my whole body as the man grabs my shoulder, and I do a two-step not to fall over with the force he is gripping my flesh.

"No?" He jerks me closer to his body, his eyes piercing into mine. "You jump from Scalera's property. *You're* Scalera's property," he sneers, revealing perfect teeth and the tip of a pink wet tongue that he sweeps over the line of his upper teeth as he waits for me to react.

"I—"

He shoves me so hard that I stumble and fall to the upholstered seat of the boat, grappling for the railing. Before I can even think, he has his knee pushed into my pelvis, pinning me to the seat as he ties my hands to the railing with a cable tie. I wince with the pain as the plastic cuts into my skin.

"*Puttana,*" he hisses, and his spit splatters my face. "*Randazzo sarà felice di avere in casa la puttana di Matteo Scalera.*"

I close my eyes, wanting only to weep. *Puttana. Matteo Scalera.* Words that need no translation. I kick at him, but he laughs.

"American whore," he says as he forces my legs open and ties them each to some hook on the boat's floor. When he's done, he points his gun at me, pushing at my wet skirts, his intent clear. I scream, but my voice is lost in the noise of the boat's engine and the vastness of the ocean.

For my efforts, I get a backhand over the cheek. My head whips to the side, and my wrists jerk at their constraints. I gasp in pain as blood seeps between my teeth, the taste making bile rise in my stomach.

The other man glances at me, a smile playing on his lips.

"Stop, *idiota*, leave the fun for later. Once Randazzo has seen her."

His perfect English rings in my ears with the force of the slap I got dealt.

*Randazzo.*

I have no clue who that is. All I know is that I've jumped into something without thinking. That I've gone from the frying pan into the fire.

These men weren't catching fish. They were spying on Matteo, waiting for a stupid woman to jump off the cliff. A woman Matteo doesn't care for. I'm just merch. Exchangeable for cash.

A virgin to be sold to the highest bidder.

For some reason I don't think that matters anymore. *"A whore for life, or a whore for one night, Tasha. Choose."*

A whore until I'm dead.

By jumping off that cliff, I've sealed my fate.

# 32

# MATTEO

"What. The. Actual. Fuck?" I bite into the phone as I close my eyes, leaning back against the headrest of the back seat. "Say that again?"

"She jumped, boss, off the fucking cliff like— like—"

Like a woman running for her life. Visions of Tasha flying, shattering, plunging into the water and never surfacing again fill my mind's eye and they make a surge of bile push up my throat. "But she got picked up?"

"Yes. Yes, boss." Burley, who is as steady and stable as a surgeon's hand with that first cut, has a tremor in his voice. He's gone soft on her. And then there's the matter of losing *my wife* while he's supposed to be guarding her. In the Don's *Il Consiglio*, that would be an automatic execution.

But Tasha's a *wife* that won't be guarded.

She actually fucking jumped.

She could have fucking died.

"A speedboat picked—"

"You said so already. I'm there in ten." I kill the call and strangle my phone. I don't move, I don't blink. I stare out of the window, waiting for the rage in me to still.

I don't lose control. Not when it comes to shit like this. When everybody's in a fucking panic, that's when I keep shit together. A lesson hard learned with Alex's death.

When the car drives into the estate, I glance around, looking for the security detail Dominic had diligently posted to protect me and my wife. I went rogue last night, risking it in some random hotel, but fuck knows, I couldn't come home. Not to her sassy tongue that only tempts me with her teasing. Not to her and that hot body and sweet pussy that begs and begs and then begs some more.

And now she's gone. She'd still be here if I'd spent the night.

I should have known a stint at a strip club would kill all fucking joy. Ever since I carried Natasha Armstrong with her wet little ass in that tease of a bikini into my apartment in Boston, I've been jinxed. I couldn't stand watching the strippers, never mind fucking one of them. Not when the last woman I watched stripping was Tasha, when she tried on the dresses for me, with her untarnished skin, doubting her own beauty, but her body pure perfection.

Worst was, there was something about the strip club I couldn't pinpoint that creeped even me out. Never mind the overall seediness and dirt and gunk on the floor that would give Stephano and Luca a twin heart attack, the women all had tattoos. Some had them on their hips, on their lower bellies, their breasts. There were two who were already naked, tattoos on their cunts, piercings everywhere.

I understand tattoos as well as the next guy, but these were all the same. They were the markings of possession, of ownership. It was only when I pored over the smaller details, as I went through the envelope the mole gave me, that it clicked. One photo was of that specific tattoo. The marking is Randazzo's seal.

I spent maybe half an hour at the club before I had to get

the hell out of there. My driver found some backstreet hotel where everybody would suspect me of spending the night with a whore. This guaranteed me some peace, and I spent the next six hours memorizing and poring over the details of Randazzo's compound. I'm as prepared as I'm ever going to be, but now I've got to deal with Tasha's disappearance. An unexpected snag if ever there was one.

She'll surface. The locals working for me will know where to look.

The car stops in front of the old stone house and I get out, buttoning my jacket. I wanted to change for my meeting with Randazzo, and that was the only reason why I headed back here in the first place.

As I stride through the house, it's clear they've lost the fucking plot. Massimo, the butler, isn't anywhere, and far off, through the French doors and past the veranda, I see men gathered. Staring like a bunch of idiots into the ocean.

I make my way over the lawn to where Burley is on his phone. As soon as he sees me, he ends the call and the rest of the men, who'd stood idly by, scatter.

"Boss—" He breaks off, knowing me well enough.

I climb over the small wall and look out to the ocean and then down the cliff. I have no fear of heights, but this isn't something many people do on a daily basis. She's fucking gutsy and, in my mind, I salute her. *Well played, kitten.*

"She's crazy, boss. I couldn't stop her. One minute I'm still drinking my coffee and the next she's sprinting like an Olympian down the lawn. She didn't hesitate. She just looked to both sides and then flew over the edge. Nobody dared shoot at her, what with her being *your wife.*" He takes a deep breath. "Who the hell jumps this, boss? Who the hell..."

"Alex. Alex would have jumped this." I glance at him and that shuts him up. I turn and head back to the house. "You're tracking the boat that picked her up? Where are you going to intercept them?"

Burley falls in next to me. "That's the thing, boss. The local men who stood guard on the cliff... they recognized the men. They say those guys were Randazzo's."

My hand shoots out and grips his throat. It's thick and muscled but he doesn't flinch as I squeeze. "Randazzo's men?" I growl, my earlier rage erupting.

Burley nods. "Yes."

"And you choose to tell me that *now*?" I squeeze.

"Matteo," he groans. "It all happened like half an hour ago."

"They've been watching the house." I let go of him. Randazzo knows I'm here, but he's also not taking chances. "Best we don't waste time. And you're coming along." With Tasha no longer here to guard, I'm going to need Burley by my side. He can choke Randazzo until his eyes pop. Seeing and reading between the lines of the information the mole gave me, I don't want to even think—

I don't know what's worse; Tasha dropping to her death from a cliff in Sicily, or Tasha being kidnapped by the Sicilian.

# 33

# TASHA

We're heading back to land, the water spraying in my face. My wrists bleed where the cable tie has cut into the skin, salt water stinging the wounds. I gasp in relief when the boat finally slows as we head close to shore. There's no harbor or town in sight. We're basically in the middle of nowhere. Our captain switches the engine off and is on his phone, speaking in Italian. The words are indistinguishable except for *Scalera*, which comes up several times.

I drop my head as the man who hit me comes to stand next to me. "Randazzo wants to see you." He cups my cheek where the painful sting of his palm feels swollen. He lifts my face up, forcing me to look at him. "Lucky girl."

His spit has mingled with salt water on my face. The least I can do is return the favor. I spit at him, but my aim sucks and it hits him in the chest.

He laughs. "You are going to have the time of your life, *mia cara*."

The boat's engine starts again and I jerk away, but he gets in a last brutal squeeze of my chin.

We head even closer to shore, the crystal blue water an

idyllic daydream to my nightmare. The shore is thickly lined with palm trees, promising a lush oasis behind them. The pebble beach is narrow, but it's there. As the boat gets as close as it can to the shore, I blink in the stark sunlight. Men are coming through the palm trees, holding guns.

When the captain hands the spitter a knife from a small cubbyhole, I strangle a scream, but he only comes closer to cut my cable ties.

"You should scream," he says, conspiratorially. "Randazzo likes that."

I shake my hands as the cable tie finally shoots loose and bring my legs together as soon as one leg is free. The urge to kick him in the face is there, but I suspect it's only going to give him more fodder. The last person I want to see again is this man in front of me. He is pure, undiluted evil.

As one of the men comes out onto the beach and wades into the water, I know it's futile. I'm hauled to my feet by my hair and made to stand. The exchange is clumsy, but soon I'm tossed over this massive guy's shoulder, and he hikes me to shore. I'm not sure why he's bothering, as my dress is wet and ruined.

He doesn't put me down and I hang limp, fighting the nausea of the boat ride and my new situation as we enter the shade. The pressure on my stomach isn't helping. I can't spare him. I puke, my eyes tearing. The man curses as my breakfast stains his black trousers like a waterfall.

He drops me and I stumble, but already another gun is in my face. "Walk," the command comes, and I hobble forward as I remember for the first time that I left my ballet flats under the breakfast table.

The path leads up at a steeper incline than I expected and soon opens to a breathtakingly beautiful villa. There's a massive swimming pool to the side, but we're heading in the direction of the veranda. A man is sitting there, working on his laptop, breakfast still laid out on the table. A ginger cat is baking in a stretch of sun, and it lifts its head with a lazy blink as we pass.

We're almost at the table when the man closes his laptop and looks up at me. "Tasha Scalera. Matteo Scalera's wife. This is unexpected." He waves at me to join him at the table, and I'm pushed into a seat at gunpoint.

He studies me and I glare back. An old man, brushing seventy, possibly older if it weren't for money used to hide his age. Watery brown eyes and a diamond earring that looks out of place. A cut in his ear as he turns his head to ask someone something in Italian.

"He's not my husband," I say as the gunman taps my elbow. I put my hands on the table where everybody can see them.

My hosts blinks at me and his gaze drops to my hands where I'm wringing them together.

"Yet you're wearing Bianca Randazzo's engagement and wedding rings." He smiles at me. "I should know; I was best man at the wedding and the ring bearer."

Crap. I've jumped from one Mafia stronghold into another. Ever since Matteo walked into my life, I can't catch a break. Someone holds a silver platter out to me with a wet facecloth and a green shot of something. I take it gingerly, sniffing the wet cloth surreptitiously before I wipe my face. I've taken too many drugs involuntarily lately and eye the green cup with unease.

"Mouthwash."

I don't relax under this pretended kindness, but I rinse and spit into the cup provided. It's as if I'm at the freaking dentist. "I'm not Matteo Scalera's wife," I repeat. "I'm just someone he brought with him to Sicily. I'm innocent." In more than one way.

He studies me for a few seconds, then takes up his coffee cup and empties it. He puts it back in its saucer with care.

"Here's the thing. Whether or not you're married to Matteo isn't key. What is his, is mine. You're his, in some way or another, which means, you're now mine."

I sink into my seat, wanting to drain out to the ocean. That must be Mafia math. And equals *I'm done for.*

"If you're his wife, he will come for you. If you're his whore—" He raises his hands in a very Italian way. "—well, then you've come to the right place." He lifts a finger, and another goon stands closer. "Tell Mara to come over immediately. Mark her as one of mine. Put her to work."

A gun muzzle pushes into my back, and I'm forced to stand. My legs are so shaky, I barely manage.

There's no need to read between the lines here.

Everything is crystal clear.

# 34

# MATTEO

I should have chartered a helicopter. Driving is fucking killing me right now, especially since Tasha traveled on a speedboat where there's no traffic to contend with.

If Randazzo has been keeping an eye on my place, the most logical thing for him to do when he captures a rogue unit jumping randomly off a cliff is to take her in for interrogation. Now the clock is ticking, with her probably being tortured, while I'm stuck behind some fucked-up camper van that drives half the speed limit. My driver understands the urgency, but crashing won't help Tasha either.

I've calculated everything to the T for this meeting, and now have to deal with a curveball I didn't anticipate. Never mind dealing with the Sicilian once and for all, my focus is on saving Tasha first. The last thing I want for her is to become one of the women at the club last night. Without a doubt, Randazzo will slot her right in, drugged until it's the only way she can function, her spirit broken.

I have to get Tasha back. Should I get to eliminate Randazzo in the process, I'll consider myself lucky.

I have the best luck.

And Burley is here. He's been stretching and fisting his fingers a thousand times since we clambered into the car. He has murder on his mind. I might adjust the initial plan just to accommodate him.

There's a gap and the driver speeds past the camper van, and suddenly the road is open. Two other cars are backing us up; men I would have had with me in any case.

By the time we approach the compound an hour later, every scenario has replayed in my mind. I have to keep my cool. Stick to the original story. I'm here to sell the family farmhouse, I brought my wife on our honeymoon, the Don wants to have a clean cut with his past. I've been sent as emissary to come in peace as the Don is dying.

A security checkpoint at the gate keeps us for twenty minutes as they search every fucking nook and cranny of the car for weapons, the undercarriage for bombs and scan us for weapons too, airport style. They confiscate our phones and I protest, but I expected this. My phone is only a decoy, but Randazzo clearly lives on the edge. He must be a nervous guy.

We drive on, the house coming into view behind an artificial hill, landscaped for maximum privacy. The sea is right there, an escape route we've considered but the mole told us that it's too risky.

The driver parks in the circular driveway and I pop the car door open with a final nod at Burley. He'll be right behind me. Randazzo won't deny me all my men. We're the fucking Mafia, after all.

I button my jacket as I wait for Burley to circle the car, taking in the place. It's a classic Italian villa, glaringly white in the warm summer splendor, with a shocking pink bougainvillea in full bloom stretching over a pagoda, reminding me of Tasha's ripped dress.

*Tasha*. When the fuck did she happen?

Another armored guard appears at the front door and nods

at us to follow. We don't speak as we enter the lion's den, but then, Burley and I don't need to talk to communicate. As we walk through the house, my gaze flits over the interior, making connections to what I studied last night. I've clipped two weapon caches to my memory by the time we've walked the sprawling mansion to the back veranda.

A grey-haired man is sitting at a table, a closed laptop in front of him, staring at the expanse of the garden. He is wearing a black polo shirt and chinos, as if he just got back from a round of golf. That diamond in his lobe and the ear notch confirms my target. He doesn't even look in my direction, not until I'm right in his peripheral.

When our gazes meet, I'm flooded by this feeling that I know this man from somewhere, from some previous life. Those eyes, the dark brown of my own, so Italian, but the shape… it's like looking into my own eyes.

Can't be.

"Matteo Scalera," he says, studying me keenly. "I've been expecting you."

"I did make an appointment." So yes, it follows that he's been expecting me.

Randazzo chuckles. "Sit, *mio figlio.* To think Don Scalera took so long to send you to me."

"Don Randazzo," I say, following his lead and not shaking hands, but rather sitting down next to him. Burley has my back, and in the corner of my eye I see the mole, there where he guards Randazzo from the shadows.

"I'd stand to embrace you, but my leg—" He waves in general. "An old bullet wound is playing up more and more nowadays."

Good. "I'm sorry to hear that." And I'm not a fucking hugger. I had an arsenal of small talk prepped to lure this man into a false sense of security, but now there's only one thing I want to know. "I believe you have something that belongs to me."

He laughs, and the sound makes me want to crush his throat with my fist. "She claims she isn't your wife. Fresh-faced and feisty by the looks of it. Something to tame. It's always been my preference. It runs in the Randazzo blood."

I shift in my seat, plugging my rage. "I'll do the taming. And for that I need to see her and take her home."

He shrugs, bobbing his head as if he is hemming and hawing. "I wasn't under the impression that you were coming to see me because I have your wife."

"And I won't tell you my business until I'm sure she's safe." We're negotiating. Soon there's going to be a middle school staring contest, which I'll blast the fuck out of him once I have a gun.

He nods. "Fair enough." He pulls his laptop closer and opens the screen. "Let's see how your pretty little *wife* is doing. A wife who jumps off cliffs to get away from her husband. I'd love to hear what you did to her to make her do something so drastic."

I close my eyes, forcing myself not to tense up and show my hand. The man is a fucking psycho, but I knew that.

"Here she is." Randazzo turns the screen to me, and my eyes home in on Tasha. Gagged. Hands tied above her head. Legs tied to something straight out of a gynecologist's toolkit, spread with a head leaning in between her thighs. The head looks up and a tattoo gun comes into view.

That perfect sweet little pussy, marked.

Behind me, I feel every muscle in Burley's body tense to snapping point.

I splay my fingers together as I rest my elbows on the tabletop. I press my forefingers to my lips, forcing myself to breathe. "You've gagged her," I say, softly, calmly.

"She was screaming, ruining my peace and quiet."

Which means she's here, in the compound.

"And then you tied her up."

Randazzo shrugs. "For the tattoo artist's sake. The girls aren't always willing, and I like things done… neatly."

"I see. So do I."

He beams. The decrepit fucker actually beams. "Another sign—"

"Mostly." I interrupt him, not wanting to hear another word from his mouth. "I think you won't appreciate this then. It isn't going to be my finest work." I pull back and with all the force in me, punch him in the face.

His nose cracks and he rears back, shocked. Nobody moves except Burley. The mole doesn't come to Randazzo's aid. Shutters roll down, blocking the guards on the inside of the house from rushing out. The guards in the garden are too far off to realize there's a commotion. The two other guards in the vicinity are on the mole's side and only look on. Already Burley's thick hands are around the Sicilian's neck, pressing, blocking any sound but a strained gargle that comes from his throat as blood seeps from his nose into his mouth, staining his bared teeth.

Randazzo reaches for Burley's hands to pull him off, but the old man is no match for this giant. I stand and go to Randazzo's side, blocking what's happening from view on the garden's side. We are efficient and quiet. The garden birds haven't stopped chirping, music in his final minutes.

The mole comes out of the shadows and hands me a knife. I pinch Randazzo's notched ear and start to slice. He buckles in his seat, but if I were him, I'd save my oxygen. Already his face is flushed an unhealthy red.

"That's for gagging my wife," I say as I put the ear in my side pocket. Still he struggles as I reach over and slice off his other ear. "That's for tying her up." With the pressure on his throat, the blood pours out at speed. His eyes are bulging, and I dip in the tip of the knife and dig one out. "That's for looking at my wife's pussy."

I pocket his eye, wondering if I should bother with the other. The man is so to say dead. Still he fucking gargles, as if I care. That brown eye stares at me, bloodshot now, incredulous and petrified. Staring at me like every victim of his must have stared death in the face. Meh. They come in pairs. I dig the other eye out and pocket it. "And that's for inking her."

I nod to Burley and he intensifies his hold. Blood is oozing out of every hole I've made. I stare at the hand, the desperate grip that's weakening. I pick out his little finger, the one with the ring bearing his insignia, the fucking mark he had tattooed on Tasha's pure skin. With a surgeon's precision, I cut it off, final proof for the Don.

Randazzo heaves and shudders one last time. Burley relaxes.

I stand back and look at my handiwork.

Murder.

Is.

Art.

# 35

# MATTEO

"Where is she?" I ask the mole as I turn to him. He's already muttering something on a walkie talkie. Old school, but I'm not on home ground. I don't have my phone and feel like I've lost a limb.

We have minutes. As soon as the guards realize Randazzo is dead, the guns are going to come out blazing. Some men will do so out of loyalty, others out of fear. And then there are those who will make the most of the shift in the hierarchy.

"Follow me." The mole nods and we rush along the side of the house. The hurricane shutters are closed over every window, in lockdown.

It's only when we reach the end of the house that one shutter is halfway open, blocked by a piece of metal. From inside, men are calling. The guards have realized something's up. I become aware of the incessant beep of an alarm that indicates something's been breached.

They're already hunting us.

"Once inside, you have three minutes before I open the shutters," the mole says. "The cache with the bulletproof vests is in this room's closet. Your wife is next door on your right."

I nod. The whole business is risky. We could be stepping into a trap.

"Thank you," the mole says, and I notice the sheen of sweat gathering by his temples. This guy is risking everything too, but he has achieved his own goal today and has avenged his sister. Randazzo died in front of his own eyes, and I bet if I'd handed him a knife, he would happily have butchered along.

I've trusted him this far. "See you on the other side."

Burley is already clambering through the open window, his bulk hardly fitting through the small space. I follow suit, the only weapon on me the knife the mole handed me. Where there were voices before, everything has now gone eerily quiet. Burley opens the closet and quietly searches in the little light through blankets and old clothes. He tosses me a bulletproof vest. I signal to him that there should be more than one. I hope for three. Tasha will need one too.

Crashing sounds come from the other side of the house. Something had lured the guards in the opposite direction.

"There're only two," Burley mutters. He strips his jacket and pulls on a vest. "It's too fucking small."

"Better than nothing." For a moment we just stare at each other in the ill-lit room. Tasha wasn't supposed to be here. *He* wasn't supposed to be here. I had some other bodyguard assigned for today. But this is it. The moment where I make the choice between my bodyguard and friend of over ten years and the woman I've kidnapped.

"She'll have it," Burley says and he doesn't fasten the vest. "You look after Rosalia."

"It might not come to that."

"We walked in here knowing it was going to come to that."

True. I take the automatic gun he holds out to me, hefting it for weight and comfort. Then he hands me a revolver. I shove that in the back of my pants and pick the knife up where I put it down a second ago.

"See you on the other side, boss."

I nod as we make our way to the door. Burley opens it softly, barely an inch. Then he pushes it wider, opening to darkness. One door. We only need to move one door to the right.

Burley gives me a barely perceptible nod and we inch our way along the wall, our eyes slow to adapt. He's feeling his way and pauses when he reaches another door jamb. He reaches for the doorknob and twists. It's locked.

We don't have time to pick a lock. A female voice sounds from the other side and Burley shrugs. He knocks lightly, three short ones in quick succession, then a pause, followed by another knock. A muffled moan sounds from the room and my heart skips a beat. *Tasha*.

The lock twists and the door opens a bit, but Burley is already pushing his shoulder in, gun up, ready to shoot. I follow, already knowing what to expect here as I recall the room vividly from the video footage we saw earlier.

My eyes have adjusted to the dark, but it's hard to see more than shapes. The tattoo artist holds her tattoo gun as if it can save her. Burley points his gun at her temple, a finger to his lips. Tasha is still tied up and gagged and I step up to her, my heart in my throat.

I touch her cheek, which is wet with tears, as I lean into her ear. "Sshh, kitten, you're going to have to keep it together here for me, okay?"

She draws in haggard little breaths, clearly petrified. I stroke her hair, needing her to calm down. "We don't have time, Tasha," I murmur as I put my automatic gun down on her stomach. "I'm going to lift the gag and untie you, but you need to be quiet."

She nods and I have the knife ready, feeling where to cut through the cloth and the cable ties. As soon as her arms are free, she has them around me, clinging as she muffles a sob into my neck. I cup her head close, holding on to her for the merest second. "We need to get out of here."

"Yes." She lets go and reaches for the leather straps that are holding her legs in place. I help on the one side and once she's unstrapped, pick up my gun. She puts her feet down, wincing.

"Can you walk?" I whisper, trying to gauge what I can from her expression in the dark.

Tasha nods but she's in pain. I can't see where she hurts, but if I could kill Randazzo every day for the rest of my life, it would be my pleasure.

Gunfire goes off on the other side of the house. "Party's started."

"The shutters should have gone up by now," Burley hisses. "And this room has no windows."

I'd hoped to make a clean cut through the garden to the car, but now we need to go through the house. We'll be trapped if we don't leave now.

From somewhere loud banging sounds as someone hits a shutter from the outside, making it rattle, probably trying to find the breach. Shouting ensues and we don't have a second to lose. We don't even have time for Tasha to put on the bullet-proof vest.

I push the knife into Tasha's hand, handing her the only weapon she'll know how to deal with. Giving her a gun would be pointless. "Don't hesitate, kitten. Whatever happens, don't hesitate."

# 36

## TASHA

Matteo has come for me. It's all I can think of as he hands me the knife. *He has come for me.*

Gunshots go off more regularly now. Whatever is happening out there, it's real. I clutch the knife tight as we slip out of the door, Matteo first, then me, Burley at my back. While we were still in Boston, I would have given anything to have a weapon like this. Now, if I want to get out of this hellscape, I'll have to use it. *Do not hesitate.*

Hurried voices come from the room next door and Matteo rushes down the corridor as if he knows exactly where he's going.

I came through here earlier. At some point we'll pass through the kitchen. If only we could put on the lights, but the power cut out as soon as the rattling of the shutters stopped. I'm limping from where I got a kick to the thigh, the muscle stiff. My stomach hurts with the echo of another kick, but at least he didn't get my ribs.

Matteo stops abruptly and I collide with his back, but he has his arm out, pressing me to the wall, huddling me closer to him. With Burley squeezing me from the other side, I'm as well-protected as I'm going to be. We're all holding our breaths. Behind us, voices are calling in Italian. Footsteps rush towards us from the other side.

A soft glow from a skylight in the next room makes it easier to see. Matteo lowers himself on his haunches and I follow suit. Then Burley scoots past me, into the next open concept living area that's adjacent to the kitchen. He goes down behind a sofa. He covers for us, and when Matteo taps my hip, I understand. I keep low and follow him quickly as we seek cover behind the kitchen island.

I huddle with my back against the island, watching in horror in the oven's gleaming reflection as five men sweep into the open space from the far side of the house, guns raised, seeking their targets. I tap Matteo and he looks at the reflection and nods. I close my eyes, knowing more men are coming from the other side. They are calling to each other in Italian, knowing that they've herded us into the space like cattle.

Matteo brushes my arm with his hand, instructing me to stay down. I can't see Burley from my vantage point, but Matteo clicks his tongue.

All hell breaks loose.

I can hardly breathe. Shots are raining down, splintering the marble countertop, shattering the windows and glass cupboards. I clutch the knife, but my hand is shaking. Matteo is still there, calm, listening in the spell of quiet. He peers around the counter, looking for Burley. I have no idea how they communicate, but Matteo signals to me. *Two down, five to go.*

So many bullets and only two are down?

I spot movement in the oven's reflection. A man is padding our way stealthily, his reflection perfectly visible at the angle I'm sitting at. He is going to come around the island and shoot us both. Matteo is looking the other way and doesn't notice him.

My heart hammers in my throat, my body suddenly weak with the realization that this could be it.

A surge of adrenaline spikes just as he puts a leg within range. I lean around the corner of the island with all my weight and jam the knife into his thigh, right at the spot where I'll sever his femoral artery. I twist and slice away as he stumbles with a growl. His gun goes off, peppering the fridge as his leg caves, blood fountaining out of the wound.

Minutes. He has minutes.

He stares at me with a snarl as he turns his gun towards me. I scream as I press against the island, waiting for the worst, but watch instead how a bullet hits him right in the forehead. He slumps forward, his body heavy on top of mine.

Sounds zone out. Time stands still. My blood pulses in my head while I can hear every heartbeat stressing that I'm still alive.

*I'm alive.*

I need to get him off me. The blood from his leg is pooling at my feet, drenching me. If it weren't for that bullet, this would have killed him. *I would have killed him.* The rest of the shootout happens but I'm zoned out. I battle to push his weight off me, feeling sick with the rush of adrenaline. Once I'm free, I lean back and breathe, disconnected. It's only when Matteo's hand on my shoulder jerks me out of my haze that I look at him, stunned. The knife drops from my hand and clatters to the floor.

"We need to get to the car," Matteo says as he picks up the knife. "Don't leave evidence."

I'm numb, but he has me. He helps me up but instead of rushing off he picks me up and carries me out of the room, which is scattered with broken glass, bodies, and blood.

Matteo puts me down as soon as we're out of the fray and pushes me in the direction of the front door. He turns around and I do the same. Burley is coming, but it's clear he is wounded.

"Fuck it," Matteo hisses. He heads back into the room, where a wounded lone ranger is still wielding a gun. Matteo shoots him point blank, then has Burley hitched up under his shoulder.

"You should get out, boss," he huffs. "While you can."

"Fuck if I leave you here. I'll have to kill you first and I'm out of bullets."

I'm at the front door rattling the handle, but it doesn't move. Matteo waves me to the side and rips though the bolt with bullets he told Burley a second ago he didn't have. The door inches open and I freeze as I stare out into the blinding sunlight. Two new guards are pointing weapons at us, ready for the final blow.

"Go, Tasha, they're ours."

The getaway car is right there, and I clamber in. Matteo helps Burley in and then doors slam as we skid off.

It's only when we drive through the open gate and into the public road that I exhale.

I nearly killed someone. If it weren't for Matteo wrapping up what I'd started...

I intended to kill that man. In cold blood. I can't process that now. I just can't.

Focus.

*You're actually alive.*

*You were becoming a doctor. The line between life and death is thin.*

I reach out to Burley. "Where're you shot?"

# 37

## TASHA

"Right here, luv." Burley groans as he touches his biceps, where a pool of red is spreading on his white shirt. "And here." His hand goes to the side of his butt, where his pants shine with blood.

"Put pressure on his arm," I say to Matteo, who is sitting on that side, as I look down to put pressure on Burley's butt. "I'll hold on to you here. At least it wasn't your chest or abdomen. How far do we have to go?"

I glance up to meet Matteo's gaze. He looks at me with something in his eyes I've never seen before. I can't even pinpoint what it is, too conscious of the sticky wet patch under my palm. His gaze travels my face, taking in my puffed-up cheek, the bruise I must be popping on my chin, then drops to the cuts on my wrists where the cable tie sliced into my flesh. I have to look away, but I feel his gaze burning on me. Fury. That's what it is. Pure blazing fury.

"Five minutes to the barn," he says, and his cold tone makes unease cruise down my back. "It's half an hour to a boat ramp where a dinghy waits to take us to the yacht."

We're yacht people now. Okay. Whatever. "You're going to

have to hang in there, Burley," I mutter, grappling with the idea that he needs to move twice, and Matteo said nothing about going to a hospital.

"I'm hanging, luv, but I'm not sure why you're botherin'. You nearly gave me a heart attack this morning. Which is a very clean way to kill a guy if ever there was one."

I glance down at my hands, which are stained with blood, my arms splattered with it. I want to retch, but my stomach is empty. *I nearly killed a man.* When I look up, Matteo's gaze is still on me.

"I'm sorry," I whisper. I tried to stop that man from getting to *him*. My kidnapper, who I wanted to kill days ago. I'm sorry for trying to save myself. And for jumping. For my dad's crimes. For everything that got us to this point.

"You did what you needed to do," Matteo says. "We got out."

I nod but find no assurance in his words. With one well-aimed stab I've been baptized into their inner circle.

The car speeds along the road. There's nothing out here, not even a vineyard or an olive grove. It's almost desert-like with barren land. We were totally isolated, which is great if you want to make sure nobody gets close to you. Or if you want to torture and kill people.

A scatter of farmhouses appears, and next thing we are turning into a gravel road that leads to a barn.

"We're good," Matteo says as no one follows us.

The barn is open, and we drive right in. The massive door rattles closed as soon as we're inside. We're cloaked in darkness again, but my eyes adjust quickly with light coming from missing tiles in the roof. Another driver is waiting in a white SUV with clear windows, a scented pine dangling from the rearview mirror. It looks like a taxi.

"Let's get you sorted, Burley," Matteo says as he opens the door and peels off his bulletproof vest. He strides over to the white SUV and the driver opens the trunk as if on cue.

"Come on, luv," Burley says with a weak smile. "He'll expect you to do one or the other, becoming a doctor as you are."

"What?" I give him a wide-eyed stare as he gingerly eases out of the car and stands.

I clamber out and watch in fascination as Matteo spreads a sterile pad inside the open trunk. A medical case stands ready, and he pulls out everything needed for a bullet wound emergency.

"You need a hand, old man?" Matteo shoots back as Burley limps in his direction.

"Fuck you, boss. If I take another bullet in my butt for you—"

"I retire you with a very lucrative package."

"You're my witness, luv," Burley groans as he makes it all the way. "A *very lucrative package.*" He shrugs off his bulletproof vest, his arm just hanging.

Matteo is putting surgical gloves on and glances in my direction. I stand closer, thankful for the distraction. Less so when Burley unbuckles his belt in one swift movement and unbuttons his pants. "Sorry, luv," he says as he turns his back to me, drops his pants and scoots his boxers down just far enough. He makes himself comfortable by lying down, half in, half out of the car's trunk.

"Nothing I haven't seen before," I lie. I knew it, but knowing and seeing firsthand is different. Burley is built. As in heavyweight wrestling built. Thighs that flex as he settles, sculpted ass in the air. An ass to die for, except for the round bullet hole leaking blood.

I look at Matteo, but he is already busy opening a bottle of disinfectant. He splashes it over Burley's butt and the man growls. Once some of the blood is cleaned away, Matteo looks closely. "This one's a keeper." He glances up to me. "Gauze and tape to stop the bleeding."

It's as if his instructions zap me into motion. I pull on

surgical gloves and do as instructed while Matteo cuts Burley's shirt sleeve off. "You have everything here," I say as I go through the medical kit.

"Not our first rodeo," Matteo says as he tosses Burley's blood-soaked sleeve to the side. He lifts Burley's arm and inspects it. "The bullet went right through. You're good."

I shoot Burley's arm a glance. The blood is already coagulating.

"Do the same here," Matteo says. "Just stop the bleeding."

I pause midair with the gauze I'm holding. "That's it?"

"For now."

"Aren't you getting him to a doctor?" I'm weak in the knees.

"I'm good, luv," Burley chirps in.

"He'll manage," Matteo says. "Plus, you'll look after him."

"I—" Where my hands were steady seconds ago, they now quiver. "Okay?"

"Good girl. Give him some of those painkillers."

Matteo reaches for a ziplock bag and picks something out of his jacket pocket. He plops it into the clear bag.

An eyeball is staring at me through the thin clear film. Shock ripples through my body and I dry heave. Matteo drops in another one and follows it up with a finger that still holds a gold signet ring.

"What *is* that?" I breathe, managing to keep the bile down.

Matteo says nothing. Two ears join the rest and that's when I spot the diamond earring, blinking where it isn't smeared with blood.

*You're not the first order of business I'll attend to in Sicily*. Holy... holy... *fuck*.

I look up, scared to meet Matteo's eyes. He pins me down with a frank stare and a quirked brow as he zips the bag closed and tosses it to the side. "Evidence." He peels off the surgical gloves, shakes off his jacket, and takes some wipes to clean speckles of blood and battle dust off his face and hands. "I have business to wrap up, so I'll see you on the yacht."

"What? How?" It sinks in that Matteo isn't coming with us. "Where're you going?"

He picks up his baggie of body parts, this time putting it in a black shopping bag. I don't want to know what he's going to do next, but he can't go out there. Not after what he's done. Not while carrying *that* with him. He'll be hunted and slaughtered — "Don't leave?" I beg, the anguish in my voice real. "Matteo, I can't..."

He touches my chin, gently tipping it to the side to see my cheek. "Whatever you do, kitten, don't mistake me for the good guy." He rubs his thumb over my bottom lip. "And no more shenanigans, understand?"

It isn't a request. It's a command. No more cliff jumping. Look where it got me. "Yes," I whisper, caving into him, his warm touch the balm I didn't even know I needed. "Understood."

"I won't be long, and when I'm back we're going to have a little chat." The way he says it forces all the warmth to leave my body, his tone making chills run up my arms as he drops his hand away. "You know the drill, Burley."

"Yes, boss," he groans, but it sounds like it comes with an eye roll.

Matteo clambers into the black car's passenger seat and gives the okay for the driver to go. The barn door rattles open, and the car drives away into the late afternoon heat.

# 38

## MATTEO

The dinghy is waiting for me at the agreed spot and soon I'm heading towards Don Trapani's yacht. It was the right call and I have to give it to the Don. After shooting up Randazzo's place, taking a plane out might have involved too much paperwork. It was a last-minute change to my plans, but I found it easy to navigate. When people want someone dead, they are eager to help you in whichever way they can.

It's almost midnight. I planned to be here four hours ago. The yacht is hardly lit up, only a soft yellow glow coming from the helm. The rest of the yacht is shrouded in darkness, with only the navigation lights visible. As we approach, the dinghy stops next to the side-boarding platform. I bid my skipper goodnight and climb up to the main deck.

I've had feedback from Burley once they boarded the yacht. Another bodyguard is with Tasha since he felt too woozy to keep an eye on her with the pain meds he took.

We're not letting that one go rogue again. After what happened today, she'll probably think twice about trying to escape again.

I make my way over the main deck to the sliding doors that

open to a sleek lounge area. A crew member waits for me. "Mr. Scalera?"

I nod.

"Welcome. Is there anything you need? Can I prepare you something to eat? To drink?"

"My wife?" Might as well stick to the farce.

The man must read something in my expression because he indicates I should follow him. "This way." He leads me to a closed door, knocks, and opens it after a second.

I walk inside and spot the guard sitting patiently on the sofa in the ring of a reading light, as if bodyguarding in times like these isn't the most boring shit you can get paid for.

"Matteo?" Tasha is in bed but sits up and rips the covers off.

"Leave us." My tone stops her from getting out of bed. She looks like a deer in the headlights.

The guard stands with a nod, a curt "Mr. Scalera," and heads out of the suite, closing the door behind him and the crew member.

The cabin has a lounge and counter that serves as a bar. I need a fucking drink. I take the two tins of sardines from my ass pockets and put them on the counter. They're still lukewarm to the touch. I pour myself a stiff whiskey and add some ice from the bucket.

Tasha is right behind me. I heard her getting out of bed, the sheets rustling, her footfalls soft on the thick carpet.

"I couldn't sleep. Not until you were back," she says softly as she comes to stand next to me.

I take a sip of my whiskey, the gold liquid burning my tongue, not looking at her.

I need distance.

"You changed your clothes."

Jeans and a white T-shirt scream *playboy on summer vacation* and not *Mafia pawn who just got the job done* like my blood-splattered and torn suit did.

I ignore her, walk to the sofa, and sit down.

"These are pretty," she says, the confidence draining out of her voice with each non-response from me. She's picking up the designer sardine tins, my little memento from Sicily for the Don.

"Not for you, kitten. Whatever you do, don't open it."

Tasha puts the cans back on the counter. "I don't want to know."

She turns towards me, and I study her body. She's wearing a limp grey T-shirt, and probably only that limp grey T-shirt. My plans didn't include trapezing her wardrobe from the farmhouse to the yacht.

"Whose shirt is that?" I feel a fucked-up pang of jealousy thinking that she's wearing another dick's T-shirt. Mom's wedding and engagement rings still bling on her finger. Good. She's keeping up the farce too. I take another deep sip of whiskey, then put the drink down.

"I got it from one of the crew. My dress is ruined."

Trapani's crew won't talk. And I saw what she looked like earlier. *My wife* will never look like that again.

"Take it off." *My wife* will not be wearing another man's shirts.

*My wife.* Fuck knows why I like the sound of that so much.

She pads over, comes to stand right in front of my legs and peels off the T-shirt. It's such a surprise that she doesn't backchat me, that I only have a short second to sweep my gaze down her naked body before she sits on my lap and curls up against my chest like a kitten.

"I only feel safe when you're with me," she whispers, her voice breaking as her hand wraps around my neck. "Please don't leave me behind again."

Her body is a warm drug against mine as my arm goes around her back to support her. She's sobbing now and I can't stop myself from holding her close. In one simple move she's disarmed me. Stripped me completely of every defense I ever built up against this exact situation. And my defenses are strong and high. But ever since I held her like this on the day I kidnapped her, she's been drilling a hole into my bedrock. Now she's hit my core.

"Where did they hurt you, baby girl?" I murmur as I nuzzle her temple. Her face is pushed into my neck, hiding. I run my palm over her thigh, trying to calm her. Here is a budding bruise. Looks like a kick to the leg.

I've been brimming with fury ever since I saw her on Randazzo's laptop, gagged and tied up, strapped open and helpless. Now she's here, and all I want to do is kiss her and make her forget. *I want to kiss her.*

Some things you never forget.

Like what would happen to her if she's auctioned off as a virgin.

For all I know she's no longer one.

The idea of somebody having raped her earlier is too much. "Tell me where they hurt you, Tasha."

I shift so that she's forced to sit straight on my lap. Her hair covers her face and I need to sweep it away. Those lips, those perfect lips that I've been studiously avoiding, are trembling.

*Fuck.*

I cup her face and force her to look at me. "We killed that fucking asshole."

She nods.

"And we killed all his men who were in the house. There was a shootout amongst the rest. They're all dead." Except for my mole and his team. "The place has been torched."

Tasha quivers, tears streaming down her cheeks. "I—I—I stabbed that man with intention," she sobs. "I would have s-stabbed him again. T-to k-kill him."

Here it is. The physical pain is always secondary to the psychological. She hurts because she did something she thought she'd never do. Yes, she was trying to save herself, but that was a lost cause from the start for her and she knew it. She stabbed him with the aim to kill and to stop him from killing me.

*She saved my life.*

"It was you or him, sweetheart. Anybody would have done the same." I stroke her cheek. "And you didn't hesitate. You listened to me for once."

She cracks a smile between her tears, but bites down on her lip as if that's not allowed, then buries her face back in my neck. "Matteo—"

I hold her, giving her time to grieve the girl she once was, while I wrestle with the reality that if she hadn't delivered that stab, neither of us would be sitting here now.

Things went off the rails today, and I don't know when or where, but they have, in more than one way too. Here I am holding the one woman in my arms that I should never allow in, but I can feel myself slip, opening up for her invasion. *She saved my fucking useless life and it's never felt more undeserved.*

Ever since we went our separate ways this afternoon, her actions have been eating at me. Now I'm holding her as close as a man can, and she smells so delicious. Clean and fresh and warmly feminine. My cock, always on high alert around her, is already painfully hard where it's pressing into the soft curve of her hip. "Let me see what they did to you, kitten."

"They didn't touch me beyond—" She breaks off as my hand slips between her legs.

"I want to see what they did here," I murmur as I carefully caress a knuckle down her sex. A tremor runs through her at my touch. Her skin is smooth, freshly shaven, a canvas prepared. By the feel of it, a wet canvas.

"I told him we weren't married, but he didn't believe me. And yet he wanted me marked like his other women and put to *work*. Even as your *wife*. He said that because I belong to you, I belong to him, and he could do what he wanted with me."

My hand stills, pressing lightly against her inner thigh, my thumb pausing its sweet teasing. That logic—

My brain short circuits. That's no longer how it works. For us Scalera boys it's never worked that way. We don't share, we don't degrade, we don't love. And I know why none of this is sitting right with me. I'm doing this for Alex, for my own fucking heartache which time and again escapes my chokehold where I have control over it, but Alex would never have sanctioned any of this. Alex would have been better than me and denied the Don this last request.

I swallow down the bitter pill, knowing I'll never live up to my younger brother's moral strength, and take in a deep inhale of her subtle scent. If Randazzo hurt her today, I'll never forgive myself.

I nudge her inner thigh and her legs ease open. I prepare myself for the worst. Her sweet mound tarnished by Randazzo's seal. Black on white, red rimmed from an unwanted ink invasion.

But there's nothing. It's only Tasha as she was before. My soul sags into the sofa with relief.

"They had to call the tattoo artist in, and I don't know where she came from, but she was late. She didn't get beyond prepping and stenciling out the design before the power cut."

A shudder runs through me, and I run my thumb in circles over her skin in relief. She's so fucking soft. So fucking perfect. What I saw was only the prep drawing, with no ink. She is pure. Untouched. *Mine.*

*Never. This woman can never be mine.*

I shift my hand away. My final solution for Peter Armstrong's retribution can go on. I could never have auctioned her off with the seal of Randazzo. To tie the Scalera operations to one of the biggest sex trafficking rings in Europe would be suicide.

Her lips press against my skin, softly, inquisitively, in slow kisses she trails up to my jaw. She rolls her hips into my touch, making my thumb reconnect with her sex. I can't stop myself. I need this too. I respond on instinct, caressing her, and she sighs a little erotic moan that only makes me harder.

She wants this. It's all I'll ever be able to give her.

"You're going to come for me, kitten?" I circle her wet clit with my thumb, our mouths a mere inch apart.

"Yes." She rakes her fingers into my hair, guiding my head so our lips finally meet.

Our kiss is soft, gentle, a total antithesis to the chaos of the day and the way I want to fuck her. But this is what she needs. We kiss deeper, slower, our tongues connecting in an erotic dance, while her pussy meets my hand with every circle of her clit. She moans now, her release rising to the surface.

Her fingers dig into my hair, clutching, her body shuddering as she moans my name into my mouth. Her release comes as a total surrender, her body mastered by my simple touch.

We don't stop kissing. She's a drug that I've tasted and now can't get enough of. My body is primed for its own release, and when she slides her hand down my chest and underneath my shirt, I don't stop her.

Against all logic and common sense, I let her touch me.

When she shifts to straddle me, I groan. Some battles aren't worth fighting. Not when her beautiful breasts are a temptation no man can resist, her nipples begging for attention. I caress the sides of her breasts, watching as her expression darkens as she leans in to kiss me again. She tugs at my T-shirt, and I sit up and edge forward so she can peel it off.

The way she moans as she finally slides both her hands over my bare shoulders and down my pecs, her tongue dancing with mine, is almost enough to push me over the edge, what with her pussy pressing into my cock, seeking friction again.

My kitten is a quick learner.

Her hands are at my belt, tugging. I should stop her, *need* to stop her. I still her hands with a firm grip. “Kitten—”

“I’ve been dreaming of this, Matteo, please, let me—” She breaks off and looks me in the eye. “*Teach me.*”

Teach her to suck my cock? With that begging siren’s tone?

I’m fucked.

# 39

# TASHA

I'm not lying. Ever since the day I threw his phone across his apartment and he pressed me against the wall, telling me he'd be tearing the world down to find me and make sure I was safe, I've been having visions of us.

Of me, serving him.

Of him succumbing to me.

I know it's messed up, but he kept his promise. He came for me as if I were his. My feelings for Matteo have been oscillating between pure hate and some type of warped infatuation, but now they're stuck in another corner, and they won't budge. Admiration and respect twisted with something I won't admit to myself—ever.

We're still staring into each other's eyes as he releases his grip on my hands. I'm finally getting to touch him. I unbuckle his belt. His cock strains against his jeans, and it must be uncomfortable. I deal with the button and the zip, strip him open to graze my fingertips over the silky flesh.

Matteo sighs as I caress him again, this time circling a fingertip over the wet head. He closes his eyes and drops his head back with a strained chuckle, as his cock pushes into my touch. "Get on your knees."

I slip from his lap and settle on the floor, submissive, waiting for the next instruction. He leans in and cups my cheek. "I'm not giving you more than this, kitten," he murmurs as he strokes my lips. "Understand?"

I don't want to understand. He is denying *us*.

He stands and towers over me, studying me for a moment, his hands running the waist of his jeans as he toes off his loafers. "You're too fucking beautiful to be ruined by the likes of me."

I want to protest, but he eases off his jeans and kicks them to the side, distracting me with his muscles' grace in the fluid movement. My heart flips at the sight of him, his body fully exposed to me for the first time, the visual of his tattoos from this angle, his cock jutting out.

"Is this going to be enough for you, kitten?"

I don't know how I'm going to do it. Never mind my mouth, how is that to go in down there? And no, being with him like this now will never be enough. I suspect I'm going to crave Matteo Scalera for years to come.

That's a future-me problem. Right now, all I want is to touch him, so I stroke my hands up his legs, resting my hands on his thighs, but not doing more.

"You understand this isn't going further," he grunts as he grips my hair, tilts my head and forces me to look him in the eye. "Answer me, goddammit."

"Yes." I blink at him as I inch my hands higher, stroking his strained balls with my fingertips.

His cock twitches at my touch and Matteo smirks as he pushes a thumb into my mouth and circles it over my tongue. "So fucking eager."

He grips his cock, his one hand still controlling my head by my hair, and pushes the tip into my mouth. I close my lips and suck, and he grunts as he drops his head back. "Gently, kitten. I want this to last longer than seconds."

I moan as he pushes in deeper, already feeling the strain on my throat. He pulls out and drives back in, controlling every movement with his hold on my hair, while I grip the back of his thighs. He goes deeper with every thrust, eventually hitting the back of my throat. I splay my legs, sinking into a new rush of desire building up in my core. I never knew this would be such a turn-on. No wonder I've been dreaming of it.

He thrusts even deeper, and my throat closes up in protest, my eyes tearing, but I don't let go of his thighs, not willing to back off even half an inch. I need to hold on, accustom my body to taking all of him.

As if he reads my mind, he holds still. "Told you you'd love gagging on my cock." He steps into me and bends my head back to open my throat, then gives me the smallest of thrusts. "Sexiest fucking thing ever," he grunts as he does it again. "Breathe, baby, almost there."

Tears are running down my cheeks, but I manage to inhale, my body protesting the strained position. He is so tall and like this I'm a little bird feeding on his cock. He rocks into me several times, and I feel his release about to erupt.

Instead of coming down my throat, he pulls out and ejects his cum down my neck and onto my chest. He heaves a muttered *fuck* as I stare up at him, his eyes glazed over in pleasure.

Matteo softens his grip on my hair into a gentle caress and my body relaxes. He gives me space but keeps his gaze on me. "That was perfection, kitten. You won't need another lesson."

I wipe at my mouth, basking in his praise, but also knowing he is a man of his word. There won't be a repeat and he won't give me more. He takes my hands in his, helping me to stand. I feel wobbly on my legs, but he sweeps me up in his arms and carries me to bed, where he gently lowers me down.

"Don't go," I murmur, reaching out for him to hold him back. "I need you with me... to sleep."

"Trust me, kitten," he says as he humors my touch, "after that you'll sleep pretty well."

I wonder what he'll do if I tell him honestly what I want. "After that I want to come again," I whisper, heat rising to my cheeks.

He quirks an eyebrow, a smile toying on his lips which I only want to kiss again. "Not only is she pretty and clever," he murmurs, "but she's insatiable too." He gently eases my fingers from where I've circled them around his neck. "I can't give you what you need, kitten."

"What more do I need than you staying here, being with me, doing what we did before?" I'm going to be losing all self-respect if I beg like this, even more so if he dares give me the silent treatment like earlier.

"You need cock, kitten. Lots of it. Until you've had it, you won't be satisfied. And I can't give you mine."

He walks away to where he has kicked his jeans, giving me the perfect visual of his sexy ass and that tattoo that covers most of his muscled back and chest. His words don't shock me. I've started to suspect that this empty longing in my core is for *him*. For all of him.

I sit up, reaching for tissues on the nightstand. "Don't tell me it's because I'm *merchandise* and you're still planning to auction me off at some hideous virginity auction like a piece of meat."

"And she's back. All sassy and ready for a cock to gag her. Should have lasted fucking longer, but that sweet little mouth of hers was too good." He isn't looking at me as he speaks, taking time to dress and monologuing as if I can't hear him.

He walks to the side table where he left his whiskey and picks it up. "You can't have me, kitten, because I can't have you.

You're a whole bag of emotions I'm not allowed to have. Get fucking used to it."

I crumple up the semen-smeared tissues. "And who decides what you're allowed to have and not have?" He just stares at me, not answering, and it pushes me over the edge. I throw the ball of tissues in his direction. "Just leave already."

He picks up the tissues and drops them in a bin by the bar counter. "Such a pity. I liked the smell of sex on you." He raises his glass at me as he switches off the reading light. "Sweet dreams, kitten."

I slump back on the covers and push my face into the pillow, strangling a sob, hiding my tears. He is such a fucking asshole.

When the bedroom's door clicks closed, I scream my frustration into the pillow.

# 40

# MATTEO

I've needed distance since the moment I walked in on her, but I never needed it more than I do right now. I find it increasingly impossible to say no to this woman, and then she tells me that I shouldn't go... that she *needs* me? That she *wants* me?

Fuck.

I need to be cruel to be kind. Whatever feelings she might have for me now, they will be obliterated when she learns of *Il Consiglio's* hand in her mom's and brother's deaths. I didn't mastermind it or give the go-ahead for the car wreck, but from her perspective, it will all be the same.

She is too fucking beautiful to be ruined by the likes of me. Men like me don't get to have women like her. The risk is too big. This is set in stone, and having a woman like her will ruin me for my own status quo forever. I'm that guy who fucks and leaves. I won't be able to do that with her.

I make my way back to the deck to find a crew member. The same guy who showed me the way earlier is still on duty. "Tell the captain we're ready to leave," I say as I walk up to him.

"Right now?" he asks, not questioning but confirming.

"Right now." I finish my whiskey and put the glass on the counter. Time to get away from the scene of the crime. "First show me where Burley is sleeping?"

"Sure. This way."

I follow him down another passage to where some smaller cabins are situated. With a nod for the crew member to go wake the captain up, I knock on the door. There's a grunt, so I open the door and walk in.

"Welcome on board, boss," Burley huffs as I walk in. "Glad you could join us."

"You managed to get some sleep?"

"Yeah, mostly."

"How're you doing?" I go to stand next to the bed where Burley is sprawled out on his stomach.

He rolls over to look at me. "At least they didn't get me in the bollocks, so I'm good."

I smirk. "Your arm?"

He rolls his shoulder. "This one's fine. Tasha did a good job."

"I bet she did."

A stretch of silence follows in which I swear Burley sniffs out her body's scent on me. He fucking knows that I've been messing with the merch.

"You spoke to Rosalia?"

"Yep," Burley says, taking my segue in his stride. "She's good."

It helps that Rosalia is from our world. That's one thing Tasha will never be. "You're good to stick around until we fly back together on the jet? Or do you want to go home earlier? You can fly over with the jet, and it can be back in time to pick us up."

He scoots up to be more upright and puts a pillow under his lower back and leg to ease the pressure off his butt. "I know you don't need me in Cannes, what with Stephano and his men there, but hell, I want to stick around and see how this unfolds."

"How what unfolds?"

"You know..." He rolls a hand in the air as if he isn't committed to a straight answer. "This thing with Armstrong's daughter."

I'd be an idiot to think these two haven't formed some bond. She's been in his company a lot, got him on this yacht by the looks of it and not the other way around. She even apologized for jumping off a cliff on his watch.

The only reason why he'd refer to Tasha as Armstrong's daughter is because he wants to remind me why we're on this mission.

The Don's second request.

I'm the guy who gets the job done, whatever it takes.

I need to focus. Tasha Armstrong is just another job that I'll wrap up and deliver, completed. No more getting my kitten off whenever she asks for it. Fuck, not caving in to her earlier when she asked me to make her come again had been one of the hardest walk-aways in my life.

*And who decides what you're allowed to have and not have?*

I don't want to dissect her question now, or the whiplash that came with the underlying accusation in her words. *I'm not the one who decides what I'm allowed to have or not have. Like her, I'm just a pawn.*

"If you're asking for a bullet in the other buttcheek," I say, inwardly shrugging off her words, "know that I don't aim that well."

Burley chuckles; a good laugh at my expense.

I harden my resolve and steel myself for the inevitable. "The plans are made and going ahead." Right on cue, the yacht's engines switch on with a low hum. "We'll be in Cannes by tomorrow night as scheduled."

I walk out, not wanting to hear another word from him. He can read me like a fucking book and that's the last thing I need right now.

Once in the corridor, I make my way back to the main deck. There's more crew around as the yacht is set to cruise. I can stick around here until daybreak, catch some sleep on a sofa somewhere, but I've left Tasha unguarded.

Without a doubt, she's probably awake and plotting her next escape. With the yacht's engines going, I wouldn't put it past her to jump butt naked into the ocean, with only those rings on her fingers, to get away from me.

I rip a whole string of curses as I make my way back to my *wife's* cabin. This is the last night I'll ever have with her. I open the door softly and push it open. In the moonlight that comes through the windows, I see her body etched under the covers.

She stirs, then looks up at me. "You're back?"

Her tone says it all. I'm something that the cat dragged in. Definitely awake and plotting then. I pad over to the other side of the bed and toe off my loafers. "I went to check up on Burley." I consider taking my T-shirt off and hesitate. The jeans can go, the jocks must stay.

Maybe not get naked with her at all.

"Oh." She lifts onto her elbow. "How's he doing?"

"He's fine."

"What are you doing now?"

"Coming to bed."

"Here?"

"Where else?"

"There's a whole yacht with a gazillion bedrooms—" She breaks off, then inhales sharply with realization. "I've sorted myself out, if you think you can stroll in here after—"

"Good girl," I say with a smirk. "Next time I'm watching."

"There's no next time," she mutters as she rolls onto her side, giving me her back.

No, there's no next time. This is why I have to be here, to be with her like this. I stay fully clothed, get under the covers, and edge closer to her.

"Matteo—"

"Just this, kitten. Nothing more." My hand slips over her naked hip, nudging her close to me, her sweet ass snuggled to my groin, my chest flush against her back. I run my thumb over her hipbone as I slide my other arm under her pillow. "So you can sleep, remember."

"More likely so you can keep an eye on me." Her head comes to rest on my biceps, and I inhale her delicious scent with a chuckle, storing it away for some future session with the wank bank. She doesn't move, her body stiff and unwilling against mine.

"Relax, kitten, we both need to sleep."

I can feel the tension seep out of her as she stops fighting me, takes my hand, weaves our fingers together and presses them between her breasts. "You know what your problem is, Matteo?" she whispers into the night.

"No?" I press the softest kiss below her ear, and she purrs softly in response. "Tell me my problem, kitten. Tell me all my problems."

"Here you are, *cuddling* with me. Because *you* want to cuddle with *me*, not for any other bullshit reason you might come up with." She lets go of my hand and turns into my embrace. She cups my cheek. "You won't allow yourself to be a good guy, but you are one."

She presses the softest of kisses to my lips, then she snuggles her head under my chin, hooks her leg over my hip, and sighs the contented sigh of a woman who got in the last word as she settles against my chest. Totally *cuddling*.

"Say that again?"

"You heard me the first time," she murmurs as she pats my

pec. "To me it feels as if I've been let into a secret. Now go to bed."

The secret of Matteo Scalera. *I'm a good guy.*

Fuck.

I'm not going to sleep a wink.

# 41

## TASHA

When I wake up the sun is already high and beaming into the cabin's wide windows. I don't feel rested, but it could have been worse. If it weren't for Matteo, I wouldn't have slept at all. Last night my mind was in a tailspin, trying to get away from flashbacks of the shootout. The resistance of the man's body as I stabbed into him still echoed in my arm, and the sticky heat of his blood all over my legs and arms wouldn't go away. I washed everything off in the barn before I set out with Burley for the yacht, but it was only after a very long shower that I felt even remotely myself. Seems you can wash off the evidence, but the blood still stains my mind.

I only fell asleep once Matteo was with me but had a nightmare at some point. Helpless, soaked in blood, trying to scream but being gagged, unable to move. Matteo was there, comforting me, holding me close. I never fully woke up, but with him there the terror passed.

He isn't here now.

I sit up and ease off the covers, only to realize I'm wearing his white T-shirt. I'm not sure when that happened. As I pad over to the washroom, I spot some clothes laid out on the sofa.

A gold bikini with the tags still on—so not my taste. A very skimpy summer dress and a pair of golden flip-flops. One of the crew did mention that they could get something for me to wear from Gigi's cabin, but not without her approval.

They didn't explain anything more, but I bet this is Matteo overriding this Gigi's vote on whether or not I can borrow her clothes. Whoever Gigi is, I hope she doesn't mind sharing. At least I won't need to walk around semi-naked, which has been the status quo for most of my stay with Matteo.

A stay that's coming swiftly to a head with the reason why I'm here in the first place. The auction is set to take place in Cannes and the yacht started cruising last night.

I'm mostly convinced that Matteo won't eliminate me after this auction, despite everything I know and have seen at his apartment. I've witnessed a murder, but I also know that guy had it coming. Matteo is fair, if a bit religious in his attempt to do everything he set out to do. This is why he won't be able to let go of this stupid virgin auction. But yesterday we went through something horrible together… and the way he held me last night—

I haven't been able to escape his clutches, and after yesterday I don't want to escape them anymore. Whatever Matteo has in store for me, it can't possibly be worse than being abducted by a Sicilian mafioso who toys with you like a cheetah with its prey. Plus, I can't thwart his plans, but I might let them play into my hand, and not into his. No man cuddles with a woman like he did last night with the end game of murdering her in cold blood or watching another man take and use her.

Well… there *are* psychos out there, but I've given Matteo the all-clear on that ailment.

After another long shower, I tug the bikini's price tags off and put it on. It's cute, but the gold makes me look in dire need of a tan. The dress fits perfectly, and I feel ridiculously sexy as I step out of our cabin and head towards the dining area. I'll find a crew member there, if not Matteo himself.

"Mrs. Scalera." A young guy meets me as soon as I step out into the hallway. "Your husband is on the deck waiting for you to join him for breakfast."

I can get used to this. Totally. *Mrs. Scalera*. Wearing a ring shouldn't make you warm to the idea of having a husband. Having several mind-blowing orgasms at the same man's hands and tongue shouldn't make you feel in heat at the idea of having *him* as a husband. Seeing the man shirtless on a deck chair basking in the sun—

I pause mid-stride. Matteo is sitting some feet away from me, in black board shorts, his long legs stretched out, sunglasses on, typing with both hands on his laptop as he clutches his phone between his shoulder and ear. His abs flex as he talks, sits up a bit in argument, leans back, his tattoo only accentuated by the sculpture of his toned body. He talks rapidly to someone in Italian, and I hold back.

But as if he is drawn to me, he pauses his typing and looks at me. He kills the call with two curt words, closes his laptop and puts all his electronics to the side. The intensity of his stare makes me blush. For all this man has seen every part of me, has kissed me in places I can't even fathom, his gaze has the power to strip me down to my core innocence and make me blush.

"Come here."

I walk over, shy as he watches me in this dress that's a bit extra. Whoever this Gigi woman is, she must be into clubbing and wearing as little as possible while doing it. There isn't a lot to undress, but I feel stripped naked by the time I reach his deck chair. All I want to do is straddle him, have my hands on those pecs and trace the lines of his tattoo with my tongue.

"Sit." He points to the deck chair next to him where a towel is spread out.

"Is this what we're doing today?" This is too easy and there must be a catch. I settle on the deck chair, the heat of the sun on my skin.

"For now." He waves at the vast open Mediterranean. "Nowhere to go."

A waiter comes arounds with a fresh fruit tray and a selection of fruit juices, and I bite my lip. I could get so used to this.

"Get her some sunscreen," Matteo says as he leans over me to take a slice of pineapple off the platter. "Do you want coffee, cappuccino, a latte? They'll bring you breakfast with all the bells and whistles."

"A cappuccino, yes, please. I'm famished."

"Thought so. Bring her the full spread," he says with a nod to the waiter.

"When did you wake up?"

He smiles wryly. "I hardly slept, kitten."

Oh. "Did I—" My stomach turns, every visual of yesterday's attack flicking on in my mind like headlights straight in the eyes. I drop my fork with the square of melon on the plate, all hunger gone. "Did I keep you up? I swear I had a nightmare—"

His hand comes to rest on my thigh, and it should tickle but he puts just the right amount of pressure to reassure me instead. "You were fine. You *are* fine." His eyes are studying me, searching, but then he lets go of my leg to pick up my fork. He holds the bite out to me. "You need to eat, sweetheart."

I'm melting on the spot. *Sweetheart*? Coming from *this* man? He must have had something with his coffee.

I take the bite and avoid his gaze. There is something sinfully sexy about everything he does, as if he knows exactly how to twist the tension in me until all I want to do is hurl myself at him.

"Whose yacht is this?" I ask between bites. The waiter interrupts any further feeding by putting down the coffee and sunscreen on my side table. "Thank you."

"It belongs to Carlo Trapani. I haven't met him yet but he's an old friend of the Don's."

"The Don?"

"My dad."

"I see." Matteo has a dad. Somehow I've never visualized him with one. How bizarre. "And the clothes?" I pick up my cappuccino and take a careful sip. *Sooo good.*

"They're his daughter Gigi's. The elder of his two girls. They have their own cabins with their things that just stay here permanently. The family uses the yacht a lot by the looks of it."

"Nice. And what does Carlo Trapani do?" Matteo's dad is a Mafia Don and Trapani is his friend. Sounds all shady to me.

"Too many questions, kitten," Matteo teases as he pokes another piece of melon onto the fork and offers it to me. "Eat up."

"And shut up?" I squeeze in before I take the bite, my eyes wide and innocent as I stare at him.

Matteo shakes his head and chuckles. "You understand me perfectly lately." His phone buzzes, and he picks it up to kill the call.

I'm not sure whether he doesn't want to take the call in front of me, or whether he is being polite. Whichever it is, when the waiter arrives with a hot breakfast on a tray, my hunger returns in full force.

"Do you need help?" Matteo asks as I pick up my fork.

"Maybe." I love him like this. Teasing, easy, not all messed up and growly. His phone rings again and he cusses. "I'll be fine."

He stands with his phone and walks off to the railing. The call lasts the duration of my breakfast, but I don't mind. I'm at leisure to watch him talk as he walks the deck, turns, and crosses back to the other side. I only catch the odd word but at least it sounds mostly like legitimate business. Nothing about what's happening next.

The day is perfect, so I strip off the dress to get some sun. The waiter comes and takes my empty plate away. Matteo watches our interaction, then ends any friendly interchange by killing his call as he walks back in my direction. "We're not to be disturbed."

He still watches me as if I can't be trusted. And yet, I woke up alone this morning. No space for shenanigans here, what with no land in sight. The waiter walks off with a nod and Matteo reaches for the sunscreen. I look up at him, expecting him to smear some on himself.

"So, what's happening next?" I want to know where we're heading and have some timeline of my final demise. I have no clue how long this cruise is going to take and no means to find out except to ask him directly.

"This. This is what's happening next." He squirts a dollop of sunscreen onto his palm. "Onto your stomach, kitten. I'll start with your back."

# 42

# MATTEO

I'll do anything to touch her. Here, where it's just us, I can feed my need for her.

Tonight, I will hand her over to Stephano and I will walk away. I gave my word to the Don.

I couldn't sleep because the very thought of going through with the auction repulses me. It takes a lot to disgust me, but Armstrong's debt for Alex's death was settled twice over. What are two million dollars given that this woman saved my life? I'd write it off without thinking. The Don, on the other hand—he likes seeing people broken, ruined, *dead*. He wasn't in that shootout and would never believe me when I told him Tasha stabbed someone and gave me those few crucial seconds between life and death. There were too many of Randazzo's men. If it weren't for her, we would've been outnumbered.

Tasha's hair falls over her back and shoulders as she eases onto her stomach, and I gently sweep it away, turning my touch into a caress. I suppress the temptation to kiss the length of her spine as I tug the bikini straps loose. This body was made to be worshipped, every inch of her that of a goddess. As I press my palms to her skin, my touch turns sexual; there's no stopping me. I want this woman, *all of her*, and that contented little sigh whispers back that she'd let me take her, ravish her, now, here on this yacht, for all to see.

I keep massaging the sunscreen into her skin, going lower and covering her whole back.

"Matteo," she murmurs, as I carry on down to her legs, making sure she can't miss my intention as I sweep my thumbs low over her butt and deep into her inner thighs.

"Yes, kitten."

"Can you—" She breaks off as she shifts her leg up, giving me the access I crave.

I lean over her, one knee pressed onto the deck chair, and kiss her neck, then lower my hips to her body and press my straining erection into her sweet ass. "You want this?"

"You know I do."

What would happen if I just took her now? Make her mine. I close my eyes as I ride into her, savoring the pressure of her tight ass against my hard cock. The scars on my back pulse as I feel every crack in my ribs of his *discipline*.

Instead of stripping off my board shorts and fucking her as I want to, I slide my fingers between her thighs and shove the bikini bottoms to the side. She's open and wet for me, always so ready. I caress her softly, as I've come to learn what she likes. She reacts to me tenfold, splaying both her legs and pressing her sweet pussy into my touch. She needs this. I drag her release out, watching her face as the arousal blushes her cheeks, as her breathing becomes more strained. She's holding back too, biting into her bottom lip to ride out the wave for as long as she can. This time I can't stop myself from dipping a finger into her and watching her reaction. Her hands curl into fists as she twists the towel as she starts to come. I pull my fingertip out, rubbing her clit again, wishing it was her G-spot. She moans softly as she pushes her fist to her mouth, and I press a kiss to her temple, almost coming undone.

I'm not looking for proof. I didn't doubt her word when I saved her from Randazzo's compound, but for Stephano's sake and reputation, I won't let her go without making sure she's still a virgin. Her reaction tells me everything. No man brutalized her while I didn't have her under my protection.

*Soon, kitten, you will know what it feels like. And even if you don't come, you would have had this one from me.*

"I have to get some work done," I murmur as I press a final kiss to the corner of her mouth. "Have a nap."

Once she's taken after the auction, she won't get to sleep at all.

# 43

# TASHA

Matteo left me hanging, and I didn't see him for the rest of the day. I was left to my own devices, and reminder: I don't have any. I ate all my meals alone, and the crew didn't engage in any conversation with me beyond pleasantries. Whenever I wanted to go explore, someone was on hand to block my way. I was allowed to see Burley, but even though he let me stay for five minutes and check his wounds, he made it clear that Matteo wouldn't tolerate me 'hanging out' with him.

I had too much time to think, which isn't always a good thing. I waded through everything I've seen Matteo do, his reactions, his choices, and I've concluded that this mission of his with me, with the guy he killed yesterday, were orders he was fulfilling. Orders from his dad, the Don.

Which means that auctioning me off is maybe not what he wants, but he'll go through with it to wrap up the business he set out to do. The Don won't let him off the hook if he doesn't comply; he will only send someone else to finish me off. I'm still torn, uncertain what to do. I want to push Matteo's buttons so that he finally succumbs to me, but I also don't want to reach the auction's final destination.

It's a risk I'm going to take, praying all the way that nothing goes pear-shaped.

We've entered the Cannes marina and docked. The captain dealt with immigration control earlier. I saw that fake passport of mine in the officer's hand. We seem to have the all-clear, and soon I'll have the opportunity to jump and run, but then I spot Stephano walking down the marina, coming to meet us. Two men are in his vicinity, suited, with avatar sunglasses. Bodyguards.

I rather enjoyed the relative freedom being on the yacht gave me today. Nobody breathed down my neck.

Matteo comes to stand next to me, staring down at his brother with an expression I can't read.

"Hey," I say, suddenly even more nervous. He doesn't acknowledge me, and it's as if a cold wind comes from him. "Matteo?"

"I'll speak to Stephano."

"About what?" I ask, but he ignores me again as he goes to the bar counter where a waiter has been on standby since lunch.

I watch as he orders a double shot of whiskey, my annoyance with him budding. I want to say something, but a woman in high heels who waves at me as she hurries along the dock draws my attention.

"Ciao!" she calls out, with a smile and a wave. She's so focused on me, where I'm standing at the railing, that she bumps into Stephano as she rushes past him. He steadies her with a hand on her elbow but their interaction is swift and already she's homing in on me again.

She has long, lush dark hair, golden bronzed skin, and legs for miles in a summer dress that fits her like a glove, showing off some serious cleavage. Her sunglasses are pushed up on her head and she is smiling widely at me.

*This*, I realize, with equal amounts of dread and hope, isn't part of Matteo's plan. The woman deftly pulls off her high-heeled sandals before she boards the yacht, clearly used to everything as if it belongs to her.

Matteo comes to stand next to me and leans in to watch her. "Fuck."

"Who is that?" I ask, but I already have my suspicions.

"Gigi Trapani. Must be."

At last, another woman to converse with, or not.

Matteo waves at Stephano to come on board, just as Gigi's face appears from the boarding stairs.

"Ciao, cousins! All the way from America!" She opens her arms as she strides towards us, ready to embrace.

"We're not cousins," Matteo mutters as he intercepts her, so she can't engage with me first. "Gigi?"

"*Si*, Gigi Trapani, my dad told me he has important guests on the yacht and that you will be cruising here. I was already in Cannes so when the captain let me know you were arriving in the marina—" She breaks off, her smile wavering as Matteo makes no attempt to pull her close in an Italian-style, familial greeting.

"Matteo Scalera," he introduces himself, stretching out his hand to block any closer contact. He doesn't include me in the introductions as Gigi takes his offering and gives it an uncertain shake.

I sense in my gut Matteo's cold greeting is about to backfire. Gigi's gaze flicks to me, then to my hand where I'm still clutching the railing and the massive bling on my fingers. "And your wife?" She looks at me, and then her eyes swerve over my body, taking in the dress, the straps of the gold bikini that peek out at the neckline, the golden flip-flops on my feet. *Her clothes.*

But that's not what's giving her pause. Her gaze homes in on the abrasions around my wrists where I was bound to the speedboat. I didn't cover them up, wanting them to heal in the sun. The bruise on my thigh is also visible as this dress of hers is so short. At least the slap I got to the face didn't turn into a bruise for her to stare at.

I watch Gigi's face transform as she smells a rat. Then she takes a step closer to me, but Matteo blocks her with his arm.

"*Cara*," she says in a rushed tone as she slaps—actually *slaps*—Matteo's hand away. "Are you held against your will? Have they hurt you?"

If she knew what I know she wouldn't be slapping at Matteo. I'm so caught off guard at how quickly she summed up the situation that I'm gaping like a fish.

"Gigi—" Matteo warns with a firm hand on her shoulder, but Gigi shrugs loose just as Stephano appears on the deck.

"Need some help there, Matteo?" he asks casually, not realizing he just stepped into a shitstorm.

Gigi's face lights up with fury and indignation. She turns on Stephano and hisses, "I don't care who the hell *you* are, but you're getting off my yacht, right now."

Stephano's jaw ticks. "I don't care who the hell you are, angel, I'm not going anywhere."

In two steps Gigi has crossed the deck and slaps him too, this time full on the chest in an attempt to push him away. "Leave!"

Stephano takes it, too dumbfounded to do anything else. But then he shoots into action, grabbing her wrists, making her drop her sandals, and twisting her into an armlock that has Gigi wincing.

All my blood drains to my feet as I watch in horror, having been in a similar situation. They are too deep into the yacht for people on the marina to see, but Gigi just needs to scream—

Stephano covers her mouth with his hand and looks at Matteo calmly. "Jesus Christ, Matteo," he sighs. "Can you stop collecting hoydenish shrews? It's bad for business."

"Fucking curve ball," Matteo grunts. "Bring her inside so we can talk without an audience."

He takes me by the hand and leads me inside the yacht's formal lounge, passing a dumbstruck, wide-eyed waiter in the process. Stephano follows with Gigi, who is kicking and screaming for all she's worth. Her voice is muffled, and Stephano is laughing all the way as he carries her as if she weighs nothing.

"Leave us," Matteo says to the crew who suddenly surfaced, coming to Gigi's aid, but at Matteo's authoritative tone, they scatter.

Yikes. Some people are going to get fired, judging by the wrath shining in Gigi's eyes.

Matteo indicates that I should sit as he pushes his hands into his pockets and leans against the bar.

"I'm going to let you go, angel," Stephano murmurs in Gigi's ear as he makes his way toward me. "Try not to bite, okay?"

As soon as Stephano lets go of her, Gigi shudders as if she's totally grossed out. "Get your filthy Mafia paws off me."

She doesn't pay him another second of attention but turns to me and reaches for my hand. "*Cara*, what is your name?"

"Can I gag this one?" Stephano asks, reaching for his belt buckle. "It will give me endless pleasure."

Matteo sighs a world-weary sigh. "Nobody is getting gagged. Gigi, what goes on here is none of your business."

"You're on my yacht. *She's* on my yacht. It *is* my business."

Matteo grinds his jaw, as if he just knows he's in for it now. "Yep. *You* being on this yacht wasn't exactly the plan."

Stephano smirks as Gigi purses her lips, annoyed, but then his attention jumps to me. "There's some damage to the merch, Matteo."

"She did it to herself."

At this point, Gigi is clinging to my hand, studying my wrist. "Oh, no, please, don't tell me you tried to cut your wrists!"

The rings on my finger flash in the overhead lights and Stephano steps closer, his eyes narrowing. "Are those Mom's rings? On *your* hand? The senator's daughter?" He straightens and stares Matteo down. "What the actual fuck, bro?"

# 44

# MATTEO

Stephano's tone says it all. I've gone a step too far. Everything about Mom is holy in a way. When someone dies in childbirth with her stillborn daughter, after the doctors warned she should never get pregnant again after having had the twins, well... That Mom survived Benedict's birth was a miracle, but after him she had no luck left. We might be hardened Mafia, brutal and cruel adults now, but in us live five boys who would forever look up at the stars and think there are two angels looking down on us. Mom and little Gabriella.

"Take them off," Stephano commands Tasha as he holds out his hand. "Never mind the fucking sacrilege, you can't wear them tonight."

"Tonight?" Gigi clings to Tasha's hand, refusing to let go.

"None of your fucking business," Stephano growls at her, and by the looks of it, Gigi would spit at him if it wasn't beneath her.

"Tonight is cancelled," I say, dropping the bomb. Gigi just sped up the whole conversation I planned to have with Stephano. This isn't the approach I wanted to take; I would have gone about it more diplomatically, but I don't have time to argue with him.

"What?" Stephano says, a red flush creeping up his neck. "Tonight's auction? Cancelled?"

"Yes. The debt's settled."

"Is it now? How?"

"That's none of your business," I say, not ready to admit that Tasha got into some serious trouble, then ended up saving my life.

"I can tell you what my business is." Stephano steps up to me, his face inches from mine. We're both tall men and see eye to eye. "I've been working on this fucking auction for your sake for the past two months. I have nine VIP clients here who jetted in for this little one's sweet ass. Now unless you fucked her, and messed with the merch, for which I will fucking kill you, brother, I won't let you fuck with my reputation."

The silence that follows his tirade makes me only more conscious of my pulse beating in my temple, but I stare back, not giving him an inch.

"Oh my God," Gigi whispers, her gaze jumping between me and Stephano, then back at Tasha, who hasn't said a thing. "Is it true? You-you—oh God—you... you—"

"Thank fuck something has put you at a loss for words," Stephano bites back at Gigi's stuttered shock. He has his hand on my chest, fisting my shirt. "Did you fuck the merch?"

I want to strangle him, but Stephano has every right to be irate, so I calmly dislodge him, forcing myself to keep cool and in control of the situation. "The merch is untouched."

"I'll verify." Stephano pumps his fist in my steel grip.

"Fuck you. Take my word for it. You touch her, you die." As the words spill from my mouth, I realize they are no idle threat. I don't know when it happened, or how, but this woman has gotten under my skin.

"Matteo checked this morning." Tasha's voice is soft but

sure, and unexpectedly calm. "In any case, your brother is a man of principle. He would never—"

"Oh my God! You're auctioning off your virginity! Is this for real? Are they forcing you? Is it your own choice?" Gigi is back in full force as she jumps up to stand between Tasha and us men, clearly the biggest threat in the room. Her fucking mouth that's on a run is more dangerous than anything here.

But she knew. Tasha knew what I was doing this morning when she asked me to get her off and I used the opportunity to confirm what she already told me, as if I didn't trust her. I know it's all a bunch of bullshit and even that doctor's letter confirming her virginity is phony as fuck, but Tasha's reaction to my touch this morning told me everything I wanted to know. No one touched her while she was under Randazzo's roof. *Sorry, kitten, I wanted to make sure nobody hurt you.* I've been battling my decision for days now, this thing between her and me... *I can't.* I can't let another man touch her, never mind *have her.*

"Good," Stephano says as he rips free of my grip. "The Don will be watching on the livestream I've set up."

Fuck. I have no illusions about how this works, or how far the Don will go to get what he wants. If he could watch the night she shares with the winning bidder, he'd go that far to make sure it's done *properly*. Sick fucker.

"Don't do this," Gigi begs, her voice urgent, but Tasha slips her hand from her grip and stands.

She pulls off Mom's rings from her finger and holds them out to me. "I've been promised a virgin auction," Tasha says as she meets my gaze, her voice steady and sure. "I want my virgin auction."

"What?" She's been trying to run away from me from the start, to escape this very thing, and now she's *asking* for it? "Kitten—"

"No, Matteo, I have a right to clear my father's debt. If this is the only way to do it, I'll go through with it."

"Please—" Gigi reaches out for her but Tasha steps up to Stephano.

"I'm ready to go if you are," Tasha says softly, demure. *Virginal.*

"Tasha," I say, refusing to let her do this. "You don't know what you're getting into." Stephano has his hand on her lower back, and I want to implode. "Brother, if you know what's good—"

"Nobody is going to kill anybody here," Tasha cuts in. "Understand?" She glares at me, finally using my own go-to on me. "You're lucky enough to still have a brother, to have each other, so stop making dumb threats."

Stephano blinks at me, then at Tasha, and I blink back. She doesn't know *Il Consiglio* is the reason she no longer has a brother, but with those words she's just leveled us to the ground. Never will I be worthy of this woman.

"What the lady wants, the lady gets," Stephano says. "Stop fucking around, Matteo. The clock is ticking, and she needs to get ready. If you're so eager to have her, you can place a fucking bid like the rest of them."

"I'll never degrade her by bidding on her," I hiss. How can there even be a price on someone like her?

"God, you're a bunch of creeps! She isn't property!" Gigi yells now, pulling at Tasha's arm.

"Can you all stop talking as if I'm not in the room?" Tasha shrugs Gigi off. "It's okay. Stephano will take care of me."

My brother will take care of her? My blood boils. I see fifty shades of red. But I don't do anything as I watch them walk off because I will commit murder.

Gigi attempts to follow but Stephano growls between his teeth, "You. Sit. Stay."

That stalls Gigi midair, her face a picture of fury, but what do I care.

*What the lady wants, the lady gets.*

I know that *this* isn't what Tasha wants.

And to give her what she wants, I'll have to break the vows I made months ago.

Hated vows I made not knowing what I was getting into.

While I wasn't watching, she sliced right through me, straight to my heart.

# 45

# TASHA

It's almost nine at night and I'm starting to doubt my choices. Matteo hasn't come for me.

Through a double French door that sections off one part of the presidential suite, music is playing, men are talking, drinking, networking. Around the price of a virgin.

It would seem Stephano has a regular client base that's into this type of thing, and they like to flex by getting together like this and riling each other up. Apparently, my starting bid is one and a half million dollars, and Stephano aims to triple that tonight.

I'm all primed for what has to be the most exclusive virgin auction I've ever conjured up during the long boring days. After Stephano bundled me into his car, we came straight to this five-star hotel and the presidential suite. The beauty team was here, treating me as if I'm getting married in the morning. Head to toe exfoliation, waxed everywhere, nails done, hair done, make-up done, and now I'm dressed in the white strapless dress I tried on in Matteo's apartment. That feels like months ago now, and as I stare at myself in the mirror, I want to burst into tears.

Matteo wanted to cancel tonight. I insisted on this. I've

made my bed; now I'm going to lie in it with some prick whose hands—

I can't bear thinking of it, and I can't cry. Stephano has been with me all the time, and losing face in front of him is the last thing I want to do. He has been working on his laptop, always within earshot, but not watching me, only making sure things progress without me speaking much. My French isn't up to scratch and the women who worked on me seemed to have been selected based on their lack of English. Stephano is totally disinterested beyond getting this auction done. At some point, he showered and got dressed in a tux, but I can't recall when. We've hardly exchanged two words that weren't an instruction from him, and me an obedient little dog.

One of his bodyguards knocks on the door jamb and Stephano stands. He takes a boutique tote from the man and peers inside as he walks in my direction. I'm not allowed to sit because it will crease my dress, and already my heels are killing me.

Stephano drops the bag to the bed and takes my hand. "Did Matteo do this to you?" He runs his thumb along the fading red marks on my wrist, then meets my gaze.

"No." I quiver at his touch, but it's not him, it's my nerves.

"Want to tell me about it?"

"No."

"Matteo said the debt's settled?"

"I don't know what he meant by that." I bite my lip, wishing he'd let go of me, but I force myself to keep steady. I need to get used to unwanted touches from a man I don't know.

He lets go of my hand and shakes several jewelry boxes from the bag onto the bed. They fall open to reveal two wide chainmail bracelets with a matching golden necklace that looks like a collar. "Normally I wouldn't put something like this on you, but I can't have you go on auction with these marks. Here."

I hold out my arm for him and he wraps one bracelet

around my wrist. It's malleable and soft against my skin, structured to fit any size. I turn my palm up so he can close the little hooks, so it fits snugly. He does the other one and grasps my fingers for a second. "Do you want something to calm you down? You're shaking like a leaf."

I chuckle, but it's nervous. "You're offering me drugs?"

"Yes."

"By the time I'm done with you lot I'll be an addict."

"I take it that's a no."

"It's a no, thank you. I'd like to be fully present."

He reaches for the collar and steps behind me. My hair is in an elegant updo, accentuating my neck and bare shoulders, and all I can do is watch in the mirror as he completes my look. Once he's done, he meets my gaze in the mirror. "You're good to go."

I look like a million dollars, but I've never felt cheaper. "What's going to happen now?"

"We go next door. You get to mingle. It's a silent auction and once there're no more electronic bids on our app, the winner will do a transfer and he will take you to the suite next door. You'll be alone with him until noon tomorrow. I'll be here the entire time. There're cameras almost everywhere except next door. I have guards at the elevator, so don't try and escape. I'll meet you tomorrow after the fact and then we'll make our way home."

I get to go home? That sounds too good to be true.

"And Matteo?"

Stephano shrugs. "He isn't here, is he?"

It's been five hours. Five long hours of torture, a lifetime to contemplate what's coming my way.

And Matteo isn't here. My heart falls, and for the first time I realize how fragile it is. It's going to hit rock bottom and shatter into a thousand pieces.

# 46

# TASHA

Stephano leads me by the elbow to the French doors, where a bodyguard has been standing the whole time. The man opens the doors for us, and as soon as I step inside the suite's circular foyer several pairs of eyes turn to me.

Someone wolf-whistles and I'm choking on a new terror I've never felt before as I take in the scene in front of me. I'm trapped. Three men, dressed in tuxedos, stand with drinks in hand; two more sit further away in the living room on a half-moon shaped sofa; and a poker table is going with four men, one on each side. Male waiters are attending to their every need by the look of half-eaten plates of steak that are pushed to the side, but trays of finger foods are also doing the rounds.

My heart pulses in my constricted throat, my whole body quivering. I should have taken Stephano up on his drug offer, but there's no going back now.

"Smile for the camera." Stephano points to where a laptop is discreetly placed so whoever is watching can see my entrance, but not the other guests. "That's the Don looking on."

I swallow, looking at the camera but not smiling. "To think I still don't know what my dad has done that I deserve this."

"Matteo hasn't told you?"

"Nothing much."

"Your crooked dad copped out of a deal, blew the whistle on our location and *that* killed our brother Alex. Then he never settled his opportunity costs. That's why you are here."

Tears burn behind my eyes, but I nod. That photo Matteo had in his closet, of him with a teenaged boy his age. *Alex. Dad, how could you?* "I'm sorry for your loss." I know the pain of losing a loved one. How it balloons in your chest out of nowhere, suffocating you.

"Our brother has been atoned for, and this auction will cover the rest." Stephano pushes me toward the men who are waiting. "I'll introduce you to our guests. Smile and wave. Play nice. Leave the claws for the bedroom, kitten. They'll like that."

I feel the red heat staining my cheeks at his words. *Kitten*. I know Stephano heard Matteo call me that, but nobody gets to call me kitten except Matteo. "I'm not your *kitten*."

I try to shrug loose from his hold on my elbow, but Stephano's grip firms as he turns slightly to face me. "He isn't here, *princess*. You're under my watch now, and soon you're going to belong to one of these men, if only for half a day. I suggest you start playing along so I'm not forced to turn our classy evening into a vulgar sex slave market."

"What do you mean?"

"Tie you up, strip you naked, put you on a pedestal with a gag and blindfold so you can only moan your displeasure instead of shooting deathly glares at everybody."

I close my eyes. I asked for this; I took a risk that hasn't panned out. I blink and take the first step toward the group of men who are standing, patiently waiting for us to come their way. They're enjoying the show we're putting on; all of them are smirking as their eyes strip my body.

I shudder. Soon I'm going to be sold to one of these perverts. And then—

Behind us the door to the suite opens and footsteps fall behind me. "Party's over. Bidding's closed."

I stall as I hear his voice.

That voice that I've come to love.

That voice that can command my body as if it alone is its master.

My legs want to buckle, but Stephano has me steady.

"Oh my God!" another voice chimes in, high heels clicking on the porcelain tiles. *Gigi.* Gigi Trapani has come for me too. I don't know if I want to laugh or cry. She carries on hissing things in Italian which I don't understand and don't care to either. All I want is Matteo.

"I'll take over from here," Matteo says as he comes to stand where we're frozen, his presence filling the room. The other men only look on, waiting to see what happens next. His hand slips around my waist and I lean back against his chest in relief.

Stephano lets go of my arm and as soon as I'm free, I turn into Matteo's chest, clinging to him. His arms wrap around me, and I've never felt safer, more treasured in my life.

"What took you so long?" Tears that I've been holding back by a mere thread spill over.

"Gigi," he says. "That one doesn't sit and stay. She killed the WiFi and ordered the captain to sail out to sea, practically kidnapping me to do a hostage exchange for you, kitten. Then she forced me to bring her along to see that you don't come to any harm. She's got guts, that I'll give her."

One day I'll thank her for caring so much that it was almost too late.

Matteo presses a soft kiss to my neck, and I shudder at the sudden warmth and pleasure of it. Him. This. Us. It feels so right. "Where's the livestream?" Matteo asks Stephano.

I peek at Stephano, and the fury on his face is almost comical. Gigi is standing toe to toe with him, every challenge in her stance.

Without breaking the staring contest going on between him and Gigi, Stephano points to the camera where a minute ago I was supposed to smile at the Don, the evil orchestrator of this whole mess.

I watch as Matteo casually flips the bird at the screen, then bends down and throws me over his shoulder. I shriek and laugh and cry at the same time.

"Let's get out of here before shit hits the fan," Matteo says as he heads to the front door.

"Where're you going?" Stephano says, his voice clipped.

"You'll figure it out." Matteo calls back.

"Thanks for the fuck-up, brother," Stephano hisses. "And leaving me to deal with... this."

By *this* he means so much more than Matteo's gate-crashing his virgin auction. Gigi is in his face, and she isn't going to take any bullshit.

"I'll make it up to you." And with that, Matteo strides out of the suite, down the corridor to the elevator, which waits, a bodyguard holding it open.

Matteo walks in with me, presses the button for one floor down and I giggle all the way as we make our escape to a suite he must have booked. A bodyguard is there and opens the door for us. It swings closed with a decisive click.

One thing is for certain: I'm going to lose my virginity tonight, and to the only man I ever wanted to give it to.

# 47

# MATTEO

I slide Tasha down my chest until her feet touch the floor. I hold her close, and her hands are gripping my neck, still clinging. She looks stunning, radiant with a sparkle in her eyes, still wet from tears.

"Did you really think I wouldn't come for you?" I ask as I squeeze her butt with both hands, pressing her soft curves into my hard erection.

"It was an awfully close call."

"I'll always come for you, kitten, whatever it takes. Know that now and forever." I tease my hands up her back, fighting the urge to tear this dress right off her and have her here against the wall. On top of the dainty console table, rocking into her so hard that the flower vase crashes to the ground. Part of me wants to go at her like a beast, but that other half, the half that I buried for so long, wants to take its time, torture her in other ways and make her wait for going against me when I said the auction was cancelled.

"I—did you..." She trails off, her voice uncertain.

I cup her cheek and wipe at a tear with my thumb as I make her look up at me. "What?"

"Did you bid on me?"

I firm my grip on her jaw. "Didn't you understand when I said that I'd never bid on you?"

She swallows, her eyes on my mouth, her tongue peeking out as she licks her lips. "I just want to understand under what agreement we're here."

"We're here because I want to fuck you until you can't walk." *Amongst other things. Things that take time but will have her come again and again.*

"Oh." Now she's biting her lip, her eyebrows hitched in concern.

"If that's what you want." I ease my hold and caress her jawline with a fingertip, tracing a line down her neck, over her necklace and down to the bit of cleavage her dress shows. It's rather demure, perfect for tonight. Goosebumps follow in my wake, and when I press a kiss to her neck and make my way to her ear, I whisper, "Tell me what you want, kitten."

"I..." She drops her head to the side with a moan, exposing her neck for me, and her hands fall away from where she clung to me, opening her body completely. "I want it all. I want everything."

"Good girl. So fucking greedy for my cock." I'm ready to plunder her body, holding back with steel force, for after tonight this girl will never be the same. She'll give herself to me without knowing who she's really getting into bed with, and I'll play along for as long as I can. She might want me, but there'll come a day when she won't. Once she's learned the truth. But by then it will be too late. I've altered my course completely because of her and there's no going back.

I cup her face with both hands now, my fingertips gentle as I guide our mouths closer. Her lips are open, and she moans as I swipe my tongue into her mouth, hers answering in equal languid passion. So fucking sweet, but I know there is a wildcat in there. But this is just it, we both want it so bad, but at the same time, we both want this moment of anticipation to last. I'm the first and last man she'll ever have.

My fingers slide down her chest and I cup her breasts without breaking the kiss. Her nipples are hard and as I run my thumbs over the tips, she pushes into my erection with a groan. "Are you wet enough for me yet, kitten?" I murmur against her lips.

"I've been wet for you from day one."

Her admission is like fire in my blood, an extra chamber to my heart. *From day one.*

Yeah, I've been a good boy doing everything the Don asked me, all his dirty work that came with the expectations he has for his *heir apparent.* I'm fucking done. I get to decide what I want and I'm starting with making this merch mine.

I find the side zipper and tug at it, holding her steady against me with my other hand on her hip. I picked this dress and Stephano made it happen as if he knew. As it comes undone, the built-in corset still holds the dress in place. I want to curse, but Tasha is like a present I've waited years for, and opening it is as much a turn-on as the wait I subjected myself to.

"Hold on to me, kitten," I murmur as I let go of her hip, and her hand comes to rest on my shoulder. Her eyes are closed but she lifts her other arm up so I can get to those little hooks. When the dress at last falls away from her chest, I ease it down over her hips. "Fuck," I groan as I help her step out of it. "How the hell did I manage to resist you for so long? You're too fucking beautiful. Too perfect."

She's left in nothing but high-heeled sandals, a thong that without a doubt has a slit in the crotch and jewels I'm not sure from where. I miss those rings on her fingers. *Not for long.*

I slide my hands over her hips, her skin smooth and soft

like silk. She smells so good, and I want to lick every inch of her. I hook my fingers around the thong's bands and rip hard. As expected, they come away with ease, and I tug at the thong, letting the fabric slide between her thighs.

"Oh—" Tasha breathes, her hand clutching my shoulder tighter.

"I swear if you just came because I ripped that through your slit," I grunt as I bundle the thong up in one hand as I cup her neck with the other, using a firm grip on her hair to make her look up at me, "I'll have to punish you."

There're a few seconds of silence as she takes my measure, her chest heaving, her nipples brushing against my tux. This one is something else, I swear she's been *made* for me.

"What if I didn't come, but I still want to be punished?" she teases, peeking at me from under her eyelashes.

I take my time to press her wet thong to my nose, letting her wait. Fuck. She's so ready for me... "Well then, kitten, you're pretty fucked, aren't you?" She laughs but I cut her off with a dominating kiss to the mouth, toss the thong to the floor and cup her sweet ass to lift her up against my cock. "This is what you're coming with, nothing else."

With long strides I walk through the suite and her sandals fall one by one. When we get to the bed, I drop her, not very gently. She bounces a little, but it comes with a giggle as she settles on her elbows, watching me keenly to see what's going to happen next.

"You look so hot in a tux," she says as I stand at the foot of the bed, staring down at her.

"Yeah?" I pull at my bowtie. "Want me to take it off?"

"Hmm... yes, you're even hotter without it."

I smirk as I drop the bowtie, shrug out of my jacket, and head for the shirt buttons next. "Splay your legs, kitten, and show me how you get off when you're alone."

She blushes, her eyes shy, but I slip my belt from its loops and curl it around my fist. She runs her tongue along her lips, waiting, so I press a knee onto the bed to lean over her. I slide the leather over her tummy, and her eyes widen as she realizes where I'm going the strap.

"Matteo."

"Come on, kitten," I murmur as I dip and drag the tip over her sex. "Don't double your punishment by not listening the first time around."

When I tap the belt gently against her pussy, she jolts and groans in pleasure at the same time, and I just know...fuck it, as if I didn't just know from the moment when she defied me that this woman will match me on every level.

Her hand reaches up to my chest, where my shirt hangs open. I pause, and when she touches me it's with some reverence, her fingers ghosting over my skin, the lines of my tattoo, over my abs to my pants button, hypnotizing me with her touch. "Be quick, Matteo, with you like this..."

And suddenly it's the last thing I plan to do. I want to drag this moment out and give her memories of her first time that will wipe out every other nightmare this whole mess has sparked. Whenever she thinks of these weeks, this night is all I want her to remember.

I take her hand and guide it to her sex. "I've got you, kitten." I stand back and wait for her to touch herself, and when she eventually circles that sweet clit with a fingertip, I drop the belt and begin to strip again, her eyes on me. I take my time, wanting her to be as ready as she can be. When I finally release my cock from its constraints, she arches into the mattress with a moan, and I lean in and pluck her hand away. "Not yet, kitten."

She slumps back in soft protest, and I straighten to strip the rest, watching how her gaze roams my body, how her fingers quiver as they slide over the duvet to her breasts so she can toy with her nipples instead. Fuck, she's a tease, but I should have known. Inwardly, I'm burning to have her, but once I'm naked, I just stand there, drinking her in as she drinks me in.

"Matteo..."

"Just let me look at you, Tasha."

"You've seen all of me already."

"But not like this."

Not with the eyes of a man who has finally decided to take control, who has caved in and will be taking what he wants. And what he wants is to worship every inch of her body and make her feel what she does to him.

Our eyes lock, and in that moment, all jokes and teasing are pushed aside by this intense desire and need that have been waiting in the wings. I sink onto the mattress and glide my hands over the smooth length of her legs. Goosebumps follow and she purrs as she arches again in anticipation, splaying her legs even wider.

To have her like this, open and begging, feels like sin, but I block the thought as I drop down to press a single kiss to her mound. She quivers, even more so when I trap her hands away from her body so I can lick and kiss my way to her breasts, circling each nipple with my tongue as I weave one hand with hers.

"Matteo—"

"Shh, kitten. I want to take my time." Because this is my first time too. The first time to make love to the woman who has captured and conquered every part of me.

And I take my time, kissing and nibbling and touching her soft skin until the heat of her arousal has glazed her inner thighs, until her fingers tug desperately at my hair, and I can't hold back anymore. It doesn't matter how ready she is, this is going to hurt and the last thing I want to do is to hurt her.

I balance on a hand and guide my cock with the other, sliding it over her wet slit until I pause at her entrance. "Eyes locked with mine, kitten, so I can see where you're at." I've never had this intense need to look after someone like this, to be this gentle, to let her pleasure guide mine.

Talk about pussy whipped.

I'm the guy that fucks and leaves about to become that guy that makes love and stays.

# 48

# TASHA

I stare into his eyes, a deep earthy brown, and I know I'm about to landslide into love with this man. There's something in his gaze that I've never seen before. He is always so stern and cold, every word calculated. He never speaks when silence can go so much further, but now, he murmurs my name as he pushes the tip of his cock into my body, his gaze soft, as if he is sliding with me.

He is perched on one hand, his other holding mine, and I grip it tighter as I caress his jaw. He is taking it slow, giving my body time to adjust to him. Just the pressure of his weight, the feel of him making his way, is like a heady drug. I pull him closer, and he dips down for a tender kiss.

"This is going to hurt, kitten," he murmurs against my lips.

"I want it to hurt," I whisper back. "I want to feel how you're my first."

My words seem to pull a trigger. Matteo drives into me, and the pain that comes with it makes me gasp as I dig my nails into his hand and grip his hair. I curl into him, but he pulls his cock out and slams it right back into me. I cry out, blinking at him, but he has shifted his weight so he can hold my jaw, forcing me to look up at him.

"Good girl," he praises. "Did I hurt you real bad?"

"No," I lie. *You just tore a slit in my soul with your cock and climbed right into me, becoming part of me forever.* "It's fine now."

"You feel so fucking good, Tash. One more time, sweetheart, just one more time."

He pulls out again, and this time it's better. When he rams back into my body, I moan with pleasure, because suddenly it all makes sense. *You need cock, kitten. Lots of it. Until you've had it, you won't be satisfied.*

*And I can't give you mine.*

And yet... here we are. Matteo holds still, fully sheathed, and I can only look into his eyes as tears sneak out of the corners of my own. *Only two tears. No more.* He broke all the rules to be with me, and I'm falling, a pile of emotions for this man I never knew existed coming straight down with me. "You feel so right," I say as I hook my legs over his ass, hugging him close.

He wipes at a tear with his thumb, the gesture so tender and caring that I'll weep if he does it again. "I promise to never hurt you again." He lowers to kiss the tears away, his lips soft and gentle beyond measure. "You're so fucking tight, kitten," he whispers against my cheek, then perches up on his hand again to look me in the eyes. "You sure you're fine?"

I nod, my body already only wanting to rock into his. "I want more. I want to come on your cock."

He repositions himself to go slow and easy as he thrusts into me. "Thought so."

He dips his head and kisses me, his tongue diving into my mouth, slowly out, a mimic of what he is doing with his body. It ramps up everything in me, and as I was on the verge of coming earlier, it doesn't take much to summon back the rise of the tide that's going to take me there.

"Matteo," I whisper against his lips as his rhythm becomes more urgent, more focused.

"Come with me, angel," he whispers back as he drops his head next to mine. His torso presses down on me, but it makes everything more intense. The crash of my orgasm shudders from deep within me along with my feelings for him that keep ballooning out of control. As I come, I cling to him, never wanting to let go.

"Tasha..." He groans my name as he peaks. He pauses and his pleasure vibrates through my body into my core.

And still I'm coming, a release that's born out of finally being with him like this. With Matteo in my arms, I'd be happy if I were to die right now. This is why I waited; I needed this man to be my first. Not some high school fumble with a boy who doesn't know what he's doing, not a college dorm romp with a random jerk who's had three different girls in his bed that week already, used condoms on the nightstand. I needed a man who controls his pleasure as much as he controls everything else around him.

I turn my face to his and we kiss between heaving breaths, my orgasm subsiding. He eases off me, slowly, our lips still touching, tasting, teasing. And then my legs, weakened by the intensity of my orgasm, slump to the side. Matteo slips from my body, but already he is kissing me, worshipping his way down my neck to my chest as he had earlier, a hand on my breast, kisses to my nipples. I close my eyes and arch into him, wanting to do all of this again. His hands slide over my stomach and to my hips, and I feel his cum seep out of me, and then his fingers are there, touching a sweet line through my slit. I'm sensitive, but I don't protest as I watch how he dips his finger and drags it over my skin, all his attention on what he is doing. The last of the summer evening light spills in from the large windows onto him, making him look godly. Again and again he repeats the motion, writing something on my inner thighs with his fingertip.

Matteo stands, looks down at his handiwork and shoots me a naughty grin that melts me on the spot. "I'll get something to clean you up."

I watch him walk to the bathroom, then peek down at what he has written on my legs. It's tiny. It's hardly legible.

On one thigh he wrote *mine.*

On the other thigh he'd made a little heart with my virgin blood mixed with his seed.

I've been claimed and bound to him. To this god. There's no other way I can think of him now. He is a god and tonight he's claimed me as his goddess.

# 49

# MATTEO

When I walk out of the bathroom with a wet facecloth, Tasha is exactly where I left her. She looks radiant, well-fucked, and so goddamn beautiful my breath catches. And she's waiting for me... *waiting for me* as she toys with her hair, which has come undone. A few hair clips are tossed to the side and the final thing I want off her body are those jewels. This woman needs nothing to adorn her, neither does she need to be dolled up. She is perfect as she is.

I slide the warm cloth from her ankle up to her inner thigh and she sighs. "That's nice."

"We can shower later," I say as I wipe away at the little heart I drew. Cute. So not my usual exit. Right now, I just want her cleaned up and to hold her close.

"It's messy," she murmurs as she lifts onto her elbow to watch as I soothe the warm cloth over her sweet cunt.

"It's perfect." *Mine*. I wipe at the word, knowing I'm going to have to make her all of mine soon. There's no other way. I've never considered having a wife. In my world, it's too risky. Women are always the soft target, the easy way to get to someone when you're not man enough to battle the beast behind her. The only way anybody is ever getting to this woman, is if I slip up and expose her as an easy target. I can't afford to slip up.

I toss the facecloth on the floor as I climb onto the bed and pull her close. She snuggles onto my shoulder and eases a leg over mine. A fingertip trails over my stomach, does a little turn around my navel and then travels up the line of my dragon's tail. She leans in to press a kiss somewhere, but I intercept her with one of my own. She cups my face as she leans up into this kiss, which is tender as her hand keeps on exploring. Her caress stops and she pulls away to look down at where her finger has hit the spot of dead scar tissue.

"Is this Alex?" she asks softly as she splays her hand over the body of the dragon, the one falling, escaping the talons of the other dragon.

"Yes," I murmur, gathering her hair from her face as she circles his closed eye.

"And this is you?" she asks as she glides her hand over to the face of the other dragon. "You were with him when he died, and you couldn't stop it from happening."

Astute. I don't say anything, but when she presses a kiss to the wounded warrior and then to his brother's body as it falls into the abyss, I swallow.

"I'm sorry," she whispers into my neck as she makes her way to my lips.

"It was a long time ago. Twelve years."

"Sometimes that doesn't seem long ago at all," she says, her nose caressing mine.

"No." I rake my fingers into her hair and bring her closer for another kiss. *Sometimes it feels like yesterday, kitten.* She kisses me back, as if we have all the time in the world. When she comes up for air, I hold her close. "Marry me," I whisper against her lips.

"What?" Tasha pulls away slightly to meet my gaze.

I'm not asking. She doesn't have a choice, but it might make it easier if she thinks she has one.

As if she can read my mind, she says, "For real?"

"For real, kitten. It's the only way I can protect you."

For a moment she just frowns at me, then she drops back to my arm and stares at the ceiling. Clearly not the marriage proposal she dreamed of since she was a little princess aged six or something. What do I know of a woman when it comes to this, in any case. Facts are facts. "You know too much, kitten," I say as I pick a strand of her hair to play with. "You've seen too much. And you sort of partook in our shootout frenzy at Randazzo's place."

She would have killed a man if I hadn't finished him off for her before he bled out.

For a long while it's quiet between us, then she turns back into my embrace, a devious smile toying with the corners of her lips. "So… what would marriage to Matteo Scalera be like?" she asks, her fingertips back on my pecs, toying with my nipple.

"There will be bodyguards…" I start, then clasp her hand to still it. This is a very serious conversation and to get a hard-on now would derail this plan I've set in motion.

"I'm used to that," she says. "And?"

"There will be events that you need to attend as my wife…"

"In pretty dresses."

"Only in pretty dresses." I plant a kiss on her head. "You'll be allowed to sass me once a day and I won't mind," I tease, glad that we're moving away from Alex and everything that happened twelve years ago.

"And what would happen if I sass you more than once a day?" she jokes back, her hand traveling south.

"We'll see. It depends on the degree of sass."

"I didn't know sass had degrees."

"Oh yes, it does." I roll onto my side and her head moves onto the pillow as I still her with a hand on her hipbone, my hand big enough to let my thumb stroke the side of her breast. "You'll live with me." That is non-negotiable. Obviously.

"In *that* apartment?"

She doesn't hide from me, her face open, and in her eyes I see every panic and horror she lived that night we made Greg Martinez pay for his sins, the other thing she witnessed that binds her irrevocably to me. "We can find something... cozier."

"Okay." She bites her lip and my heart pounds at seeing a sparkle in her eye. "Cat or dog?"

"Goldfish?" I chuckle.

"No!"

We both laugh, and she pushes up against me in protest. I'm on my back and she sneaks a thigh over my hip, caressing my hard cock with her leg. Consciously or not, it's fucking sexy. She takes hold of my wrist and pins me to the mattress. I want to crack up laughing, because why does she even try?

"What about my studies?" she asks, very serious now.

This is a no-brainer. "You'll go back when classes start." *With like two bodyguards in tow and a bullet-proof car to drop you off at classes and—*

"Are you for real?" Her eyes are wide, disbelieving, her grip going soft.

"Yes. Can't let you get bored." I smirk as I slip my hand from her hold to hook a strand of hair behind her ear. "You do crazy shit like jump off cliffs. So better keep that mind busy. You're dangerous when you're bored."

She laughs and I smile. Brave, crazy girl. *Mine.*

"More of this?" She rolls her hips, rubbing that sweet pussy against my side.

I cup her neck and pull her closer. "Lots of this."

"Babies?" she whispers against my lips.

I still. I'm not ready for that commitment. Making her my wife is already a giant leap away from my original course. "Maybe. You want babies?"

"I want to *make* babies."

"There will be a lot of that, maybe without the end result for a while." That's a situation that's going to call for serious logistical and safety planning. We have time. As for tonight, Stephano has a care package for her in the morning with pills that will nip anything in the bud.

"Can we start now?" She kisses my jaw.

"Insatiable. You're not too sore?"

"No… I don't think so."

"So that's a yes, kitten?"

"Yes," she whispers and then bites my earlobe. "But only because you asked so nicely."

That's novel. Nobody has ever called me nice.

I'm losing my touch. Or maybe I'm becoming a *better man*.

Shudder.

And then her hand wraps around my cock and I draw in a deep breath. *Mine.*

# 50

## TASHA

The sun's shining bright into the bedroom when I wake up in Matteo's arms for the second time that morning. When we first woke up it was only a slow-changing midnight blue laced with a tinge of orange. Now the sun is warm on the bed, and I stretch languidly. Matteo stirs too at the knock on our door.

"Kitten," he murmurs as he nuzzles my neck and I close my eyes with a shy smile. What a night. What an early morning...

*What a proposal.*

My head's still spinning. From day one my chances of getting out of this mess were limited, but the deeper I got in, the narrower the way out seemed. Now I'm stuck, and to be honest... I'm loving it because I'm in love with Matteo.

He's never once mentioned love. It's a chip to my heart, but if I can have him as he is now, it will be enough. Even if he is only marrying me because he doesn't have it in him to kill me.

Maybe over time he'll come to love me? He'll surely have no problem making me fall deeper in love with him, not if last night was a taster of what's to come.

"Who's knocking?" he groans, sounding about as sleep-deprived as me.

"I'll go check." I glance at the electronic clock on the nightstand. "It's eleven already."

"No wonder. Must be Stephano."

I pad over to the door, feeling the heat of his eyes on my body. I'm sore. And stiff. And deliciously sated in a way I've never known before. Matteo lived up to the 'agreement.' The one where he fucks me until I can't walk anymore. One more time would have done it.

I peek through the peephole. "It's breakfast." And just like that my stomach growls.

"Good. We need to get going. Start the shower in the meantime; I'll let them in." He stands and I can't help sweeping my gaze over the length of his body. It's magnificent, muscled, his cock hardening as I can't pull my gaze away from the beautiful art on his chest. Whoever the tattoo artist was knew what they were doing. "Where're we going?" I ask on a swallow. I can't believe I want him again. Already.

"Keep staring like that, kitten, and we're not going anywhere," Matteo says as he opens the closet and reaches for a robe. "We're going home."

My heart flips. Home?

*Dad.*

I force my expression to be neutral but I'm quivering inside. It's surreal. "Okay. So soon?" Not that I have any say, but I wouldn't have minded a few more days being sex-stunned by my future husband. My fake husband who's going to become my real husband. It's all too much and I don't know why. Everything that's happened since Matteo appeared on that veranda at our house in Boston has been extreme... but I'm not ready to leave this bubble yet. There're some harsh realities waiting for me back home.

"I have business to wrap up with the Don."

How weird that he keeps on referring to his dad as the Don.

*Dad.*

My dad and the Don. In business together, of sorts. It's a tough pill to swallow.

*Mom. And Kevin.* Twelve years. I can't break down now. I walk towards the bathroom door and as Matteo passes me, he grabs me around the waist, kisses me on the forehead and squeezes my ass. "We'll have a real honeymoon at some point," he whispers in my ear, as if it's a secret promise.

I chuckle. "Okay."

I head to the bathroom and get into the shower, waiting for Matteo to join me. But when Stephano's deep voice sounds through the open bathroom door, it's a signal that our time here is over. Especially when the brothers' voices get raised in argument. By the sound of it, Matteo was out of line yesterday... but he came for me. I blink at the tears that surge up, not understanding why or where they come from. Yes, any conversation surrounding Mom's and Kevin's deaths always triggers me, even hours after the fact. And yes, last night was intense, but it was also easy, and fun... and full of joy I didn't expect to find so addictive. *Matteo* is addictive.

I wash my hair and try to ignore my rambling thoughts, then stand under the spray for a long time, hoping it will ease my tired muscles everywhere else. Eventually it's too hot and too long, and I step out of the shower and towel down. There're more robes here, and since I once again don't have any other clothes in this room than my discarded white dress, I put one on.

Stephano's angry voice still comes through the open door and now I wish Matteo had walked over and closed it. For all I know, he is keeping an ear on me if not an eye. I walk out of the bedroom into the dining area of the suite. Matteo and Stephano both look up and I blush. It's one thing to know something privately, but with Stephano knowing exactly what happened and what got lost last night, I just can't help it.

Matteo holds out his hand for me and I take it. He pulls me

onto his lap and presses his nose into my neck with a deep inhale. "You smell divine."

He smells of coffee and sleep and I smile, suddenly shy.

Stephano pushes a white gift box with an elaborate pink bow in my direction. "Your morning after-care package," he says. "A suitcase with clothes for you." He points to the door where a cabin bag is pushed against the wall. "I'll leave you to it," he says as he stands. "We meet in thirty minutes. The plane is booked to take off in two hours."

Matteo nods and I get off his lap.

"What happened to Gigi?" I ask as I sit down at the table to finally have something to eat.

"Gigi?" Stephano repeats.

"Yes. Gigi Trapani?" Matteo asks. "The *one and only* Gigi Trapani."

I'm not sure for whose benefit they're all playing dumb.

"Nothing," Stephano grunts as he crosses to the door and opens it. "See you in thirty."

And he's gone. There's a moment of silence before Matteo clicks his tongue and inhales slowly through his teeth. "That nothing wasn't a *nothing*."

"Nope. I bet she gave him hell."

"And not the fun type." Matteo smirks. "You treat a woman like a dog, don't be surprised if she comes and bites you in the ass."

"Wise words, husband," I tease, feeling lighter.

He smiles down at me and cups my cheek. "You don't bite, kitten, you just scratch."

Hmm.

"Here, put this on again. It's safest on your finger." He picks up his mom's engagement and wedding ring set from the table and slides them on my finger, then lifts my hand to his lips for a tender kiss. "I'm going to shower."

"Okay." He lets go of my hand, and as he walks away, he drops the robe.

Right there on his lower back... oh heavens... red nail tracks where I scratched him in passion.

*Kitten indeed.*

# 51

# MATTEO

We're finally on the jet and flying back to the States. Four hours into the flight and I start to relax. Job one: check. Job two: botched in the best possible way. Tasha is sitting on the other side of the plane with noise-cancelling earphones, pretending to watch some movie, but I know better. She looks up often and stares out of the window, without going back to see what she's missed. She might be tired, or her mind is simply drifting, like mine is.

These past few days had too much action for me to get my head around everything that happened in Sicily. A lot of questions have formed in the back of my head ever since I dealt with Randazzo, and the fact that he felt like someone I knew, or should know, beyond his history with the Scaleras. The Don never doubted Randazzo's eagerness to see me, and to get a meeting with him—one of the most secretive and elusive capos in the European Mafia—was way too easy. And then there were his eyes...

"Matteo, you're not fucking concentrating," Stephano sighs. "I know you're pussy-whipped—"

"Yeah." I can't even get angry at him because he's right. I

shift in my seat, tearing my gaze away from Tasha. Stephano is keeping his cool, but I know he's annoyed with me. He's even more annoyed that Gigi Trapani was there last night, but I can't get anything more out of him as to what happened with her—with *them*—once we left. He has nothing to show for months of work, plus he's out of pocket with all the expenses he incurred to get the show on the road. He can do me a favor and get over it. They're all *Il Consiglio* expenses and in the bigger scheme of things insignificant. One man getting the prize is the natural outcome of any auction, and none of his clients need to know the final bid: zero.

We're trying to run through some numbers while we're together in an attempt to move on from what happened in Cannes, but my mind isn't in it. I close my laptop screen and Stephano does the same.

"What's your plan with her now?" Stephano asks.

It's a loaded question. Tasha looked on as Stephano dealt with Tatiana's assailant, Greg Martinez. I might have planted a bullet in his head, but Stephano would want some guarantee that Tasha will never talk. When it comes to that, dead is best.

"When we get off this plane, we're getting married." There. I've said it. Made it public.

"What? Why?" Stephano keeps his voice low, but it's still shocked.

"It's the only way I can really protect her."

"Not from me," Stephano grunts. "But why the rush, dude? It's not as if she's going anywhere."

"No, she isn't." Whether she likes it or not, Tasha has been sucked into our world. She has no choice really, but when things start falling into place... At some point she's going to realize how our pasts intertwine, connect those dots between Alex's death and her mom's and brother's.

"Just fuck her until you've had your fill and let her go like you always do. It's easier in the long run—"

I lean over the desk and fist his shirt. "That's enough." One of Stephano's bodyguards makes as if to stand up, but this is between brothers, so he hesitates. "You speak of her like that again, and I will fucking damage you beyond repair."

"You've lost it, bro." Stephano strangles my wrist and tears my hand from his shirt. He's strong, as he should be.

I shrug loose and fist my hand in frustration. He is right, but he doesn't get it. I've never felt this way about anyone before.

Stephano shakes his head with sigh. "Be careful, Matteo. The Don is dying and the last thing we need is you losing your common sense because of a woman. *That* woman in particular."

"I don't care. Best you let the others know how to treat her."

"You're the one with that reputation, Matteo. Not us."

"As if yesterday's performance on the yacht was something to look up to," I snap back. How I was in the past with women is just that: the past. "If Gigi gave you hell, you deserved it."

"Fuck me," Stephano grunts as he stands. "I need a drink."

When he comes back minutes later, we've both cooled off, if only on the surface. I'm no longer in the mood for his company. At times like these, a private jet feels like a cage.

I take my laptop and shove it back into my backpack, careful to slot it in next to the two cans of sardines I've been hauling along for the Don. I take the offered whiskey and walk over to where Tasha is sitting. She looks up and takes the earphones off.

"What are you watching?" She's opted for the smaller seat screen and not the massive one on the wall that cordons off the bedroom. Burley is occupying the bedroom with bullet butt, giving me no privacy to initiate Tasha into the mile-high club.

"*Ghost*. I've watched it like a hundred times." Her gaze follows me as I sit down next to her. "It's comforting."

"You like horror movies?" Didn't peg her as one of those.

She blinks at me, her jaw going slack. "It's not horror... it's... it's like the *most romantic* movie ever."

Should have known. I'll put it on the to-watch list. "Come here, kitten," I murmur and as if she reads my mind she comes to curl up on my lap. I don't know when this woman has gone from invading my mind to easing it by just sitting on my lap.

"What's up?" she asks as she cuddles into my embrace and plays with a shirt button.

"We're getting married as soon as we arrive in Boston."

"Like on arrival?"

"At city hall—it will be after hours, but an official is waiting for us." Money makes the world go round.

"Oh... that's very soon." She doesn't pull away but seems to want to get even closer to me. "I was hoping my dad could be there."

Really? Hasn't she realized by now that her dad is a fucking loser idiot? The beat of silence between us stretches way too long. "I don't want him there."

She presses on my chest to sit upright, and now she has tears in her eyes, and they wreck me. "I can't be estranged from him, Matteo. He is the only family I have left." She wipes at her face. "Up until you... we were each other's everything."

"I don't expect that, kitten," I say as I brush at a tear she missed. "Just don't expect me to invite him over for Sunday brunch." Or for him to ever see his grandkids.

Thinking about Peter Armstrong's grandkids comes out of left field, and I blink. A wave of protectiveness fills me like a rage, and I press Tasha to my chest again, hugging her close. The Don is another grandfather that will never see his grandkids. Funny thing: cancer is going to take him before it ever comes to Tasha having my baby, but if it didn't...

There's no chance in hell that the Don comes anywhere near my children. Never mind holding my first—*his* first grandchild—I won't allow him to set eyes on them. And to guarantee that, I'll kill him.

# 52

# TASHA

That was the longest flight of my life. I was stuck with too much time to think clearly now that my life is no longer in danger.

And this has just been the shortest wedding ceremony I've ever attended. Impersonal, functional, and so far removed from my dream wedding that it was like taking a bathroom break. There was a *yes* in there somewhere, and a reassuring kiss from Matteo, but now that we're driving through the familiar streets of Boston, my stomach is in a knot.

Everything is hurried, surreal, and emotionally I'm just trying to stay on an even keel. Questions have been building in my head, each one of them a brick, pushing down on my heart. I'm weighed down with unanswered questions, and even though I know Matteo can answer them all, I don't want to hear the answers from him.

*Dad*. At some point, when this whole debacle started, it was clear that if either of us did something wrong, the other would die. Now, and maybe from the start, holding Dad at gunpoint was just a smoke screen. I need to see him, but I don't want to see him. I'll have no peace until I've had the truth from him, but after everything I've learned while being captive I don't know if I want to know the truth. It's going to change my life. It's one thing to grow up and know your place in the world, see your dad in society's hierarchy and understand where you fit in. It's another thing altogether to have that whole structure shattered, leaving you hanging with bated breath to see where the pieces will fall.

My life has changed so drastically I don't even recognize myself anymore, but not recognizing the place I left behind is going to be a mind-bender.

"Where's Burley going?" I ask. He's been with us all the way, but once we landed in Boston, another SUV picked him up.

"He's going for some x-rays to see if they can remove the bullet." Matteo squeezes my hand where he's holding it on his lap.

"Which hospital?"

His lips quirk. "It isn't an actual hospital. It's off grid."

Fantastic. Matteo's network spans wide and over many industries. He even has a medical team on his payroll that make bullets disappear without anybody ever knowing a trigger got pulled.

"When we get to your apartment—"

"When we get *home*, kitten. It's home for now."

I draw in a shaky breath. "When we get home, can I have my phone back? I want to call my dad."

"Dominic has it. I'll get it from him in the morning."

It's late, and Matteo doesn't offer me his phone to call Dad either. We're quiet the rest of the drive to his apartment block, and even the elevator ride to the penthouse is quiet, what with the bodyguards that we have with us for now. As soon as we reach the foyer that leads to his front door, Matteo disarms the alarm, and the bodyguards bid us good night.

I'm not nervous but going back inside this apartment will flood me with memories I'd rather avoid. I don't think I'd be able to sleep here if Matteo weren't with me.

"Do you need anything?" he asks as we walk inside.

"No, I'm good." The flight was catered with delicious food, and I've wanted for nothing. "I'm just tired."

Matteo studies me in the soft light coming from the entry hall. "This isn't how you imagined your wedding would go, is it?"

"No." Why lie, it's not going to change anything.

He hasn't let go of my hand and squeezes it as he tugs me deeper into the apartment and the open plan area with the living room and execution square.

I burst out laughing when he switches the lights on and even Matteo chuckles. Giant helium balloons in white and gold are everywhere and floating gold letters that spell out *Congratulations!!* are tied down to the sofa. A bottle of champagne waits on the coffee table with two glasses and what looks like hundreds of red roses everywhere.

"Who did this?" I ask, somewhat stunned.

"Rosalia," he murmurs as he pulls me into his arms. As if on cue, music starts to play—*Thinking Out Loud*, the wedding song of all wedding songs. "She loves doing this type of thing."

Now I don't know if this was Matteo's idea or Rosalia's and I don't ask. Ignorance is bliss. All I know is there's been no mention of love. Even our vows at the city hall where a bleary-eyed clerk did the necessary only included an unconvincing *to have and to hold, for better or worse, for richer or poorer, in sickness and in health till death do us part.* We somehow skipped the love and cherish part altogether. Stupid, insipid vows.

They're better than nothing. In his arms, I feel safe. I'll see less of Dad, but one thing is certain: Matteo won't kill his father-in-law. I bite back tears, refusing to be weak in this moment where I can hide against his chest.

"The wedding might have been a disappointment," he murmurs in my ear, sending a spark of desire down my spine, "but the wedding night won't be."

No, it won't. I smile and inhale deeply, taking in a calming breath of his scent I've come to love. If nothing else, we have off-the-charts chemistry. It's the perfect distraction and I can live off that alone.

For now.

# 53

# TASHA

I wake up alone. From the bathroom comes the splatter of water. Matteo is in the shower.

*Alone. Without me...*

*Sneaky.* I slip out of the bed and head that way, but the water turns off. I peek into the bathroom only to see him tug a towel off the rail. Water droplets glisten on his chest, making the dragons' scales sparkle and bringing his tattoo to life. I could stare at him the whole day.

As if he senses me, he looks up. "You're supposed to sleep in," he says as he wraps the towel around his neck.

My gaze drops. I can't help it. He has zero body confidence issues. Doesn't need to have.

"Like what you see, kitten?" he asks as he saunters over.

I bite my lip. "Hmm, yes?"

He wraps his arms around my waist, and I shriek. "Eeek! You're freezing!"

Matteo laughs and lifts me up, cold fingers splayed on my naked butt. I get squeezed against his cold pecs and abs, forced to wrap my legs around his hips. My hardened nipples, still tender from last night, relish his cold skin like a balm. I wrap my arms around him, useless in resisting him. I love that he's so easy. So playful like this and so different from the man that's hardcore Mafia. I bury my face into his neck. "You take cold showers. Crazy, crazy man."

"Only when you're not with me, kitten."

"Thank God."

He makes me stand on the bed and my feet sink into the mattress. Like this I'm a head taller than him and my breasts are basically in his face. He cups one and sucks a nipple and I drop my head back with a moan as I dig my head into his hair.

"Fuck it, kitten. You smell of sex... of us."

"Can I warm you up?" I ask.

"So tempting..." he murmurs as he trails his lips over my chest to that little spot below my ear. "But I need to meet with Dominic."

"Surely you can be five minutes late."

He cocks a brow at me. "You're suggesting I fuck you in five minutes?"

I shrug. Matteo is one hell of a confidence boost for me, in everything. "I'd like to send my husband off to work in a good mood."

"I was already in a good mood," he smirks, "but I like your thinking."

He doesn't need to be invited twice. Next thing I'm on my hands and knees and his cock drives into me. He rocks hard into me where I'm already sore and sated. And yet... when he leans over my back and slips his fingers between my legs to stroke my clit, I'm there with him.

"You're too fucking hot for your own good, kitten. Totally irresistible," he says as he fists my hair to pull my head to the side, opening my neck for his lips. Those words are like an adrenaline-level boost to my wet and needy sex. Hearing him want me like this is the strongest aphrodisiac. When he sucks and licks open-mouth kisses down my neck, I explode in orgasm, triggering him to come with me.

How easy it is to learn the signs of his body; how easy it is for mine to succumb to his. He groans as he rips into me, stroking my hair tenderly. For a moment we hold still, probably a bit shocked at the intensity of our mutual need. Then he slips from my body, and I drop forward, trying to avoid the dripping cum that tags along with his cock. Nothing matters anymore after last night. If bedsheets could be read like tea leaves... well, these would correctly predict a sex-laden future.

Matteo gives me a soft slap on the butt, and I roll onto my back to watch him. He dries his hair and wipes a bit here and there, then drops the towel to the bed for me to use. I'm still catching my breath.

"I'll be out most of the day, but Rosalia will be here."

"Is there any news of Burley?" I ask.

"I haven't checked. She'll know."

It's already ten in the morning. I did sleep in. To be honest, I'd much rather be in a state of sex-induced fog than think of anything, but I suppose Matteo has work to do. I had an internship for which I never arrived. If only I had access—

"I'll bring your things later."

"And my clothes, from home?" I have some favorites that will make moving into this apartment feel a bit more like home.

"Sure, you can fetch it later this week."

"Can I see my friends?" I'd love to see Vee for one, but everything seems to be on hold until Matteo gives me the green light.

He doesn't answer for a long time, and my spirits sink. This is one silence where it isn't a yes.

"There's a lot to sort out on my side, Tash." He has his boxers and pants on, and now slips into a white button-down. "Let me deal with a few things first before I give you the all-clear, okay?"

"Okay."

When he's dressed and leans over to kiss me, I kiss him back. No regrets. There's time enough to figure everything out and I suspect the only way I'm going to stomach it all is in bite-sized pieces.

"I'll see you later, kitten."

*I love you*, I want to say, but bite my tongue. Instead, I only watch as he leaves and listen to the sounds that come from the apartment. Voices. Matteo's and Rosalia's. When it's quiet I get up and reach for a T-shirt and my panties from yesterday. Rosalia will know if there are still some of the clothes Matteo bought on a whim in the apartment.

When I walk out of the bedroom, I look down to the open plan area. Rosalia is there, busy gathering the balloons. I don't have the stomach to ask her if Matteo had any hand in this, because I don't want to be disappointed.

She glances up at me. "Hi," she says with a smile. "Welcome back. And congratulations."

I chuckle as I take the stairs. "Do you think I can talk to you now?" We're alone without a bodyguard in sight.

Rosalia only grins, her doe eyes softening. "Suppose so."

"Where's Burley? And how is he doing?"

"He's next door. The doc took the bullet out last night so he's a bit grouchy."

"Thank heavens for that. I've been worried."

"Thanks for looking after him." Rosalia heads to the dining table, where she ties the balloons around a table leg. "Do you want some coffee and breakfast? I can make you something?"

"Only if you join me."

Rosalia laughs. "Don't push your luck, Mrs. Scalera," she says, but heads to the kitchen and waves at me to sit down at the island.

Rosalia has just drawn the line in the sand, but she's the

only person I have access to, and she'll know things. "I have so many questions," I start, not even knowing where to begin.

"I bet." She places a pod in the coffee machine. "I'll answer what I can and may answer."

"Okay." I smile at her, suddenly nervous as all hell. "Firstly, how do you fit in?"

"Easy. My mom used to work for Don Scalera, Matteo's dad, as head housekeeper. She's retired now but I met Burley at the Don's house, you know... working."

"Ah. Okay. And you've been married for...?"

"Almost a year."

"And how many bullets has Burley taken for Matteo?" This comes across as a light question, but I need to know what level of danger my husband really functions in.

"Oh, it's a standing joke between them. He's good at dodging bullets. Mostly." Her voice cracks just the tiniest bit at the end and she looks away. The coffee machine is done, and she busies herself with getting sugar and cream and everything I don't take with my coffee. Rosalia has lived through a close call, like we all have, but she didn't answer my question. "As for Matteo," she continues, redirecting probably to avoid bursting out in tears, "the last time he took a bullet was when his brother Alex died, and that was before Burley started working for him."

"Twelve years ago." That number bugs me so much and I can't shrug it off. "Was Matteo in any other shootouts since then?" Bar the one I was in, from which I still wake up at night in a cold sweat, until Matteo's arms fold around me, his reassuring whispers calming me.

"I don't know all these things." Rosalia meets my gaze, holding hers steady. "*Il Consiglio* functions on a need-to-know basis. And to be honest, the less you know, the better. Trust me."

I sense her clamming up. I'm not going to get much more out of her. Rosalia is guarding her secrets as she doesn't trust me yet. Fair enough, trust is earned, but I'd like to take some shortcuts sometimes.

There's no other way. I'm going to have to be frank. "What does it mean, in *Il Consiglio's* frame of reference, when someone's death has been atoned for?"

She blinks at me. "You know the quote an eye for an eye?"

"Yes, the one from the Bible."

"*Il Consiglio* doesn't do that. Rules for crime rings are different from the rules they have for civilians on the sidelines of their operations." Rosalia shrugs as if all of this is par for the course. "The rule is simple and effective. Plus, it makes people think twice before coming for them or snitching. If you've killed one of theirs, they'll kill two of yours. And you wouldn't have seen it coming."

*You wouldn't have seen it coming...*

My stomach turns as I grip my cup. Two for one.

No. It can't be. I can't believe that. I won't. Because then it means—

My vision swims and heat prickles over my skin.

Alex has been atoned for. Stephano had said so himself.

Two for one.

Mom and Kevin.

The bodyguards I got saddled with after their car wreck. Dad losing his mind over security because of the tiniest things, turning my life ever more introspective, closeted within the walls and safety of our house. Me, being watched, guarded, all the time.

It wasn't an accident at all, was it? I stand so violently from the chair that it falls over. I rush up the stairs to our room, where I reach the toilet just in time to throw up.

Cold sweat swamps my brow when I eventually stand up and wipe at my mouth.

Mom's and Kevin's deaths were pure revenge.
And Matteo... What if he had a hand in it?
Then I've married a monster.

# 54

## MATTEO

"She's not from our world, Matteo," Dominic says. "How—" He throws his hands up in the air.

"Isn't she?"

"No—" Dominic breaks off. "Whatever her world was in the past, this is a very different future for her."

"I'm not so sure."

"Why the fuck did you go and marry her? Honestly. I get the feeling the Don wants both her and her dad wiped."

The Don can go fuck himself. I won't be killing Peter Armstrong for him. That third loose end which the Don will only reveal once the other two are completed has been like a skin tag. Irritating, but easily dealt with and gone soon enough.

I ignore Dominic's question about why I married Tasha. I don't expect any of my brothers to understand, so why bother telling them that I'm a lost cause when it comes to her. "How's Dad doing?" I ask instead. Ever since the Don announced to me that he is dying, I've been slowly suffocating the idea of him in my head. I barely think of him beyond these last things he asked me to do.

"Fuck if I care," Dominic says with a shrug. "He's dead to me already."

And has been for some time. Maybe this has been the Don's agenda all along. Make us hate him so much that our brother bond will just be stronger, securing his legacy.

"I need her things." This meeting is wrapped up. There's been no crisis at work while I was gone and for the rest, it went about as expected. Nobody is going to be thrilled with having Tasha Armstrong as a sister-in-law. They don't know her as I do. Not yet. She'll have them on their toes soon enough.

Dominic unlocks the safe hidden in the wall behind him. "I've kept her busy and out of town." He hands me Tasha's electronics. Her phone lights up with probably a thousand notifications.

"Good."

"When are you seeing the Don?" Dominic asks.

"Tomorrow." I need to get this shit behind me and move on with my life. After Sicily I have so many questions, but whether I'll get answers I don't know. All I know is that I'm done. I have a new life to look forward to, with my wife.

As I walk out of Dominic's office, my phone vibrates. Burley. Hell knows why he's phoning me. The guy needs to have some downtime.

"Boss," Burley says without preamble. "Your wife just walked out of here. Thought you should know."

I freeze in my steps. "What?" And then, as visions of Burley's call in Sicily when Tasha jumped off the cliff flood back, I turn back to Dominic. "How?" I hiss.

"Boss." Burley sighs. "She had breakfast, then went for a shower, got dressed from the stash of clothes left in the spare room, from what I gather. Rosalia came to check in on me and Tasha took the gap. Looks like she found your car keys and picked the Maserati."

"She's driving herself? And nobody thought to stop her?" I

snap, my eyes locked with Dominic's. "Check my place's footage. Tasha's left."

"Matteo," Burley groans. "She's your wife. You left zero instructions. She dangled the keys, telling whoever is on guard that you gave her permission. They were still trying to phone you to check when she burned rubber getting the hell out of there."

Fuck. I'm going to go on a killing spree. If anything happens to her...

"I told you it's bad practice to have your sports cars in that garage. The exit is way too easy." Dominic is quick to open my house's security footage on his computer and rewinds the latest footage so that we can follow.

Well, fuck me. When I had the set-up installed, I didn't have a wife who has a creative mind when it comes to escaping. Now I watch in fascinated horror how Tasha strolls out of the apartment, takes the elevator to my private garage, almost flirts her way to the car, past the guards in place. As if she owns it. Which she does. We haven't spoken about much, but when I left this morning, I didn't get the feeling that she was that impatient to get out of there. Something must have triggered this move on her side.

"Is she running?" Dominic asks. "Because if you want a team out—"

"No, she isn't running. There's only one place where she'll be going."

"Home?"

"Yes." To Peter Fucking Armstrong so he can poison her head. "You have a team at Armstrong's house. Let them know they can let her in. Don't let anything happen to her."

"Done," Dominic says as he unlocks his phone. "You want me to come with you?"

"No, this is going to be some housekeeping that I prefer to keep private."

Dominic sucks through his teeth. "Oof, I hope she's up to your discipline."

"We're well matched." But fuck, if she does this again, shit's going to get real.

I walk out of there, her electronics in my hand, sensing in my gut that Tasha has figured us all out.

She'll never trust me again.

# 55

# TASHA

It's so weird to be behind a wheel again, and it takes me a good ten minutes to figure out the car. Now I understand why Dad insisted I learn how to drive stick shift cars. This one is highly strung and crazy fast, and definitely not the best car for my current state of mind. I'm jittery with having made it out of Matteo's apartment, but I bet he has ten people on me already.

Not that I care. My fear has been wiped out by my need to know the truth. Plus, I haven't been scared of Matteo for some time now and he would never hurt me. That doesn't mean this move isn't going to piss him off big time.

I drive through the city, finding comfort in being in this familiar place, even though part of me feels like a stranger with everything that's come to light. When I eventually hit our exclusive suburb and the wall that surrounds our house, my heart is like a rock in my throat. Heavy, beating, ready to be vomited onto the pavement.

The gates open and I drive in, somewhat suspicious that it's so easy. The new guard that opened the gate isn't one I know, but for the rest, everything looks exactly the same. I park in front of the garage and for a moment clutch the steering wheel as if it's a life buoy. The front door opens and when Dad steps out into the sunlight, I blink at the rush of tears. I can't help it... whatever happened, he is still my dad.

I'm out of the car and run up to him, into his arms, and we're both weeping.

"What did they do to you... what did they do to you, honey?" he sputters between tears. "My sweet child. I—"

"I'm fine, I'm totally fine," I try to reassure him, but I pull away to look into his eyes. "What have they done to you?"

"Nothing. Absolutely nothing. I've been under house arrest of sorts. It's been torture not knowing where you are, or what... how? How did you get here?" he asks, his hands on my shoulders, squeezing to make sure I'm real. "Are you free?" He glances around, nervous.

I spot two bodyguards in my peripheral, guns in hand, ready to pull a trigger. "Best we talk inside."

"They'll listen in either way." Dad is trembling, but we have each other by the hand and go inside the house. I swallow as I blink into the well-lit interior, so foreign now, and ignore the bodyguard who is by the front door, watching us.

"I don't have a lot of time," I say, wanting to get to the point. "How did we get here, Dad?"

He leads the way to his office, and as I walk inside, it's clear it's been stripped of all electronics. Dad's been cut off from the rest of the world just like I have, and that right here at home.

"I don't know where to start," he says as he sinks into the leather sofa.

"Start with why you got into dealing with these people in the first place." The mess surely started there. My knees cave and I sit too, although I have the urge to pace the room.

"Ah, honey, you'll never understand—"

"Try me," I bite out, tired of being treated like a little girl. "Can we cut through the bullshit?"

He's shocked by my word choice, but then, I never used to

swear. Now the cuss words want to flow like a river right out of my mouth and it's liberating.

"I thought I paid. I did pay, for everything." He sinks his face into his hands, and now he sobs.

"Did you pay in cash?"

He doesn't answer and for a long moment he just sits, shoulders shaking. *Hiding*. "What happened, Dad? All I understand is there was a deal that went wrong or something, that you blew the whistle on them and Scalera's son died."

"Alex. He was only twenty years old." He looks up at me, his eyes red-rimmed. "Natasha, understand that I was only trying to get ahead, but by the time I realized where the deal was going, it was too late to pull out. *Il Consiglio* had invested a lot of money to get illegal goods into the country, and... and I smoothed their way with the paperwork. They promised me a cut, a *significant* influx of cash, but then—" He pauses and wipes at his face.

"But then?" I prompt, needing to get everything out of him now.

"I realized how narrow the tightrope was, how deep the crevasse. I'd just been elected senator, and suddenly all eyes were on me. I couldn't risk it and had to get out. I thought the deal still offered an opportunity for me to make my mark. For the better of the state, and the city."

Suppressed hate finally bubbles up in me. Him, it's all about him and his career. "What did you do?"

"An anonymous tip off to the police department."

"That backfired? Alex and Matteo were there, in a shootout—"

"If I'd known Scalera's boys were going to be at the warehouse, I wouldn't have tipped off the police."

His gaze locks with mine as if he is forcing himself to look me in the eye, that sign of honesty, but suddenly I'm not so sure. My dad's a politician, and what they say about politicians is true: they're all self-serving liars. This one is no different. He would have tipped off the police, regardless of who was in that warehouse... even if it were me.

He swallows and puts a fist to his mouth. "Turns out the tip-off wasn't so anonymous. Scalera somehow found out and... and—"

I bite my lip, unable to face the truth. "Two for one. Mom and Kevin—"

"No! The *two for one* is just a rumor, Natasha. There's no truth in that at all."

I jump from my seat, too agitated to sit still. Tears are flowing soundlessly because I wept and mourned my mom and brother for years. These are tears for something else. "How could you be such an idiot? They're the fucking Mafia!"

"I was out of my depth. As soon as I realized it, I did what I could to cut ties. Mom and Kevin's car wreck was an *accident*."

"And yet it happened a month after Alex Scalera got killed, at your hand, if indirectly." This morning, as I raided Matteo's closet, looking for anything to connect me to the outside world, I had time to look at the photo in his closet. Of him and his brother, in that special frame that had Alex's dates of birth and death engraved on the back. A month. It took a month for them to plan and act out their revenge.

When I did that math, that's the moment when I really panicked.

"You have never wanted for anything," he says. "How exactly do you think that happened? Spoiled brat."

I close my eyes and turn my back on him, anger ripping through me. Material goods mean nothing. This hollow house is an empty shell of the place it used to be, the laughter and love gone for twelve long years. "I wanted—I *needed*—my mom. And Kevin was only fifteen!"

"You're not the only one who lost them," he bites back.

I can't be in the same room as him anymore, unable to

digest his idiotic stance that their deaths weren't related to his shady dealings with *Il Consiglio*.

But then the truth of the whole situation flares up in my face. "You didn't fight for me that day when Matteo kidnapped me," I croak out as I turn to face him. "You didn't bother to send anybody after me. You sat this out, waiting, like a freaking coward. Too scared for the rest of the world to see what a criminal piece of shit you are. You're so freaking weak, you'd rather let me die than face the music." I need to deal with the new reality that my dad is a self-serving, narcissistic idiot and I'm not safe with him at all.

"Watch your tongue." My dad stands and steps toward me, wanting to grab my arm, but I sidestep him and make for the door. I stall mid-step, a dark shadow I know too well blocking my way.

"Nobody calls my wife a spoiled brat, puts a hand on her, or tells her to watch her tongue. Least of all the scum who raised her."

# 56

## TASHA

"Your *wife*?" Dad spits out as he stands. He shoves his hands into his pockets, as if he might raise his fists to fight Matteo and has to constrain them somehow. It's laughable. He didn't fight for me one inch that day Matteo and his men came to kidnap me. Everybody could have spared me the circus; Dad would have let me go without blinking. And I would have walked out willingly, doing anything to save his life. I'm not sure that sentiment is reciprocated.

Thing is, it was Mom and Kevin in that car wreck, but it could have so easily been all three of us. Or me and Mom. I'm just a body. Nothing.

I glance at the one, then the other, suffocating. On one hand I have the man who claims to love and care for me, my dad, the only family I have left, for twenty-four years the center of my life. On the other hand, I have the man who says things like *I'll tear the world down to find you*, and then goes and does just that. It makes me want to wrap myself around him and cling for dear life. But he's also the man who probably killed my mom and brother, and who's forced me into a loveless marriage for more revenge.

Matteo steps into the office, fury radiating off him. "Kitten."

His tone gives away every layer of his anger, but I just can't deal. I rush past him, pressing him away as he reaches for me, and make a beeline for the stairs. I ignore every guard and make it to my room where I kick the door closed, lock it, and fling myself onto my bed.

Voices sound from the rest of the house. Angry. Steps. Up the stairs. They die out on the soft carpet on the landing. I'm holding my breath as tears seep into my pillow.

The doorknob twists.

"Tasha." Matteo sounds calm, patient, but I can visualize him bracing the door jamb with his hands, resting his forehead against the door as he breathes to control his anger. "Kitten, open up or I break the door down."

I don't move. Let him break this house down. See if I care.

A minute later there's a loud bash, followed by another that comes with the crack of wood. A third try splinters the doorframe and I flinch where I've buried my face in the bedding. I can't see him, but I feel him. His presence fills the room.

When he touches my hair, I startle. He sneaked up on me. I roll over and squirm away from him, back against the headboard, legs up and hugging them close, making myself as small as I can.

Matteo just stands there, all suited and sexy, jaw twitching as he looks at me. Not a word, just silence.

"Tell me the truth," I say when I can't take his eyes on me any longer. "This two-for-one thing *Il Consiglio* has going: did you kill my mom and brother in a car accident? As revenge for Alex's death?"

He sighs. "No, I didn't." For a second, I'm relieved. Matteo isn't the monster here. "I was incapacitated with two bullet wounds that nearly killed me." He looks away, and although there's hope, it drains out of me like everything else. "The Don did."

I'm trembling, fear and hate and disgust pulsing through my veins, mixed with the wretched knowledge that Mom and Kevin died for nothing. "God. You're so fucking evil." I wipe at my face, but it doesn't help. I'm a quivering mess. "Tell me, *husband*, would you have done the same?"

He doesn't hesitate. "At the time, yes."

"My brother was a kid!" I bawl out, sobs ripping through my chest.

"So was mine!" His voice trembles but he inhales and hisses the breath out. "To be honest, we both were." He turns his back on me as he walks to my bedroom window, which overlooks the garden. "It was our first gig for *Il Consiglio*. Our baptism. It should have been clean and easy. In the end we lost six men. We only got out because we had an extra escape route that we didn't share with your dad. Just in case."

*Just in case* my dad couldn't be trusted. My dad was the domino that triggered everything, but I still can't bring myself to see him on the same level of evil as Matteo and his kin.

Matteo turns to face me. "I never pretended to be a good man who sticks to the rules, kitten. You got to know me exactly as I am."

Yes. And even worse: I got to fall in love with him exactly as he is. I bite down on my lip, wondering what it would take to kill every last feeling I have for him.

"Now be a good girl and pack the stuff you want from here so we can go home."

"What?" *Home*? *With him?*

"You heard me the first time, Tasha. We're leaving in five minutes, whether you're ready or not."

"Fuck you," I scream, tossing a teddy bear at him, but he only catches it and flings it into the corner.

"That type of shit stays. You're no longer a little girl."

"I refuse to go with you, back to that apartment," I hiss.

"You do? You're my wife." He lets this statement hang a

moment. "I'm not leaving you with your *creep* of a dad. In fact, you're never to see him again, understand?"

"No! *Understand* that you won't fucking stop me from seeing him."

"I'll do what the fuck I want. You are my wife, and I will protect you in every way I deem fit. Trust me, kitten, it will be for your own safety. Now..." He quirks a brow at me. "I've carried you out of this house before, and I'll do so again. This time, I'll be less gentle. Your choice."

He doesn't wait for a response but turns to my closet and goes through my clothes. I never knew hate and love could intertwine so tightly together, one a parasite to the other, and it's just a matter of time to see who kills whom.

"Do you really want some of the stuff in here?" Matteo sighs. "We can just get everything new—"

"Screw you." I scramble off the bed to salvage what I can from home. One thing I've learned is that playing along gets me further in this game than anything else ever has. I grab a sports bag from the bottom of my closet and shove things in, random things that I used to love. Evidence of a prior life, now just a vague memory.

Matteo stands back, giving me space in my fury. There is something calming in the systematic process of packing, but my head is running through every option I have. Bottom line: I'm going to walk out of here, willingly, but I'll never let this man touch me again. I will not be the *wife* he signed up for. I will defy him every step of the way. There will be no children born into this hellscape of a family. None.

Matteo said he wasn't ready for children, but we've been having sex without protection. Everything constricts, the tense twist in my stomach wringing tighter. It's too early for signs of a pregnancy. I still have time to deal with one.

Maybe he'll even give me a divorce. Wow. Not even two days married, and this is what I want. When I'm done, I pick up the bag and walk out of the room, not even looking to see if he follows me. I head down the stairs and straight out of the front door.

I might never see Dad again, but right now, I can't face him either. He's in denial about Mom's and Kevin's deaths. Matteo has admitted it was *Il Consiglio*'s doing, as I suspected. Dad's playing dumb and that's one thing I can't stomach, because indirectly it implies that he thinks I'm too dumb to see the truth. *His* truth.

Why do I suspect I haven't even scratched the surface on that one?

# 57

## MATTEO

Tasha has pushed herself into the corner of the passenger seat, as far away from me as possible, staring out of the window. At least she's no longer crying because that shit shreds a man. It's one thing to swoop in, yank the carpet right out from underneath her with everything that happened in Sicily and Cannes. It's another thing altogether to bring her home, only to watch her look on as her world disintegrates, knowing you can do nothing to ease the pain.

If only I could hold her, soothe her, things would seem better, but she's turned cold and stoic. I don't blame her, but the truth is out now. I no longer have to hold my breath, wondering when she's going to realize how closely connected we are. I'm in for a ride which I refuse to get of from, whatever comes my way. I will bend her to my will. She will learn to love me. She will stay mine. That's the only way I can protect her. It's the only way I can have her.

When we drive into the apartment's underground parking, I pull up to the security booth. "Mrs. Scalera doesn't leave the premises again. Not without a security detail, understood?"

The man nods as he peers into the Maserati, straight to where Tasha can't be bothered to look in our direction.

"Understood, Mr. Scalera."

With an inner sigh I drive deeper into the building, allowing the two security SUVs to pass and get to the parking area ahead of us. Just in case.

It's only once we're in the elevator to the penthouse that I finally relax. As long as Tasha stays put in the apartment, she'll be safe. As long as she doesn't escape... well, she's a cat with nine lives.

I have her bag in my one hand and my laptop bag over my shoulder as we walk into the apartment. Rosalia won't be here at this time of day and it's for the better. The rest of the world will be having dinner soon, while I will be having a staring contest with my wife.

"Kitten."

She turns to me, arms folded over her chest, protective. She's wearing one of those damn dresses. One of the rippers. Like the pink one she wore when we flew to Sicily and I ripped when she sassed me. This one is a bright yellow which makes her look like sunshine. Those legs would look stunning in a pair of heels, but she wasn't allowed any. Nothing like a spike in the temple to cut life short, and she'll know exactly where to hammer it in.

"Husband." The way she says it mocks me.

Oh boy. Discipline. "That was your one sass for the day, kitten, done." Her lips twitch, but not in a way that makes me think she finds anything funny. "Go unpack your things. Rosalia made room for you in the master bedroom's closet. I'll get dinner ready."

I hold out her bag for her. She really didn't pack a lot. I'll make sure someone goes and fetches everything else for her at some point. She takes the bag and heads for the stairs. I go to the fridge to see what options we have. Everything in doubles.

Nice. Rosalia doesn't need instructions, unlike my wife. I heat up the meals and wait.

And wait.

My patience is running thin as it is. Fuck it. I scale the stairs two at a time, even though I know she can't escape from the second floor. When I walk into the bedroom, she's on the bed, staring at the ceiling.

"You're wearing *that*?" I say. "In *our* bed?"

"You have a problem?"

She looks like a fucking middle schooler in red and grey plaid pajama pants and a grey sweatshirt straight from thrift store hell. *In summer.*

"I don't give a fuck what you're wearing, kitten, because you won't have it on for long." Her eyes widen. "I'm more concerned about how the clothes you're wearing make you feel." And I bet that mess makes her feel like shit, compounding her shitty day.

"If you think you're ever going to touch me again," she spits out, "I have some news for you."

"Is that so?" Challenge accepted.

With a shrug she rolls onto her side, her back to me. Not that it helps; the floor-to-ceiling mirrors are there for a reason. I shrug off my jacket, slip off my gun holster and gun, careful to put it right there where my kitten can be tempted. I unbutton my shirt, toss it to the floor, and carry on with my belt. Tasha's never been one to look away, and she can't resist me now. Soon I'm naked, erect, and ignoring my blushing bride as I head to the bathroom.

I take my time in the shower, shave again, then towel dry. I put on cologne for good measure, then step out into the bedroom, a towel around my waist. I drop it as soon as I'm in her line of vision, letting her see everything. My need for her isn't shy, and there it is... that little swallow and the lick of her lips telling me everything I need to know.

I ignore her as I walk to the closet and open it up. I get dressed in a fresh suit, taking my time.

"Where're you going?" she asks as I make to slip on the jacket.

"Since none is to be had at home, I'm going out for some company."

"Company?" She sits up and I quirk a brow at her.

"Yes." She doesn't need to know that I plan to hang out with Benedict. You can go to his place and not see anybody for days as he hides out in his dungeon.

"If you're going to go soil your cock with some whore's cunt tonight, like you did that night in Sicily, I swear to God I'll... I'll..."

I want to burst out laughing but bite my tongue. When did sweet Natasha Armstrong learn to use all *those* words. In *that* tone? Jealous much? And that night in Sicily? Fuck, I didn't know that pissed her off this much. This one's a keeper.

"You'll what, kitten?" I wait, but she's gaping like a fish out of water. The gun's right there, loaded. All she needs is to cock it and shoot.

"I'll... I'll..." She's breathing short little breaths now, angry, infuriated with being unable to give me a sharp comeback.

"You'll kill me?" I prompt. "Can I remind you how that went the last time?"

She glares at me, the anger in her eyes sparkling with lust. "Don't you dare—"

"Dare what, kitten?" I toss the jacket onto the bed, reach for the gun and drop the bullets out. Won't risk things going wrong here. I place it back on the nightstand, waiting for her next move. Now she looks like she wants to slap me, scratch me, and let out all her anger and frustration.

And I'll let her if it helps. Up to a point. What she needs is to be comforted, to know that whatever happens next, I'm here.

Hand over every part of her to me and allow me to take care of her. Submit to me—completely.

I'll give her everything she needs and more. She can break apart a thousand times, and I'll pick her up and gather her close a thousand and one.

I step up to her side of the bed and cup her face. "Dare what, sweetheart?" I slip my fingers to her neck, into her hair, slowly in that way that makes her burst out in goosebumps.

"Dare to give me a lesson in anatomy again. I know all that stuff," she huffs softly, already weakened by my touch. Or maybe it's because I called her sweetheart. She softens to a marshmallow whenever I call her that.

"I have a lot of things I can teach you," I say as I gather her hair, dipping my gaze to her hardened nipples. That godawful sweatshirt is thick, but not thick enough. "*Must* teach you, in fact." I twist her makeshift ponytail in my hand, firming my grip on it and manipulating her head so she's forced to look up at me. "Like how to stay put when you're asked and bloody well know I expect you to stay put."

"I'm not a *thing*, Matteo, an inanimate object."

"No, far from it." *You're on fire, battling every human emotion out there.* I place a knee on the bed and lean in, crowding her with my body as I brush my lips along her temple. "You're a needy, jealous wife who is going to give me a hard time, aren't you?"

"You deserve it." Her hands are on my shoulders, trying to push me away, but I grip that sweatshirt and tear it off in one swoop. "I hate you," she hisses. "I hate the vows I made! I hate—"

"Yeah?" I toss the offending sweatshirt into a corner as I stand again. Hate is one emotion I can totally relate to. "If you hate me so much, give me more of what you think I deserve." Her chest is heaving, her tits fucking glorious in her arousal that she can't hide from me.

I take her disgusting pants by the hems and pull, and with satisfaction watch as she struggles to stay upright, then fails and falls back as I rip the seat from right under her. She's on her back, kicking at me, but the pants slide right off to reveal a pair of panties with kittens on them.

*Fuck.* She wore those for me. Little cocktease, thinking she can get away with shit like this.

I'm fast, and she's so easy to overpower. I catch her wrists and tie her hands together with the pants' stretchy fabric. She struggles, out of breath, ripping an array of curses as I knot her tightly to the headboard. Handy. And such a vivid memory from that night I had her just like this with my gun. Little did I know I was a lost cause already. I fell for her the moment she flung my phone across the apartment, defying me.

Fuck, she's gorgeous. *She's my wife.*

She's a fucking wildcat, still kicking, but I catch her legs by the ankles and press them open, trapping one with my knee, holding the other firm. I give her a moment to stop fighting, to catch her breath, staring into her eyes. "Calm down, kitten," I purr, as I slide a fingertip down her chest, circling her navel, then along the edge of her panties. I trace her panty line several times, until all there is between us are her shallow breaths, her gaze begging me to do more, and my erect cock, straining against my pants, battling to get to her sweet pussy. When I caress her lower, tracing a gentle line over her slit, she quivers.

"Matteo..."

I trace the panty line by her inner thigh, right there where she is so wet, I can smell her. "Yes, sweetheart?"

She swallows and closes her eyes, rocking her hips into my hand. I sneak a fingertip under the panties' crotch, feeling how much she wants this. I press a knuckle to her clit, with just enough pressure for her to rub against. She's slick, and when I push a finger into her pussy, she gasps and contracts into my hand. Always so ready, always so easy and close.

"I think these kitten panties are the only thing I'll allow you to keep," I say as I extract my finger, leaving her hanging on the ledge. I stand and adjust my raging cock in my pants. It's uncomfortable and there's only one way I'm going to deal with this. "Understand that I'm only going to ask you this once." I let a beat of silence hang for her to grasp that I'm fucking serious. "Do I stay, my darling, or do I go?"

# 58

# TASHA

*My darling...*

The way he said those words was filled with so much tenderness, such love that I'm struggling to breathe. This man doesn't love me, but his actions speak more than a thousand words. I shouldn't buy into them as much as my pounding heart begs me to, because Matteo Scalera plays dirty, filthy games. He's left it up to me to invite him in, knowing what the alternative is. I can't watch him walk out... and then he had me right there on the verge—

"Stay," I whisper. "Please."

I can't believe I just begged him to fuck me senseless, but I'm confused, and lost, and I've never wanted anything more than him. Like this. *Mine. Only mine.*

I can tell myself it's just sex, but women aren't programmed like that. *I'm* not programmed liked that. I need to be held in the comfort of his embrace, locked with him in a type of intimacy I never knew existed, or that I needed so much. I hate him because I need him. I need him because I love him. I love and hate him in equal parts in this moment, flipping like a coin. It can land whichever way it pleases.

I'm splayed open, naked except for my panties. Matteo stares down at me, his own need reflected in his eyes. He starts to strip, slowly, teasing me by revealing his body bit by bit. His chest and abs as he unbuttons his shirt, his tattoo, which is like a secret which I've been let into, it's meaning inked in heartache —*our* heartache.

He strips the rest and when he drops his pants, his cock juts out. I wish I wasn't tied up so I could reach out for it.

"Soon," Matteo murmurs as he glides a hand up my inner thigh, loops two fingers around the crotch of my underwear and pulls. I lift my hips and he slides the thong off, then drops them to the floor. When he gets on the bed, he parks his hands next to my head, planking over me. He lowers his hips and his cock's wet tip glides over my mound, in the most intimate caress, controlled, like everything he does. Just a bit of pressure and the heat flares in me again. He dips his head and kisses me, slowly, tenderly, every kiss a vow of the love that should be between us. I blink, unwanted tears surfacing out of nowhere.

"It's okay, sweetheart," he says as he kisses them away. "I've got you."

Matteo continues his trail of kisses down my neck, to my chest and nipples, one after the other. I close my eyes, sinking into every feeling he evokes. Safe. I feel so safe with him, it's hard to make the connection with this man and the one that killed my family.

I feel safe with him, even when fully exposed for his hands and lips, because he's treasuring me, worshipping me, all the way. When he licks the tip of my slit, I shudder with a moan, pushing my hips into his mouth. He tastes me, licks me, sucks at my clit in agonizing slow motion, making my body drunk on desire. I'm so close.

"Matteo," I beg, wanting to anchor him with my hands, wanting him to stop edging me like this.

He pulls away and leans over me to untie my hands. As soon as I can wriggle free, I cup his neck and pull him down for a kiss. It's slow and intimate, and he tastes of me, of my need for him. When he caresses my cheek, I know I can never hate him. Not when he is like this, the exact opposite of the man he becomes out there.

He rolls onto his back and pulls me along, so I'm pressed against his chest. He hooks my leg over his hips and pushes me up. We haven't done this yet. We've been doing all kinds of things, but he was always in charge. Now he has me straddling him, his cock in hand, a thumb playing with my nipple.

Every sensation is like a drug, and when he nudges me to sink down on him, I comply. His hands on my hips guide me what to do next, but on instinct I start to chase the perfect pressure. I drop my head back in the intensity of having him like this, of being in charge. "You're so deep..." And fills me up so perfectly, stretching me to breaking point, only upping my need.

"You're so fucking gorgeous like this," he says as he ghosts his fingers all over my sides and my hips, then back to my nipples.

This is going to be fast and intense as I already feel my orgasm begging to break free from deep within me.

"That's it, kitten," Matteo murmurs. "Come on my cock and tell me how much you hate me again."

At his words, my orgasm crashes down and I cry out, my hands hiding my face, unable to do anything but breathe through it. It doesn't stop, and I feel how I'm gushing out on him, squirting.

"Fuck." Matteo moves, has me in a hug and in one smooth move twists us so I'm on my back and he's on top. He pounds into me, riding my orgasm, and I cling to him, desperate for this to never end.

But he stills as his own release erupts and he buries his face in my neck with a groan. I'm still orgasming, now in the slow easing as it tapers off, and I rock into him.

"Fuck, Tasha," he whispers in my neck. "We might have nothing else, but we'll have this."

And marriages have been built on less.

"Yes," I whisper back, knowing I'll never deny him again. Even if he doesn't love me, when we're together like this, I can pretend he does.

# 59

# MATTEO

Tasha's in my arms. At some point last night, she cried out in her sleep again. Nightmares. This one about her mother and brother, her heartache ripped open again from a scar that never healed.

*Two for one.*

Fucking Don Scalera. That shit ends today.

She stirs and I slip my arm free, then press a soft kiss to her forehead. It's late and I need to get going. "Tasha."

"Hmm?" She rolls into me again and I smile.

"I've got to go, kitten." I stroke her back and squeeze her butt, knowing if I don't get out of bed now, I'm going to spend the whole day here with her. I've made up my mind and putting this off would only lead to a fuck-up I can't afford.

"Where're you going?" she asks, sleepy.

"To see the Don."

At these words she slumps onto her back and covers her face with her hands. "God, did I... did I have a nightmare again last night?"

"Yes." I ease her hands away from her face, making her look at me. "It's okay, you were with me. I had you." I know how this works, how long it takes. I can't sleep with a loaded gun next to my bed anymore, in case my own nightmares come and I shoot my wife by accident.

"Okay."

"Can you please stay put until I get home?" I ask nicely. Maybe it will work.

"Are you going to be long?"

"I'm not sure." I get up and fetch her things from my laptop bag. Two cans of sardines stare at me. It's going to be a fun day. "Here, be careful how you respond to any messages. Maybe think it over first. Take a day or two before you do."

She eyes her tablet, laptop, and phone, then smiles. "The ultimate sign of trust. Scalera style."

"Yep. Here, let me connect you to the WiFi."

Once it's done, I leave her to shower and when I come out to dress, she's just staring at the ceiling, all her options to connect to the outside world discarded.

"You're not doomscrolling?" I tease as I start to dress. I pick my suit with care, her eyes on me with every choice I make.

"I've been so long without any of it that I've lost interest."

I know that feeling. How dumb and meaningless everything becomes when you've been living from one near-death experience to the next. When you need to get your head around your new reality and the world out there seems so insignificant. I pick up the gun and load the bullets again, then put the holster on. "Give it time."

"Can I call you?" she asks when I'm dressed. "When... when—"

"You can always call me, kitten. Even if it's just to tell me the puppy's chewed my favorite slipper."

She smiles; it's small but it's there. "You're not the type to have slippers."

I smirk. True that. "Clearly we have some shopping to do." I pick her phone up and add my number to her contacts. "There.

Under H for husband." I wanted to make it HH, for Hated Husband, but after last night there might be hope for us. Today I'm tying up all my own loose ends. As long as Don Scalera and what he did hangs over us, we won't be able to move on. I lean in and kiss her on the forehead. "See you later, kitten."

It breaks me to leave her here, alone, but something shifted between us last night. She'll stay put today.

I fish my two sardine cans out of my laptop bag. I hope the Don likes my idea of evidence.

# 60

## MATTEO

As I enter the Don's compound, I know this will be the last time I ever set foot here. I get out of the car and with a raised hand show Stan that I'll go in alone. A bodyguard opens for me, but instead of going directly to the Don's office, I go to the kitchen, where I get a plate and some cutlery. Wine would be nice but it's a bit early in the day for the old man.

I make my way to the office, nodding at the guards along the way. We won't be disturbed. Not for this. The Don is waiting for me in his office as I made an appointment. I knock, then walk inside.

Bruno lies center stage on the carpet and groans when he senses me. Tasha can get any dog she wants, but we won't be getting a fucking coyote mutt.

The Don is sitting behind his desk, just like always. He's shrunk into his chair, oxygen attached to his nostrils. He bats the hovering nurse away and she gives me one look before she scuttles out of the office. Clearly the stage has just been set. I bet the Don forced himself out of bed to meet me in his seat of power, even though he looks half dead.

I close the door and lock it. "Dad," I say in greeting. I haven't addressed him like that for years.

He raises a brow at me. "*Mio figlio*," he mocks me back.

I walk over to his desk and put the plate with the cutlery down, then pull the two sardine cans from my pocket. "Evidence, as requested." I put the tins by the plate and sit down in one of the chairs facing the desk. It's time for a long overdue talk.

"Is that a wedding ring on your finger?" the Don asks.

I haven't taken the ring off since I put it on while flying over to Sicily. "Yes. I married Natasha Armstrong."

The Don starts to cackle but it turns into a coughing fit that has him shaking. I wait for it to pass. I don't stand and help him. I don't hold out the glass of water that's on the desk. He eventually manages to take a sip himself and raises the glass in toast to me. "Sometimes I really wonder. Only a real Scalera could have come up with that plan."

A quiver trickles through me. Ever since I set eyes on Emilio Randazzo, our resemblance has been eating at me. The moment of truth is now.

"What do you mean?" I prompt.

"I've raised you well to think like me. This cuckoo in my nest." He lets the words hang, but they don't shake me. This is how far I've come. "Any normal man would think you're a fool for marrying your enemy's daughter, but what better way to torture a man than to rape his girl every day, day in and day out, for as long as she lives. For him to know this, and not be able to do anything about it." He sneers at me. "Only a Scalera would do that."

Mom. Raped. Day in and day out by this man. Forced to breed his children until it killed her. Only problem is, I'm not a Scalera.

"She was pregnant with me when you married her, wasn't she?"

"Oh yes, the fucker got me there. Randazzo made sure she was pregnant with his child, planning to sign her away to me. This baby girl he stole from the streets in Naples, to bring up as his own daughter to use as collateral when he needed her. He gave her to me as his 'treasured' prize, already carrying his bastard." He sneers. "How clever of me to in turn send his own son to kill him. I bet he didn't see that coming."

Fuck, they make me sick. Women are only objects, there to serve their needs, whichever form they take. Thank God I had a mother who had twelve years to nurture me, love me, quietly on the side where this man never saw the love she had for her children, regardless of who fathered them. Her life was hell, but she lived it for us.

"Randazzo is dead. His compound torched and burned to the ground. I've completed your first request." I stand and take a sardine tin, pick up the lever and pull it open. It looks so authentic, even I shudder when an eyeball stares out of the can. I pick up the fork and poke at it, lifting it out of the tin and putting it on the plate. "Eyes like mine," I say as I lift them out of the tin and spread them out on the plate. "Ears like mine." That diamond stud is the only thing that looks good as new. I take the next tin and open it. "Fingers like mine." The little finger, slightly bloated now as it got tinned, still has the gold signet ring on it. No wonder I felt like I knew Emilio Randazzo. I was looking at myself in forty years' time as I cut him into pieces. "Help yourself."

The Don blinks up at me, and for the first time in my life, I see a flash of fear in his eyes. *Yes, you fucker, little kids grow up and bide their time.* Just like our mole in Sicily did. No wonder we hit it off so well. We got each other, no words needed.

"Good job, Matteo," he says, pushing the plate away. "You know you're Randazzo's only son. His sole heir. You can go and take over all his operations in Europe. Here you have his DNA, nobody would contest it." He speaks fast, as if this idea would be his saving grace.

The thing is, he sent me to kill my biological father, who anybody already could have believed was my grandfather. Why would I hesitate to kill this man who is nothing to me? Ever since Mom died, I've been his tool. He used me for every dirty wicked thing he could use me for, shielding his other sons. His real sons. No wonder Alex's death hit him so hard. Alex was his real first-born son. Imagine the war this man would have fueled between us brothers if Alex were still alive today. This man in front of me would refuse to let me be the Don, even though he groomed me for it. I bet he planned for Alex to kill me when we were ripe for it. Maybe those bullets in that warehouse were meant for me and not for Alex. Sounds about right.

Whatever his plans, to the last I will protect my brothers. "How many people know that I'm Randazzo's son?"

The Don leans back, lured into a false sense of security by my question. "It was only us three. Randazzo, your mother, and me."

Good. There're only two of us left to keep this secret, and you know what they say: two people can keep a secret only if one of them is dead.

"You haven't tried your meal. Do you need help?"

"Fuck you."

He reaches underneath the desk, but I anticipated it. He is weak, and I am fast. I'm around the desk and have my hand around his throat. It's thin, the skin soft and so easy to bruise. I force him back in his office chair, making it impossible for him to reach any of his panic buttons, his guns, his knives. He grips my arm, but he has no strength left.

Now that I have him like this and look down at his body, I want to laugh. He's half gone already.

"Come on, Dad, eat a bite. You look like you need it." I poke at the ear with the diamond, and a soft bit of lobe comes off on the fork with the stud in tow. I pull down his jaw, forcing it into his mouth. He gags, but I keep on pushing it down. At last, revenge for feeding me raw deer liver straight from the kill. The oxygen pipes unhook from his ears as he shakes his head, trying to avoid swallowing. It's laughable how easy it is. I pinch his nose closed so he must choose. Swallow and breathe or suffocate.

He'll be dead soon enough.

He does what any other human in this situation always does. You choose to live. With satisfaction I feel how his throat works, how he pulls in a ragged breath as soon as he can. His grip weakens and his eyes roll up to stare at me, horror in his gaze.

"More?" I ask.

He struggles to breathe and I'm not going to help him here. He shakes his head, barely able to move.

"Just for the record, I don't want any part of Emilio Randazzo's fucking sex trafficking business in Europe. Let the Bratva have it." Or even better, give Interpol all the access they need to dismantle it all together. I know someone who knows someone who has been trying to break through these rings for decades. It would be my pleasure to hand it to him on a platter.

The Don struggles but can't get a word out, so I ease the pressure a bit. "Let me guess, your third request is either to kill Peter Armstrong, or to kill you? To spare you the suffering of a painful cancer death."

"The girl," he croaks. "Alive—father—daughter..."

I squeeze harder.

"What was that?" I mock. The Armstrongs? As in plural. Father *and* daughter. *My* wife? If I didn't already have enough motive for killing him, asking me to kill both the Armstrongs would tip me over. "You? Help you along?" I sneer at him. "Know this when you die today, I'm doing it for my mother, who you killed through childbirth. I'm killing you for every son she's borne, for every brother of mine, and for that baby girl that would have been the light of our lives. And lastly," I hiss as I tighten my grip, "I'm killing you for my wife. For Tasha. Two for two, you motherfucker." I clasp my hand over his mouth and nose, holding still and blocking his airflow. He is so weak, he barely struggles.

It's done in less than a minute, his body slumping in the seat. I let go of him, not an inch of remorse.

Behind him are his cupboards and drawers filled with files. The filth he's gathered on every person he's ever worked with or wanted to bribe. It's a treasure chest, really, the most valuable of his assets. I open the cupboards, not really interested in keeping anything. We've moved on and have everything electronically. The Don was old school like this.

I pick out Peter Armstrong's file, thick and heavy. This is the last hope I have for Tasha—for us. She's not going to like it, but she needs to know.

When I turn back to the desk, Bruno is sitting upright on the carpet, probably sensing his master is dead. He stares blindly towards the Don and the Don stares blindly back from his chair. I pick up the sardine tins and empty them out completely on the plate. I pull the signet ring off the finger, wipe my hand on some tissues the Don has on his desk, and make sure the ring is clean before I pocket it.

I walk over to the dog and put the plate down, tissues and all, then pat him on the head. There's nothing wrong with Bruno's sense of smell, and he knows this is meat. He digs in, eating through the soiled tissues, eyeballs, and ears, then crunching through the little finger. Then he licks the plate clean.

"Good dog," I say. "You always ate like a king."

I take Armstrong's file and walk out of the office, not looking back once.

# 61

# TASHA

I took half an hour to scroll through my social media. I'm not sure who has been in charge of my profiles, but they did an excellent job in keeping me absently present. Apparently, I went on a surprise trip with my dad to some backwater adventure in Canada where there's no network. A perfect place to be eaten by a bear and disappear permanently. I couldn't be bothered to know more or even see what my friends have been up to.

For now, I'm in this bubble, and I don't want out of it. Not until I've digested everything, and I suspect it's going to take months, maybe years. People might have questions and I'm not ready to answer any of them. Matteo was right when he said I should take my time before I respond to any messages.

For all I know, Matteo has changed his mind about me going back to my studies. We're balancing on a tightrope and the only way to get across is by taking each other's hands and helping one another along. Beyond sex, neither of us has been the first to reach out for the other; stubborn.

I've been to check in with Burley. Rosalia has done her daily dose of cleaning. I'm channel-hopping because there's nothing else to do but wait for my husband. I hate being in this apartment alone. When he said he was going to the Don, with those two sardine cans in tow, I shuddered. That was hours ago, and I hate that I'm this worried. He's crawled so deeply into my heart in such a short amount of time. I can't imagine life before Matteo. It's as if I didn't have a life, and I guess I really didn't.

I'm tempted to phone him, but I don't want to disturb him when he's in the middle of something serious.

When the front door opens, I sigh in secret relief. This is going to be my life going forward. Waiting, wondering, praying for him to come back. His gait is something I start to recognize when he isn't soft-footing around so he can creep up on you. I get up, wanting to hurl myself at him, but hold back as he appears around the corner in the open plan living area.

This man... He was born to wear a suit. Sexy Italian to his core. From the way he spoke Italian it's clear it's his mother tongue. To have a sneak peek into his life growing up would be so insightful.

"Hey," I say, suddenly shy with the way his gaze consumes me. It's that look in his eyes, the way he touches me, the things he says that make me want to believe that he isn't indifferent to me. That this marriage, which I entered into under some duress if I look at it closely, isn't the Don's or even Matteo's ultimate revenge against my dad.

"Kitten." He looks tired, but in a good way.

"Are you okay?" I want to ask how his meeting went, but that would cross into territory I'm not ready for.

"Never better." He walks up to me and holds out a thick file. "This is for you."

I take the file from him. It's heavy. "Okay." I read the label on the side. *Armstrong, Peter.* "Oh God. What is this?"

Matteo walks to the kitchen as he strips off his jacket and throws it onto the barstool by the island. The gun and holster go too and I'm relieved. I hate having that thing around all the time. "Dirt. On your dad. Do you want to go through it together?"

My knees want to buckle with the weight of his words, never mind the weight of the file which speaks of more than just a little dirt. I don't want to know, yet I slump back on the sofa and flip the file open. I take in the first few pages and my stomach turns. Such detail. Photos. Copies of emails and other papers. I swallow at the bile that stirs in my stomach. This is just the beginning. Before I was even born.

When Matteo comes over, he puts a glass of water and one of Rosalia's fruit platters on the coffee table. The man likes his food healthy. I can't stomach a thing. "Where did you get this?"

"The Don had dirt on everybody. Mafia, remember?" He sits down next to me and leans in to see what I'm looking at.

"*Had* dirt?" I ask as I look at him. That was past tense.

"He's dead."

"Matteo—" I break off, staring at him in shock. "How? When?"

He shrugs. "He had cancer."

I know nothing of the man in front of me. So little of his past, his relationship with his dad, his family.

"Were you there, this morning? While he...?" I take in a sharp breath. "Oh, God, you were there for his last minutes?" And here I was, scrolling mindlessly through my phone, channel-hopping through some random TV.

"Yes, you could say so."

I want to say I'm sorry, but I'm not. Who knew what else the Don had in store for me. For Peter Armstrong. Another man I never knew.

Matteo seems unfazed about whatever happened this morning, so when he flips a page in the file, my attention is back on my dad's undocumented criminal activity. Evidently undocumented anywhere except here, in the tight-knit Mafia circles. I keep on flipping through the file. Details of bribes my dad accepted from big businesses, votes he bought—*bought*—by arranging partnerships and money deals under the table. The higher he climbed politically, the bigger the deals became. I can hardly breathe with the shock of it.

By the time we get to the part where Dad got involved with the Scaleras, my hands are trembling. He was in business with them for five years. *Five years* of sly dealings, getting stolen cars out of the country, getting counterfeit goods into the country, clearing the paperwork trail through Boston Harbor. Like everywhere else, Dad got in one step at a time. Until he got in too deep.

"He knew," I whisper. "There isn't a chance in hell he didn't know." Tears are streaming down my cheeks. There is no chance that Dad did business like this with the Don, being in various political positions that gave him insight to everything that happened in the crime circles, without understanding that two-for-one *was a rule, not a rumor*. "He lied to me."

"Of course he lied to you."

"You were there, weren't you? Just outside the door."

"Yes, sweetheart. I waited until he pushed me too far."

This man...

My whole life is a lie.

I'm not some great politician's daughter. Dad is nothing but a white-collar criminal who has worked the system to get rich. He's a total stranger, and I his puppet, playing along for all these years.

*I never pretended to be a good man who sticks to the rules, kitten. You got to know me exactly as I am.* Matteo's words hit me hard. For the first time in my life, someone didn't pretend.

I sob, a cry tearing straight from my soul. I turn into Matteo's shoulder and his arms are there as I knew they'd be. He came in and wrecked my world, or so I thought. No, he came in and pulled the blinders away, making me see for the first time.

"It's okay, kitten," he says as he hugs me close, pressing sweet kisses to my hair. "Now you understand why I'm not keen for you to see him again."

"Yes." Eventually, when I have some grip on myself, I go back to the file and page through the last documents. Since Dad became a senator, he kept things clean, and not because he *wanted* to keep clean: he got burned by *Il Consiglio.*

I bite my lip as the realization dawns on me. "If your dad had so much dirt on my dad, why didn't he use it to break him?" I push away from Matteo's embrace so I can look him in the eye. "Clearly his career is his be-all and end-all. You only need to dump this file with the FBI, and he'll spend the rest of his life in prison."

Matteo gathers a strand of hair from my cheek and hooks it behind my ear. "Peter Armstrong is more useful to *Il Consiglio* outside of prison. And he wouldn't last long inside. He knows we have dirt on him, and he toes the line."

His careful, tender touch sends threads of longing down my spine. "I don't understand," I murmur. "How do I fit into any of this?"

"What do you mean?"

I take a shaky breath, not wanting to ask but having to know the truth. Am I a long-term revenge strategy or is there more? "Why did you marry me, Matteo? Everything here... you have him. You didn't need to..." I taper off as he cups my cheek and seals my lips by running his thumb along them.

"Would it be very hard to believe I have a heart?" he says softly as he stares into my eyes. "And you sort of marched right in and claimed it?"

My whole body, which hung over the dark abyss of a marriage that's a farce, pulls back from the ledge. "What?"

"Come here, sweetheart," he says as he wraps an arm around my shoulders and urges me to sit on his lap.

Matteo cups my hip as I sink into him, into his warmth

that's become my anchor. He is my safe place. He is my happy place, and I don't know when it happened. "Say that again," I whisper, not sure I heard right.

"Would it be very hard to believe that the moment you threw my phone across this apartment, I started falling for you so hard, brave and crazy girl?"

"Yes. It's very hard to believe," I whisper, somewhat in awe.

"Hmm. She's not convinced yet." He is staring into my eyes, worried.

"Nope." My heart is melting. Matteo's gaze is open and soft, vulnerable like I've never seen it before.

"Okay. Let me try again," he says as he glides his hand over my thigh, slipping underneath the skirt of my dress. I break out in goosebumps just because he is touching me in that way that sparks lust to the last cell in my body. "Would it be too hard to believe that by the time you jumped that crazy cliff, I basically lost my mind until I found you?"

He tore the world apart like he promised the first day we met. He killed Randazzo. And I can read between the lines. "You killed your dad this morning, didn't you?" I'm sitting on the lap of the man who avenged my mother and brother. "You killed him for me, didn't you?"

"For all of us. It was long overdue."

"Thank you." I don't need to know more. *Il Consiglio* works, after all, on a need-to-know basis. "You said that first day that if I were yours, you wouldn't be eating dinner if I were kidnapped... you'd be tearing the world down to find me and make sure I'm safe." I lick my lips, watching as he watches me. I have to tell him my truths too. "Would it be hard to believe that it was the moment when I fell for you? I never felt so *seen*."

"Oh kitten, I saw you—all of you—since that moment you were too shy to get out of the pool. You were just so off limits with the job I had to do."

I slide my hand into his shirt where the top buttons are

open, gliding my hand up his neck so my fingers can rake into the hair by his collar. This is the only part of him that's soft, and to think I wanted to plant a knife in it at one point.

He pulls me in for a kiss that testifies to the truth of every word between us. "Would it be very hard to believe that I'm in love with you?"

"No, not when you're like this," I whisper. I love him like this, and in every other way.

"You're my anchor, Tasha. Without you, I'm afloat, pointless. Aimless. I've never felt like this before… I've never loved like this. It's scary. The idea of losing you—"

"You won't lose me," I say between kisses. "Because I love you too."

He stares at me for a long while, so many emotions flicking through his mind, revealed through his eyes. "To have more than I ever expected in this life that I'm forced to live… to have you… I'm the luckiest man on the planet," he says. "You're going to have to be a good girl for me, kitten. This isn't going to be easy. People come at us all the time and I'll have to keep you safe."

"You'll keep me safe. And I thought I *was* a good girl."

He laughs as he presses his forehead against mine. "Mostly, you're a good girl. And that was your one sass for the day."

I laugh and move so I can straddle his lap and be higher than him for a change. "I plan to sass you often, now that you've told me you love me. I'm not scared of you one bit, you know. Especially now that it would seem you have a heart."

"Good," he whispers against my lips. "And you better believe it, kitten, because it's all true. And it's all yours."

# EPILOGUE - TASHA

We're having a housewarming: an actual housewarming with family and friends in our new apartment.

It's not that big of a deal. I mean the apartment is literally one floor down from Matteo's old one and stood empty for years, but it's been remodeled and rewired for security and everything we seem to need. Most important thing though: it's never seen blood.

I'm in the car with Burley and we're rushing home. I'm late. My day was split between classes and lab work that took longer than expected. I'm so relieved that I get a break over Christmas. It can't come soon enough.

Six months. It's been *six months* of crazy with Matteo by my side, in my life, in my heart. He came in and swept me off my feet. And he keeps on doing that. I smile and sigh a happy sigh, making Burley glance my way.

"You good?" he asks.

"I am, totally. Just glad to have a break for a few weeks."

"I bet. You're busy."

Yes. But so is Matteo. Over the holidays I have to study for some exams, but tonight we celebrate. I have a handful of friends that are coming too. Let's just say, that I'm married at twenty-four is weird for all my friends. To find out I kind of 'eloped' was even weirder for them. When Vee met Matteo for the first time, she gave me a wide-eyed stare and mouthed, "I have sooo many questions."

She's still waiting for answers.

Maybe one day.

Funny thing is, I've lost my family, but I've also found a new one.

Matteo and his brothers are close. Over the past few months, they've seemed to get even closer. They hang out at our place a lot—our old place with the giant TV and vast double volumes with windows that reflect everything. That apartment is now official *Il Consiglio* headquarters of sorts, so still in use, but I never need to put a foot in it again.

I'm rather in love with our new place. It's smaller but suits us better. And Matteo's brothers are always welcome. Over the months, I got to know them bit by bit. Dominic: always sensible. Luca: a lot of mouth that I swear he only hides behind. Benedict: quiet, observant. Stephano: a true hero in his own way. I don't have favorites, but I know each one of them would kill for me, probably die for me.

The love that comes with that level of devotion from men who all slotted into my heart's holes where my own family once were, is unfathomable. Mom. Kevin. *Dad*. He's still around, but we haven't spoken or seen each other since the summer. He's sent me some emails, but I deleted them. I'm not ready and I'm not sure I ever will be. It's hard to move on from that kind of betrayal.

We're entering the apartment block's underground parking, where Matteo has his own entrance. Burley is alert as always, and so is my driver. I probably adjusted much easier than expected to being a Mafia wife. And to be honest, it's not that different from being the daughter of a politician who keeps looking over his shoulder.

We take the elevator up to our floor, and Burley sees me to our apartment. "I'll see you and Rosalia later?"

"Sure thing, luv," Burley says with a wink. "I'm looking forward to it."

Something in his eyes hints at this being more than just a housewarming. Turns out Matteo is one that likes to cook up surprises. Those balloons on our wedding night: his idea. That's what he arranged on very short notice, poor Rosalia scrambling all the way. With more time... there have been two surprise weekends away to off-grid private islands, where we're free from the ten layers of security we have here in Boston.

I walk into the apartment and close the door behind me. For a moment, I listen. Music is playing, some chill vibes playlist. Footsteps. And then he's there. His arms go around me, and I'm in his embrace as he kisses me.

My pulse speeds up, heat gathering in my belly. This man... he keeps on doing this to me.

"Missed you, kitten," he whispers as he pulls away. "Good day?"

"Busy. Yours?"

"Good. Very good." He gives me a sly smile and I quirk my head to the side. Something is definitely up. "I had big plans but I'm afraid we already have company," Matteo says, heading straight for a segue before I can ask questions.

"Already?" I murmur, somewhat deflated. "Sorry, I ran late." Matteo promised me all kinds of things this morning in bed, but none of that's going to happen now.

"It's fine. Dom and Luca came early."

"And here I thought they knew what was good for them."

Matteo chuckles. "Apparently not."

I drop my backpack in the coat closet and peel off my coat. Matteo helps me and I eye my husband. He's dressed in a black turtleneck sweater and jeans. Very informal for a man who lives in a suit. He is lickable in everything he wears... and it's going to be a long night before I can get my mouth on him.

"Let me get you a drink."

He takes my hand and leads me from the foyer to the open plan space that has the living, dining room and kitchen together.

My breath catches. This morning when I left there was nothing. Now there's a beautiful Christmas tree, over eight feet by the looks of it, next to the fireplace in the living room, with lights and decorations and... *Oh. It's Mom's things.* A hard pebble pushes up my throat, expanding with every second. "How?" I whisper as Matteo wraps an arm around my shoulders. "When?"

"I arranged with your dad to pick it up. All twenty-six crates of decorations." He kisses my temple. "We didn't do all of it. We left some for you. But Christmas is in three days—"

"It's perfect." I turn into his chest, battling my emotions. "It's just perfect... Thank you."

He chuckles. "It was a bit of a Scalera team building session."

"Who helped?" I choke out as he hugs me closer.

"All of them helped, kitten."

See? *This.* This is what he does that makes me melt. What makes me feel so loved. When I'm more in charge of myself, I let go from where I cling to him and turn to greet my brothers-in-law.

Dominic and Luca are standing in the living room, whiskeys in hand.

"Hey," I say as I walk over and Dominic and Luca smile as they lean in, gazes soft on me, giving me demure and quick but very Italian kisses on the cheek. This seems to be a thing in an

Italian family with their women, but Matteo is right there to pull me to his side, marking his territory. "Thank you for this gorgeous surprise."

"It was fun," Dominic says. "We haven't done that since... well..."

Since their mom died.

"So not our wheelhouse, but—" Luca breaks off, at a loss for words.

"I'm going to shower and get ready," I say, overwhelmed.

The men exchange glances, and I bet both Dominic and Luca would be more than happy for Matteo to head into the master bedroom with me, and I need him, but the doorbell rings.

"I'll get it," Matteo says with a warm squeeze to my hip. "You get going."

I'm already in the bedroom when I recognize Benedict's voice over his brothers' as they make some joke about *fucking tinsel* I missed. I smile through my tears. *This*. This is what I missed for twelve long years. The easy camaraderie of being with people who've known you all your life. People who care more than I could ever imagine.

And I don't want to miss out. Not anymore. Tonight is a happy night, and I won't reflect on the past. I shower quickly but my hair takes time to blow dry. By the time I've dressed and put on make-up, it's a whole forty minutes later, but I have my emotions in a solid chokehold.

When I walk into the living area again, more people have arrived. Rosalia and Burley, some other business partners of Matteo's, and Bryce Sutherland with his wife Izzy, who were the architects on this apartment's remodeling. From what I gather, they haven't been married for very long, but Izzy and I are the same age and at last there's someone I have something in common with. We get along like a house on fire.

I grin as I walk over to them where they're standing with Matteo.

"I love what you've done here," I say, somewhat giddy as I take in the living area filled with people and happiness. This is us. When you strip everything else away, *this* is me and Matteo. "Don't you think it turned out stunning with the Christmas tree and all?"

I wanted something warmer than Matteo's black marble, glass and steel look he has going on the next floor up. The Sutherlands opted for warmer, earthy tones and a light brown leather sectional, with lighting that in a dark December makes all the difference.

Matteo hands me a glass of Champagne and has his hand on my hip, stroking over the silk of my ruby red dress, which I kind of got for Christmas and this housewarming. "It turned out stunning," Matteo says. "Because I worked with the best."

Bryce smiles as he raises his glass. "We aim to please."

"You have an amazing collection of Christmas decorations," Izzy says as she raises her glass to the tree.

"It was my mom's thing," I say. "European Christmas markets. As a kid we used to go every second year."

The conversation carries on, but I glaze over. The apartment is filling up. We won't be able to host more than thirty people here with space and breathing room—not in the winter at least. In summer the balcony will give more space.

"Where's Stephano?" I ask as I turn to Matteo. I knew someone was missing.

"He'll be here soon, now that you're ready."

I hitch my eyebrows at him. "What have you plotted beyond this Christmas tree surprise, husband?"

Matteo just grins, that naughty grin I've got to know and love. *Oh boy...*

The doorbell rings and Matteo pulls his phone from his ass pocket. "That will be Stephano. Right on cue." He takes me by the hand and leads me to the sectional where he makes me take a seat. "You might need to sit down for this, kitten."

"Matteo—" Now I'm on some spiky adrenaline rush that's fueled by anticipation. What has this man done, and what is he going to do next?

There's a commotion at the door but I can't see because the foyer is designed in such a way that it's secluded from the rest of the apartment.

Benedict's and Dom's voices sound, but they're muffled.

"I'm good," Stephano says loud and clear. "I've managed all the way from upstairs, haven't I? Don't ruin the effect now."

As he comes into the room, my eyes widen. Stephano is technically hiding behind a tier of three circular boxes, from big to small, that he carries with some care.

"And the man of the moment arrives," Matteo says with a chuckle. "Told him I'd make it up to him."

"Where is she? Tash?" Stephano asks as he peers over the boxes. He seems to be very cautious not to drop anything.

"I'm here," I say, laughing now as I scoot to the edge of the seat.

I watch as Matteo meets Stephano halfway to make sure the boxes don't fall. Hmm. Whatever is in there is breakable.

"This way." Matteo guides his brother and Stephano meets my gaze.

"When he said he'd make it up to me, this wasn't what I had in mind," Stephano teases. That's our little inside joke. Apparently, Matteo is still making up a lot of things to Stephano.

"I can't imagine what would be better than hand-delivering my wife's housewarming gift to her," Matteo says with a smirk.

As if I need more than this man. This apartment is already a crazy thing he's done for me, and now—

Stephano squats down with the stack of boxes and places them on the coffee table in front of me. A distinct noise comes from one of the boxes.

"Matteo—" I gasp.

"You need to start at the top, kitten."

I glance to where our guests, most of whom I haven't even properly greeted yet, are gathered around us. I bite my lip. Matteo has definitely done something crazy. "At the top?"

"Yep."

It's the smallest circular box with a lid. I reach for it carefully after watching how Stephano carried it, keeping it level. I lift the lid.

And break out laughing. "Oh my God. What did you do?" I'm staring at a glass bowl covered with cling wrap. Inside it swims a lone little goldfish. "Matteo." I glance up at him and he sinks down next to me.

"We start here," he says, for my ears only. "Come on, let's help this little guy. He needs air." Matteo lifts the glass bowl out of the box and peels off the cling wrap, then puts the bowl down on the coffee table. "There. Safe and sound. The goldfish we agreed upon."

We didn't agree upon anything that day so long ago, we only joked, but my heart is in my throat as tears push to the corners of my eyes. There are two more boxes, and there, the distinct sound coming from the middle one. "I'm going to cry." I look up to see Dominic and Luca filming this moment on their cellphones.

"Don't cry yet, kitten," Matteo murmurs in my ear. "See how cute they are first."

I reach for the second box and lift the lid. Two huge yellow-green eyes stare up at me and it lets out the cutest little meow. My heart bursts as I pick the kitten out of the box. A tiny ginger tabby whose sharp little claws immediately dig into the long sleeves of my dress. I don't care. I just blink back tears as I hug his tiny body into my neck. "Where did you get him?"

"That one's a rescue," Matteo says as he strokes the kitten's back with his forefinger. "You look smitten."

"I am," I laugh through my tears as I hold up the kitten for all to see. Cheers and claps sound through the room and I kiss the little thing on his head. "We'll find a name for him later, unless...?"

Matteo shakes his head. "We'll decide later. This moment might be—"

"Too big? No kidding." I'm not done. There's still one box left. "Here, keep him safe."

I hand Matteo the kitten and he gathers it safely in his big hands. For a moment I just look at him, this man who has so many layers to peel off and work through. He leans back and lets the kitten rest on his chest. I just know Matteo is going to be the most perfect father a wife and children could ever hope for. Because there will be children, not soon, but soon enough. This menagerie is just our starter pack.

I lean in and kiss Matteo full on the mouth. He lets me, but then nudges me to the last box. "I think he's sleeping."

The lure of my husband with our kitten in his hands is huge, but I drag the last box closer. This one is heavier. I lift the lid, and curled up in the big hatbox, snuggled deep into a soft blanket, sleeps a darling golden retriever puppy. I reach for him, and he wakes up at my touch to look up, blinking. "Come here, you sweet little thing." I gather him up in both my hands and lift him out of the box. This one is at most ten weeks old. I raise him up for the world to see and more enthusiastic laughter fills our apartment. I'm not sure how you top a house-warming, but Matteo just did, by making it a home.

"Okay, that's it," Stephano says. "She's woken the beast. Now all hell's going to break loose."

Matteo reaches out to scratch the pup behind the ear.

"Is he purebred?" I ask. I can't be sure as he's a ball of fur at the moment, all ears and eyes and a big yawn that makes us both laugh.

"When it comes to dogs, sweetheart, I only do purebred."

I lean in to hug him, and the puppy goes to my lap only to immediately struggle to sit up straight. "You're a bit extra, you know," I whisper as I sweep my lips across Matteo's cheek to his mouth. "But thank you for this crazy surprise."

Matteo kisses me back. "That's my love for you, kitten, extra...and a little crazy. Always."

Yes. Extra and a little crazy. "Always."

# BONUS EPILOGUE - MOST LOVED VOWS

"So, Chester gets two cups of this kibble in the mornings and evenings with some of that organic shit stirred in," I say, watching how Benedict diligently takes notes on his phone.

"Got it." Benedict nods. Chester is sitting right outside the pantry, tail wagging, ears twitching as he listens to our conversation about his food, eyes following our every move. "Bit of a snob, isn't he?"

"Be careful, he can understand you," I say as I step out of the pantry. "Plus, the dog's the love of her life."

"Hmm, I thought you were." Benedict eyes Chester where he slumps down in evident disappointment that he isn't getting any snacks right now.

"Any case," I grunt. "Maui, that little fucker, has half a can of tuna or salmon twice a day, you choose, and dry kibble on standby."

"In case he starves."

We both glance at the ginger where he's perched on the back of the brown leather sofa, starring at us as if we're idiots. The side of the leather sofa is scratched to bits and the reason why I call him a little fucker. He's scrawny but he's also cuddly like a bear cub with all that fur. He isn't exactly a picky eater, but Tasha loves to spoil him. And who can blame her? Maui had a rough start to life which she's trying to compensate for. "Meh, just stick to the schedule."

Benedict types on his phone with an aggressive sigh. "You know, there're about a hundred other people you could have signed up for housesitting."

"None of them need to get out of their dungeons." Fuck knows, Benedict is the hacker from hell, but the guy needs some sun. The fact that he generates our biggest profit margin is a thing I'll never overlook, and this is the exact reason why I'm worried about him. He needs to get out more. "With Burley and Rosalia also on vacation, I don't want strangers around the place."

One truth stands: trust is earned, and in our circles, it takes more than a couple of rounds. There are some risks just not worth taking.

"Yeah. I get it." Benedict swipes at his phone. "The goldfish I'll just replace when it dies or disappears."

I crack a laugh. "If Tasha knew we're on fish number five by now—"

"You're not kidding anybody, bro, least of all Tasha. Trust me, she knows."

"Probably. Maui enjoys the entertainment of that fishbowl too much. Do what you need to do."

"Will do." He pockets his phone. "You gotta leave if you're going to be on time."

"Right." I glance around the apartment. Dog toys are scattered over the floor, house plants have brought a garden inside, and somehow it's become so much more than just an apartment. It's become the home I've been craving since my mom died. And all my brothers are drawn here like moths to Tasha's light. "Time to surprise my kitten."

Benedict rolls his eyes at me as I head to the door, Chester at my heels, tail wagging. He's become my shadow, as he spends a lot of time with me in my old apartment where I work from home. "See you later, bud. Benny's going to take you for long walks."

"Don't call me Benny. Least of all in front of the dog."

"Scared he's going to call you that, huh?" I kid with him. "See you in two weeks."

"Have fun."

Our luggage is already in the car and Tasha's shift ends in half an hour. I've arranged to pick her up at the hospital for a drive out to one of our favorite spots up the coast and dinner, but instead I plan to kidnap her. It's been a year since I walked out on that veranda and saw her for the first time in the pool. That was a Sunday, but it's a Tuesday today and it took some wrangling to arrange this getaway. I'm good at wrangling. Rosalia's packed her suitcase, I've added a few toys, and the private jet is ready for takeoff in two hours.

It's finally time for that *proper* honeymoon I promised Tasha when we got married.

---

Stan drives me to the hospital, and we hit the timing just right as Tasha walks out of the entrance, Burley by her side as always. He usually waits for her wherever he can, keeping an eye on her from a distance, but my kitten has also caught on. She doesn't step out of line anymore. I trust only Burley with my wife, and he has taken to caring for her as much as everybody else in my family.

Burley spots the car as Tasha is busy on her phone, clearly messaging me because my phone pings.

*Happy kidnappeversary, husband! Where are you?*

I grin. She's put two and two together, but I bet she isn't expecting what I've got planned for us. Burley nods in our direction and when they reach the car, he opens the door for her.

"Hi," Tasha says as she scoots to the middle seat so that she can be right next to me.

She looks exhausted. She's been up early for weeks now, and these clinical rotations have long hours. I don't know if I want her to do the residency stints that carry on for twenty-four hours once she's graduated. It's a bridge we'll have to cross at some point.

"Come here," I say as she leans into me, and I wrap my arm around her. We share a kiss and then I buckle her up before Burley gets in next to her.

"Where're we having dinner?" Tasha asks as she rests her head on my shoulder.

"You'll see," I say as I take her hand and weave our fingers together.

By the time we reach the airport, she's been asleep for a good twenty minutes. She needs this break more than me. "We're here, Tash. You can sleep more on the plane."

"What?" She looks up, dazed. "Oh god, did I fall asleep?"

"Almost on your feet."

"Why're we here? I thought..." She looks out to the tarmac and the jet that's waiting for us.

"Surprise," I say and press a kiss to her temple. "We're going on our honeymoon."

"We are?" Tasha laughs. "Let me guess... Rosalia packed my bags."

"Yep."

"Who's looking after Chester and Maui and Fishy?"

"I roped Benedict in."

"Good." She chuckles. "You're so sly. You get me every time."

I do. But then, I have a team that makes keeping surprises like this fun. Soon we've waved Burley and Stan off and we're on the plane and I'm buckling her in for take-off.

"You going to tell me where we're going?" she asks as I sit down next to her.

"Not far, just the Caribbean." And given how tired she is, it's for the better. I need to get my wife to bed.

"Have you gone and done something crazy again?" She blinks at me. "Oh dear, you did."

I love doing crazy things for her. I take her hand, which only has a simple gold band on her ring finger because of her hospital work, in mine. "Nothing crazy, just us away from the crowds."

The plane takes off and once we're in the air, the hostess brings us champagne and snacks. Tasha eats, but with little enthusiasm. Usually, she's ready to down a glass of red and a steak dinner when she's worked a busy rotation.

"I think I'm going to lie down. I don't feel great."

Fuck. She's coming down with something. Being on a tropical island in the middle of nowhere isn't the best idea if you're getting sick, and she's exposed to who knows what for long hours at the hospital.

"Come on," I say as I lead her to the bedroom. "I'll lie down with you." I close the door to the bedroom and watch as she kicks off her shoes and strips off her jacket.

She flops onto the bed "I've just been run ragged—"

"I know." And thank god she's having a break. She doesn't need to work. She doesn't need to run herself ragged to become a doctor. But she'd hate sitting at home with nothing to do, especially not when she has this burning need to do good.

I watch her while I strip off my own jacket and shoes. She thinks I have expectations. She probably has them too. I mean, making love has become part of our in-flight entertainment. "It's fine, sweetheart. We have two weeks."

"That sounds so good."

As she cuddles up, I feel her forehead. She isn't burning up.

"How long's the flight?"

"Three hours."

"Okay, just this then," she murmurs as she rolls onto her side so I can spoon her. "I promise I'll be all sparkly when we get there."

I press a kiss to her hair as I gather her close. "Promises, promises, Mrs. Scalera."

She smiles, but I can already feel her sinking back into sleep.

---

"Oh, wow," Tasha says as she squeezes my hand. "You did it again."

We arrived just in time for a phenomenal sunset. Total peace and calm descended on us as the staff welcomed us at this exclusive owner-rented house. The small island is part of the Bahamas, but we might as well be in the middle of nowhere. We took the final leg of our journey by floatplane and all the way Tasha looked out of the window, clinging to a barf bag. I get it, floatplanes can make for a bumpy ride, but she isn't usually that queasy.

She seems to have recovered as she's in my arms and kissing me. I cup her butt and she circles her arms around my neck as she perches with her toes on mine. I turn away from the lit rim-flow pool and the view over the ocean to walk us back into the bedroom.

"Shower or bath?" she murmurs as I head towards the en suite.

"Shower," I say between kisses. I plan to have her against the wall in about two minutes. When we get to the bathroom, she strokes her hands over my shoulders, down my pecs, and lower to tug my shirt from my pants. She loves doing this, and I always let her. I feel like she's unwrapping me like a gift and it's fucking sexy. I swear the way she goes about it is like every time is her first time. Button for button, until her lips can caress my skin and her tongue can trace the lines of my dragon tattoos. I drop my head back, letting my wife work her magic. Soon I'm shirtless and that's not exactly fair. I grab her hands, pin her to the wall, and press my erection into the soft curve of her belly. "Want this, sweetheart?" I murmur, needing to get into her pussy already.

"God, yes," she whispers. And it's as if the need that's been building since she woke up on the plane for landing earlier suddenly boils over. She tugs at my belt, and I tear at her shirt, to the extent that the buttons pop off. She only giggles and helps me shed the rest of her clothes. She's naked and I'm still in my pants, but I always get a kick out of still being dressed while she's wet and wanting.

"Fuck, Tash," I groan, tracing her hardened nipples. I'd die for these breasts, and as I tease a nipple between my thumb and forefinger, she pushes her pelvis into my cock, her hands on my ass. "Yes, kitten, beg for me with your body," I hiss as I hook her leg over my hip and kiss her. It opens her up and the pressure, right there, is divine.

"Wash me," she whispers as we come up for air and I don't need to be asked twice.

I lean into the double shower and open one faucet. I feel the water until it is just right, then nudge her inside. We don't do cold showers together.

"Thank you," she says with a smile as she dips her head under the water.

Double showers are honestly the best. Water in the face when you need it, water out of the face when you don't. I strip off the rest of my clothes, get in with her, and lather up some liquid soap. "Come here."

She steps away from the spray and drops her head back as I wash her down with my hands, slowly, every stroke an erotic dance over her skin. By the time I've worked my way down to her calves, she's clinging to my hair and I'm kissing and licking her pussy, her one leg hooked over my shoulder as she slumps against the marble shower wall.

"Matteo..."

"Hmmm?" I hum against her most sensitive skin.

"I'm so close... but I need you."

That translates to *I need to be fucked* so I pull away from her and stand, blocking the spray from her face with my back. What my girl wants, she gets. I grip her butt and raise her up against the wall so she's just where I need her and slowly penetrate her, every inch of her body made for me, every inch feeling like coming home. I close my eyes as I rest my forehead on hers. Our breaths are coming ever more haltingly as I find the rhythm that will get us there at the same time. Tasha clings to me, her lips against my neck, making my skin pop out in chills as she whispers *I love you so much* between kisses.

My heart is full, and my cock spurts empty into the body of the woman who made me whole. I feel her orgasm clutching mine. "Fuck, kitten, I love you too."

---

I lean over and feel for my wife. Her warm body isn't there and I blink. Light is seeping into the room but it's early. Clearly it hasn't sunk in yet that she's on vacation and her body clock is still set to get up at five in the morning. The sheets are still warm, but I don't like it. When I want my wife in my bed, I *want my wife in my bed*. This shit ends today. I don't care if I have to pay for her to work somewhere privately to get her hours and goddamn degree.

My ears home in on the sounds coming from behind the bathroom's closed door. What is she up to now? Fuck. Wrappers. I really don't need her to be on her period right now. And how the fuck did I muck up my planning like that? That's a week of no going down on her and I'm a man that needs to eat my wife's pussy on a regular basis. I sit up, staring at the closed door.

More crinkling of wrappers and then after a minute, the toilet flushes. I want to walk in on her to check that she's okay, but that sounds dumb. I mean, she wasn't feeling great last night and she's tired and now—

I pick up my phone and check the time. Five forty. Fucking hell, kitten. When a good ten minutes has passed and she still hasn't surfaced, I get out of bed.

"Kitten?" I say as I stand at the bathroom door. I knock when there's no reply. "Tash?"

"Yes." Her voice is small and somewhat uncertain.

"You're good?"

"I..."

Fuck it. I open the door only to see her standing by the toilet, hands behind her back. She's put the baby doll lingerie back on that I bought for the first night. Its white diaphanous fabric hides things, hints mostly, and makes her look almost virginal. She stares at me, eyes wide and cheeks flushed, but the way she bites her lips speaks only of mischief.

"What're you doing?"

"You're not the only one that can have secrets, you know."

Secrets? My wife has secrets. From me? "What do you mean?"

"All this honeymoon planning—"

"What have you done, kitten?" I walk up to her, crowding her against the wall, trapping her with my hands on either side of her head.

She looks up at me and laughs, and it slows down my racing pulse as I breathe out. Fuck, that I can panic in mere seconds at the thought of something going wrong with her... with us.

"More like... what have *we* done?" she whispers.

"And what have we done?" I ask as I lean in and press a

string of kisses from her temple to her ear and down to her neck. We've done a lot of—

"Tash?"

"You might want to sit down for this." I frown as I pin her with my gaze, then my eyes jump to the vanity where a small paper box lies discarded.

It tries to be discreet but… *Fuck.* It's a pregnancy test kit.

My chest tightens. This can't be real. I cage her face with my hands before running them down her bare arms, peering into her eyes. She lets me tug her hands from behind her back and I lose a heartbeat or three in there somewhere as she holds up two pee sticks, with those little lines that tell you everything. They're *positive* pregnancy tests.

"Holy fuck… kitten?"

"You'll have to stop swearing… our baby can hear you."

I sink down on the edge of the bath, drowning in a well of emotions that seems to suck me in from the bottom up. I pull her close, my hands slipping underneath the fabric to caress her naked butt, to her lower back so I can press my face into her and hide. I'm shaking. I'm physically fucking shaking. *She's pregnant. With my baby.*

"Hey?" Her fingers brush into my hair, so tender and with such love, that I choke up. "Matteo? You okay?" she asks. "Please don't be mad. I know we didn't plan—"

"Fuck, sweetheart. I'm not mad… I'm fuck—" Ah *fuck.* I take a deep breath as I slide my hands over her hips so I can circle her stomach with my thumbs. "I'm so happy I think I'm dying."

"Don't die!" she cries out, her voice breaking with happy tears. "Our baby needs a dad! One that's going to love this little one like every baby and child needs to be loved."

A dad who's going to reverse all the generational trauma he carries. A dad who has put down all his baggage and proved that he's a better man and not shaped like either of his fathers.

No wonder I'm having a moment here, for my moment has come.

Damn right. I slowly stand, meeting her gaze as she steps back, and I'm not shy to show her my tears. "When you walked into my life, I knew you were perfect, but I didn't know what perfection was. This, sweetheart, *this* is perfection."

I take her into my arms and kiss her, and she quivers with her own tears as she smiles into my kiss. "You're going to be perfect."

And with those few words, she burns all my nagging doubts to the ground.

---

Hours later we walk along the white sandy beach. I had plans for these two weeks. I memorized things I wanted to say. Since this morning's curve ball, I had to reword a few lines, and let's just say, unless there is a *fuck* in there, I'm not exactly good with words.

Tasha has been swinging between bouts of nausea and bouts of happiness. When we spoke about her studies, she waved it off with an *it will work out. Surely I'm not the first woman to get pregnant during the stupid decade it takes you to become a doctor.*

Brave, crazy girl. *Mine.*

I watch as she walks deeper into the water, bunching her skirts up so they don't get wet, then walks back to me, her hair whipping in the breeze.

She reaches up and presses a kiss to my lips. Fuck knows what I've done to deserve this woman.

"You know, I never got to do this properly," I start, my heart jumping into my throat right on cue as I gather a few rogue strands from her face.

"What? You're always so very... thorough."

I chuckle. "Kitten." I pull the rings from my shorts pocket where they've been burning for the past few hours, waiting for the right moment. I reach for her hand, pull off the plain gold band, and she watches as I slip her new wedding band and engagement ring on her finger. The wedding band is an eternity ring with diamonds that I had commissioned. The engagement ring holds one solitaire.

"Matteo, why... where?" she asks, her eyes wide as she looks from the rings up to me. "They're really gorgeous."

"For the engagement ring... I had to take my mom's and split it into parts. I mean, I'm not her only son and the others... well, we can hope that one day they'll be as lucky as me." The engagement ring's single diamond blinks in the softer early evening sun.

"Oh, God. Of course you did." She leans into my arms, and I hug her closer. "I love it... thank you for letting me be part of her."

"I'm not done," I say clearing my throat. *No fucks allowed. Well, no fucks* aloud.

"Okay." She leans back and gazes up into my eyes, all expectation. "What more can there possibly be than this perfect moment?"

"My love vows to you, sweetheart." I smile, my heart in my throat. "You're my once-in-a-lifetime person, Tash. To think I carried you out of your home and into my life as if this was planned by something bigger than us... that there's only you for me. This year, you've become more than my wife, my best friend, my lover, my rock. You're my beginning and my end and now you're going to bring this little mix of us into the world." I swallow down the emotions that have been barking up my walls the whole day. "With these rings I vow to love you and all our children deeply, to treasure you, protect you, cherish you, for better or for worse, for richer or poorer, in sickness and in health, till death do us part."

Fuck. Now I've made her cry. And I let her because the moment is swallowing me up too.

Eventually she whispers against my neck. "How do you want me to top that? To top any of this? You didn't even give me time to think—"

I press a kiss to her hair. "Just say ditto, sweetheart, and we're good."

She laughs between her tears. "Ditto, my crazy love, ditto."

# BROKEN VOWS

## GIGI AND STEPHANO'S STORY

**Are you ready for the explosive love between Stephano and Gigi? Follow me on social media or sign up for my newsletter for more deets! Release date 3 September 2024. Pre-order here: BROKEN VOWS**

For more information sign up for my newsletter on my website www.sophiakarlson.com or via this link Newsletter.

**Stephano Scalera**

I can spot trouble a mile away. Not that anybody can miss Gigi Trapani. As the son of a notorious Mafia Don, her first words to me hit a nerve. I promise to put her in her place, but instead we end up having an explosive one-night stand because we'll never see each other again.

A month later, Gigi calls in a favor and hurtles back into my life with her sister in tow. Forced to protect them, I enter an arranged marriage with Gigi. Suddenly she's in my house, in my head, *everywhere*...except in my bed.

Gigi has a pile of secrets and teasing them out of her only makes me develop feelings—feelings I'm not allowed to have.

There's a reason I've vowed to never love, and it's a demon I fight every day. What if avenging Gigi is the only way to set me free from my past and make my marriage real?

**Gigi Trapani**

My whole life I've had one mission: to escape my family's Mafia crime ring and take my younger sister with me.

When my stepbrother forces me into an arranged marriage with the new *Capo Crimini*, I'll do anything to escape this fate, even marry the man I've vowed to never see again: Stephano Scalera. Our explosive one-night stand still haunts me—our chemistry was off the charts, but it only took one night to know Stephano is the most dangerous man I've ever met.

When the *Capo Crimini* hunts me down, Stephano proves to be the husband I never knew I needed. How does a woman walk away from a man like that? She doesn't. She falls deeper in love and fights to keep him.

# ACKNOWLEDGMENTS

How many people does it take to write a book? So many...but this one happened in such a spur-of-the-moment, insane way. I never thought I'd write a Mafia romance, and if you've read any of my other books, you'll know that I don't do hardcore alphaholes. Well, not that Matteo is a hardcore alphahole entirely, but he is by far the bossiest character I've ever written.

This book was born out of desperation to save a crappy year (I don't recommend moving from Toronto to Vancouver to anybody) and the pit of low spirits I had to drag myself out of after the move. The year wasn't done, but I had nothing planned. An then NaNoWriMo came along. National Novel Writing Month happens every year in November. Around the world aspiring authors and writers attempt to write 50 000 words, or a novel as such in thirty days. My friend Amanda Holly, herself a dark romance author, suggested I should give writing Mafia romance a shot. I thought about it for a hot minute and was like "I literally have nothing to lose."

I plotted this book and then proceeded to write it in eight weeks. And I loved every single second of it. For this, I have to thank my characters, Matteo and Tasha, who literally poured out as I typed away in Scrivener, as if they'd been trapped in a cage in my head somewhere for years, and finally set free. As a reader, I bet you can see the ease with which this book was written.

Thank you to my beta readers, Leia King, Amanda Holly,

and my sister, Tilla, for her proofread. You can spot a gremlin like nobody else. As always, thank you Meg Chronis for your valuable input and gremlin scouting!

Thank you to my readers. This is the first book in an intended five- book series. Let's see where this takes us!

# ABOUT THE AUTHOR

Sophia writes sensual, emotional, and evocative contemporary romance. Some snark might sneak in. When she's not writing, she's binge-watching the latest TV series, being walked by her beagles, or planning the family's next trip into the wilds. She's ghosted Facebook, is failing at Tiktok, and has little time left for Instagram, however, she hasn't given up (yet). Check out her efforts at @sophiakarlson or @sophiakarlsonauthor

Sign up for her newsletter to get updates about new book releases and free stuff! Rest assured, you won't be bombarded! https://BookHip.com/RKDPHT

## ALSO BY SOPHIA KARLSON

**The Love Nests Series**

The Paris Apartment

The Shrink

The Neighbor

The Intern

**Ashleigh Lake Series - Small Town Romance**

One Sweet Summer

When I Fall in Love

**Standalones**

Just My Type

**Mafia Romance**

Hated Vows

**Perfect Series**

Perfect Mistake

Perfect Obsession

Printed in Great Britain
by Amazon

48296434R00189